Thus it begins . . .

Proteus fell to the ground. His teeth were gritted and his face contorted in pain. He began to *change*, as the prophetic trance gripped him. His mouth, which was no longer exactly a mouth, choked out his words.

"Change follows change, when god devours god. Titan against Titan, god against god . . . power unleashed, force undreamt . . . The gull shall weep, the eagle cease to soar, when the white mare rears her hooves and the broken willow pierces their hearts . . ."

LORD OF THE CROOKED PATHS

PATRICK H. ADKINS

ORBIT

An Orbit Book

Copyright © 1987 by Patrick H. Adkins

First published in Great Britain in 1990 by
Futura Publications, a Division of
Macdonald & Co (Publishers) Ltd
London & Sydney

ISBN 0 7088 8322 2

Reproduced, printed and bound in Great Britain by
BPCC Hazell Books Ltd
Member of BPCC Ltd
Aylesbury, Bucks, England

Futura Publications
A Division of
Macdonald & Co (Publishers) Ltd
Orbit House
1 New Fetter Lane
London EC4A 1AR
A member of Maxwell Macmillan Pergamon Publishing Corporation

For Alisha,
my bright-eyed daughter

INTRODUCTORY NOTE

The Age of the Titans, the elder gods of Greek mythology, was little known even to the ancient Greeks themselves. Our knowledge of that era is still more scanty. The only work of appreciable length dealing directly with it, the *Titanomachia*, failed to survive the collapse of classical civilization. What we know of the Titans is drawn from short summaries in the *Theogany* of Hesiod and the *Bibliotheca* of Apollodorus, and from brief references that must be sifted from works devoted to other, often nonmythological subjects.

Although a work of fiction, *Lord of the Crooked Paths* is based upon extensive mythological research. My purpose has been to shape a new, fictional story around these scattered fragments, many of which are quite esoteric and no longer have a true story context of their own. In the process I have attempted to form a coherent fantasy world from the sometimes confusing and contradictory elements of Greek mythology. Like the historical novelist, I have felt free to pick and choose among conflicting evidence, expand upon tantalizing hints that lack full documentation, and extrapolate freely within the established confines of my subject. Nevertheless, accuracy of mythological detail has been my goal, and I have sought to remain faithful to classical authority throughout.

The reader's forbearance is requested for any seeming contradictions of the mythology of the Age of Zeus. The gods willing, these will be resolved in future volumes. Only one such point need be mentioned here. The Muses are generally said to be the daughters of Zeus and the Titaness Mnemosyne (Memory), a genesis that is more allegory than myth. For this reason and others, I have overruled both Homer and Hesiod in favor of the nearly as ancient testimony of Mimnermus and Alcman, who deem them the children of Ouranos and Gaia.

The nature and manner of the gods is based primarily on Homer, while the milieu of Kronos and the intricacies of divine relationships are drawn principally from Hesiod. Latin authors have been consulted only to elucidate matters left unclear by the Greeks. The title is loosely derived from the Homeric epithet *Kronos agkylometes*. With a single exception the names of the gods have been directly transliterated from the Greek; as an aid to the reader, however, I have partly Latinized Krios to Crios, that he might not so easily be confused with Koios, his brother.

—Patrick H. Adkins

ONE

"Come, Kalliope! Melpomene—Thalia, come on!" Metis scowled, tapping her foot impatiently as she waited for the three Muses to catch up with her and Lachesis.

For more than half an hour the five goddesses had been making their way across rugged mountains and rambling foothills, walking with an ease and suppleness that belied their towering size. They seemed to glide over the rocky terrain and between the huge fir trees of the mountain forests. When the trees grew too closely together, they bent them aside. They drew up the hems of their chitons to step lightly across rivers and gaping chasms.

For the Muses the journey was a lark; the divine maidens traipsed along, singing and bantering among themselves. The young goddess Metis, no longer quite a child but not yet a youth, usually rushed impetuously ahead. Lachesis, stately and somber as ever, followed at a steady pace, wrapped in her own thoughts.

"Can't you three come on?" Metis demanded, her dark curls flouncing as she stamped her foot.

Lachesis had gotten ahead of the others and finally slowed to a stop. "Is something wrong?" she called down, her voice not quite as lackadaisical as usual.

Melpomene shook her head and held up a hand to silence them. Metis shrugged in resignation and began to skip back down the path. A few moments later Lachesis followed her.

Thalia danced toward them as they reached the group. "Quiet, child, do try to hold your tongue," she sang without the slightest hesitation, caressing Metis's cheek with her open hand; "a song is not a song, you know, until that song is sung!" She twirled gracefully away, continuing to sing as though there had been no interruption.

Metis folded her arms across her chest and waited with obvious impatience. Finally Thalia completed her last verse, swept into a pirouette, and ended with a deep bow. Kalliope and Melpomene, both laughing, applauded with enthusiasm.

Metis planted her hands firmly on her narrow hips as she turned toward Melpomene. "You promised to show us something new and interesting," she said. "You're supposed to be leading us to it, but I'm always in the lead. And I don't even know where we're going!"

Thalia answered before her sister could. "You lead, rash child, because your feet outpace your brain. A slower pace—"

"You brought your basket," Melpomene interrupted, smiling indulgently. "If we walk too leisurely, you can distract yourself among the plants that grow beside the path."

Metis shook her head vigorously. "You go too slow. You keep stopping to talk and dance—and to sing your untrue songs."

"What's this?" Thalia asked, turning to her sisters in exaggerated surprise. "Untrue songs, indeed! The child thinks we lie."

"All those things you sing about—they never really happened," Metis said. "You just make them up."

"Not at all," Kalliope said patiently. "You're simply too young to understand. We only tell *true* lies."

"True lies?" Metis grimaced. "How can you tell true—"

Melpomene was holding up her hands to quiet them. "No more, you three. We'll walk faster, and Metis can search for plants."

Metis clutched her large basket against her stomach. "I *always* look for unusual plants when I walk in the woods. I've been looking. I haven't found any."

"And we *always* dance and sing in the woods," Thalia said, patting the child's head.

They began walking again, Melpomene studying the crest of the high, rounded hill.

"Is it much farther?" Metis asked.

"Hush," Thalia said, leaning toward her confidentially. "You'll only embarrass Melpomene. She's lost, you know."

Now Kalliope drew toward them, speaking in a mock whisper intended for Melpomene to hear. "Tell the child the truth, sister. Melpomene does this all the time. She says, 'Come see what I have found'—won't tell you what it is, of course, to keep your interest up—and leads you on a merry chase for hours stacked on end. It makes a fine, droll tale to tell that night."

"I think the place is near," Melpomene said, pointedly ignoring their conversation. "We must be quiet now, or risk discovery. We mustn't scare them away. . . ."

"Ah, *discovery*," Thalia whispered. "That certainly lends an air of mystery to the affair."

"Scare who away?" Metis demanded. "*Who?* Tell me!"

Melpomene shook her head. "You must be patient. I promised you something new, and I won't break my promise. I think you'll find it interesting."

"She's got such a knack for suspense," Thalia said, still pretending to whisper.

"Whatever this mysterious thing is, at least tell us a little," Kalliope said. "When did you find it?"

"Yesterday afternoon, on my way back from Mount Helikon."

"Well, it can't be all that interesting," Thalia said, "or she'd never have kept it a secret this long."

Melpomene gave them her most tight-lipped smile. They had reached the top of the hill. All around them stark peaks and gaping canyons bespoke the unimaginable age of their world; at the same time laughing streams and virgin forest proclaimed its eternal youth. Staring out across the treetops, Melpomene scanned the smaller hills and valleys below, teeming with life. A lone red deer came down from a hillside forest, while a saber-tooth stalked it from the concealment of large rocks.

Beyond the farther hills began the moist expanse of the Boiotian plain, most of which was still covered by early morning fog. Near its edge herds of antelope and bison had begun to graze. Barely visible, Lake Kopais glinted dull blue in the distance.

"Yes, I'm right," Melpomene announced. "We aren't far now."

She pointed off to the left, where jagged limestone hills descended toward the plain. A crystalline stream gleamed among the rocks. On its way to the lake it broadened, becoming brown and shallow as it crossed a long, narrow glade rimmed by ash and oak trees.

"Is that where we're going?" Thalia demanded. "If you weren't lost, you certainly took the most roundabout route possible."

"I wanted to avoid crossing the plain. If we were seen—"

"She *was* lost!" Thalia began to dance around her sister.

"I was *not*," Melpomene protested, for the first time becoming genuinely annoyed at Thalia's playfulness. "I didn't want to cross the plain, and I didn't know the most direct way here."

"That's what I said. *You were lost!*"

Melpomene folded her arms across her breasts and refrained from answering. It took only a few moments for her to regain her normal, indulgent good nature. "I'd love to bicker the rest of the morning, dear sister, but we should start walking toward those trees. From here on we must be very quiet—I know you'll find that a chore, Thalia—and we must avoid being seen."

Thalia grinned broadly, but before she could reply, Kalliope took her arm and guided her in the direction Melpomene had indicated.

The goddesses made their way down the rocky slope. By following the valleys and passes they managed to come to the plain at a point not very far from the glade. A pride of lions, grunting their disapproval at the appearance of the towering maidens, retreated at their approach.

Melpomene brought the goddesses to a halt at the edge of an open area. She held Metis back to keep her from venturing too far into the open, then drew concealing fog from the plain. It crept toward them in drifting wisps at first, then in slow, billowing waves. The fog grew thicker, layer upon layer, completely obscuring the space they must cross.

Hand in hand, Melpomene led them forward until they crouched behind the concealment of the tall, thick trees that rimmed the glade. She dismissed the fog and signaled to the others. Following her example, they cautiously parted the branches to peer through the foliage.

Metis could see nothing. To get a better view she threw

herself on the ground and crawled forward between the boles of the trees. Before her lay the mud bank of a stream. All along it, at irregular intervals, vaguely oval mounds protruded from the water and ran up onto the shore.

Metis edged forward on her elbows, making as little noise as she could. The mounds glistened where the sunlight struck the translucent slime that coated them, and they heaved with slow, rhythmic movements. She watched in puzzled fascination for more than a minute before she became aware of the creatures across the stream.

They were tiny, but perfectly formed—not much bigger than the hand of a goddess. All were dirty, but some were caked with mud from head to foot. Much of their bodies was covered with coarse, sparse hair, and in places the hair sprouted in thick patches.

Ten or fifteen of the creatures were visible across the stream, and now Metis realized that there were more on her side. Some cracked open acorns and ate them. A few seemed to be playing. One began making high-pitched, piping cries as another chased it.

Metis backed out from between the trees to join the other goddesses.

"Well," Melpomene asked, whispering softly, "what do you think of this strange new thing? An interesting discovery, aren't they?"

"What does it mean?" Metis asked. "Except for being so tiny, they look just like us."

Melpomene smiled despite herself. "Well, no—not *just* like us. As far as I can tell, they're all male."

"And they're filthy," Kalliope said. "They've got ugly hair all over their bodies and they smell dreadful. I can smell them from here."

"Are they really little?" Metis asked. "I mean, is that their natural size?"

"I think so. That's how they looked yesterday."

Thalia was studying them, her brows contracted in thought. "Dirty, smelly little gods," she said finally as she turned toward the others.

"I think they're cute," Metis objected.

"Filthy, hairy little creatures formed in the image of the immortal gods. Grotesque little godlings, caricatures of the gods—*mockeries* of the gods!" Thalia's eyes brightened and her lips spread into an enormous grin. "And not a female among them. I love it! It's hilarious!"

Metis was pouting. "I still say they're cute," she insisted. "All they need is a good bath."

"Look at the one over there," Thalia continued, pointing. "See how he walks, watching the ground. He looks like Crios, and the one next to him could be Koios! Oh, this is a marvelous joke. The gods will never live it down."

"There's something about them. . . ." Lachesis said thoughtfully.

"Indeed there is—their odor!" Thalia laughed.

"Quiet," Melpomene warned. "They'll hear us. Keep your voices down."

One of the creatures was wandering toward them in search of acorns. Even as Melpomene spoke it looked up through an opening in the concealing leaves and branches. Its eyes grew very round and it began to cry out in shrill, inarticulate sounds. Kalliope reached for it between the trees. The creature stumbled backward, falling, and she picked it up by the feet.

At the first cry the others had disappeared among the rocks and trees and bushes. Now not one remained in sight.

Melpomene rose to her full height and the others stood up around her. They gathered to look at the specimen Kalliope had captured. It wriggled like a fish held by the tail, but as soon as it noticed their huge, peering faces, it became completely limp.

For nearly a full minute Melpomene stared at it, her head arched to one side. Finally she said, *"Man."*

Kalliope and Thalia nodded their immediate agreement.

"What?" Metis asked. "What did you say?"

"This is a *man*," Melpomene explained. "That's what the creature is called. Usually we know the right word immediately, without having to think about it. This time it took a bit longer."

Lachesis repeated the word slowly as she stared at the peculiar *man*, which was still dangling upside down from Kalliope's fingers. "It's very puny. Puny and helpless," she said.

"Let me hold it," Metis pleaded.

Kalliope gently lowered the man into her outstretched hands. Now Lachesis stood beside the child, searching the tiny form with her eyes. Melpomene pushed her way between the trees, and the others followed out to the bank of the stream. They stopped beside one of the mounds. A section of mud had fallen away near the top. Through the jagged opening they could see a diminutive, godlike mouth. It gurgled and sucked air.

"This man," Metis said, "is it a god? I mean, is it a little god or . . . or . . . only an animal in the shape of a god?"

Melpomene looked down at the tiny form in the child's hands. "It's hard to imagine that they could truly be gods," she said. "They make me feel sad, somehow."

"Sad? Why so?" Kalliope asked.

"They're such pitiful creatures. Look at them. Wretched little things . . . shaped like us, but born of slime. . . ."

"They're our brothers," Kalliope said. "We, too, are children of the earth."

Melpomene smiled wanly. "A poor joke, sister, and a cruel one. By that logic the grass and the trees and the insects are our brothers and sisters also."

"They are," Kalliope said. "Less fortune than we, but still kin, even if they have been born of mud and slime rather than immortal flesh. Poorly born, these may yet prove worthy."

Melpomene looked doubtful.

"Look at this one," Kalliope continued. "He has a good face, handsome under the grime. Look at his chin and forehead—the nose too. All well shaped, not without a touch of nobility about them. Perhaps they are gods. It's too early to say."

They moved slowly up the long, narrow glade. Across the stream little heads appeared, wide eyes following them.

"They're watching us," Metis said. "They're curious. That means they're smart."

A bittersweet smile touched Melpomene's lips. "So much the worse, if they do have any intelligence."

"Why?" Lachesis asked.

"They'll compare themselves with us. They'll envy us and aim too high. They'll smolder with resentment, and finally they'll hate us, when the futility of their efforts starts to crush them. Oh, pay no attention to me," she said suddenly. "I don't know what's wrong. My mood has turned terribly glum."

The mounds grew in all sizes. Some were little larger than

acorns; others were as big as the full-grown men watching from the trees. Many of the largest mounds had the mud broken away in places from the violent struggles of the creatures within, which seemed to be trying to extricate themselves.

"I think you're wrong," Kalliope said. "None of that matters. Even beings as wretched as these can be noble, if they strive." There was a peculiar quaver in her voice.

"But without hope of success . . . ?"

"It doesn't matter," Kalliope insisted, pointing first toward one of the mounds and then across the stream. "Yesterday they were fighting to birth themselves from these mud and slime cocoons. Today they're playing in the wind and sunshine. Who may say what they'll do tomorrow?"

Metis was absorbed in the man cuddled against her breast, and not listening to their conversation. "May we take this one back with us?" she asked.

It took Melpomene a moment to cast off her sad thoughts. "You'd better not, I would think. Not until we've received Lord Kronos's permission."

"You'd better put him down now," Kalliope told her. She lifted the man gently from Metis's hands and set him on the ground near the stream.

The goddesses continued walking, a pace or two at a time, each now sunk in her own thoughts. Metis hung back, waiting till none of the others was looking in her direction. Scooping up the man's still limp body, she hurriedly concealed him within her basket, then followed. As she looked up, Thalia was grinning at her. She had seen, but made no attempt to tell her companions.

"Why do you suppose they've come into existence now, so late?" Lachesis asked.

"Does there have to be a reason?" Thalia said.

The creatures scurried along the opposite bank, behind the trees and brush. Here and there eyes and heads were visible.

"They're so curious," Metis said. "Why don't we try to make friends with them?"

"Just how do you propose we do that?" Thalia asked.

Metis considered for a moment. "You could sing for them. Even animals love your singing. I'm sure these tiny gods will. Please sing for them."

The Muses consulted.

"Dance for them too," Metis begged.

"What shall we sing?" Melpomene asked.

"A lullaby. Sing a gentle, soft lullaby."

Metis and Lachesis drew back to make room. Melpomene began with a voice like the wind whistling through canyons and rustling among forest leaves. Her sisters danced with the flowing grace of autumn leaves lapped by the breeze.

Tiny heads appeared among the foliage on every side. Hairy, mud-streaked bodies edged forward, until all around the goddesses men stood watching and listening in entranced wonder.

TWO

Proteus, the shape changer, awoke suddenly, listening. The singing was real, though distant. It had insinuated itself into his dream, merging with the slow, rhythmic caress of the tide upon the rocky shore of a shaded cove.

He arose slowly, disentangling himself from the arms of the sleeping naiad beside him. She sighed softly at his touch, moistening her parted lips and curling into a more comfortable position. During the night she had shared her cloak with him. As he bent to tuck it carefully around her slender body, he experienced once again the disconcerting sensation he had felt last night—a sort of false memory, as though he had done this before.

Rising, he made his way out of the dimness of the grotto. Outside he paused briefly to listen, then clambered partway up the steep rock wall that partially surrounded the narrow valley. Small rocks dislodged beneath his huge feet, and more than once during the short ascent he was forced to shift his weight unexpectedly from left to right or from foot to hand. In his own environment, the sure, powerful movements of his supple muscles propelled him through the ocean depths with speed and grace no fish could equal. Here, where everything seemed to be rocky cliff or rock-strewn valley, the ocean god felt distinctly out of place.

He raised his eyes cautiously above the rim of the valley and peered out across the plain in the direction from which the singing came. He scrutinized the five goddesses, then, as he looked more closely, became aware of the small, godlike creatures partially hidden among the foliage. He drew back a little, passing his fingers through his thick black hair. The strange sense of familiarity came again, even more strongly.

A hand touched his forearm, and he turned to find the naiad beside him. She had followed him up the steep bank.

"Good morning, my lord," she said, brushing strands of long brown hair away from her face. Her mouth had a pleasant smile but her eyes kept flitting away from him.

"Good morning," he answered, trying to shake off the odd feeling that had claimed him. "You climb very quietly."

She looked out over the valley wall rather than meet his steady gaze. She found herself peculiarly flustered at the sight of his smooth, nude body. After an awkward moment of silence, she said, "I love to listen to them sing. Sometimes I stay for days near Mount Helikon, just to listen to them."

"Mount Helikon?" He started to follow her gaze, but changed his mind and looked back at her. "You know them?"

"Of course. Everyone knows the Black-Haired Nine." She hesitated. "Pardon, my lord. You must not be from here."

"It's been a long time," he said, almost to himself.

It was his eyes, she decided, that hinted of age. He was tall, neither slender nor bulky, but with sleek muscles that rippled beneath his skin with each slightest movement. "They are ladies of Olympos," she continued, her glancing eyes absorbing every detail of him. "Those who are singing are three of the nine Muses and—"

"The child," he interrupted, "she is a daughter of Okeanos?"

"I don't know her, my lord." His face was clean-lined, with a high forehead and squared chin. He looked even more handsome now than in the silver moonlight of the night before. "My name is Nalassa. What is your name, my lord?"

He had turned briefly to look toward the Muses. "What are the little creatures?"

"I don't know, my lord. I've never seen them before."

Small beads of sweat stood out on his forehead as he turned back to face her.

"You are . . . you are an old one?" she asked.

His eyes fastened on hers, and she could see amusement

lurking in them. He wiped away the perspiration. "Yes—and you are a very young one."

His smile was very attractive. Nevertheless she looked away, flushing. She kept talking to relieve her embarrassment. "You slept soundly last night. You must have traveled far."

He nodded. "Quite far, especially after chasing you."

This time she blushed vigorously. She turned her back on him and scrambled rapidly down to the valley floor. She stopped there, hesitating, then turned to confront him. "You would never have caught me among the rocks—if I hadn't wanted you to!"

Probably she expected him to follow her down, or at least to turn in her direction. Instead he stood looking in the direction of the Muses. As she watched, his hands moved one at a time from their holds on the rock face of the cliff to clutch his head. He swayed, then tumbled backward.

With a cry of surprise she ran toward him. He lay on his back, still clutching his head. His teeth were gritted and his face contorted in pain. She threw herself down on her knees beside him.

"What's wrong, my lord? What can I do?"

His face began to change first, the features blurring. She drew back as his entire form began to alter. The flesh started to run and shift, flowing like molten wax. As she watched in horror, an amphibious monster writhed upon the ground; but no sooner had the form become distinct and recognizable than it began to change again.

His mouth, which was no longer exactly a mouth, choked out sounds. She forced herself to lean over him, trying to understand the strange words. Some were clear and plainly audible, but many were slurred beyond recognition. The garbled words were interspersed with groans and sobs and weird, slobbering sounds.

More than five minutes passed while his body writhed in continual metamorphosis. The entire time the naiad, despite her fear, kneeled beside him, ready to assist in any way she could. Then, as suddenly as it had begun, the seizure passed. The god's body returned to its usual shape, the panicked breathing slowed and became normal. Finally Proteus was himself again. He stared calmly up into her face.

"You're all right now?" she asked, more upset than he. "Shall I bring you water?"

He shook his head. "I'm sorry if I frightened you. That doesn't happen often, but when it does . . . well, there isn't anything I can do about it."

She was still kneeling beside him, and now he sat up. She held his arm to steady him.

"Did I speak?" he asked.

She nodded, her eyes very wide.

"What did I say? You must tell me the exact words."

She recoiled a little at his forcefulness. "I heard you, my lord, but I didn't understand. You kept changing, so that you would say a few words that I could understand, and then the rest . . . the rest I could not. Don't you know what you said?"

He shook his head. "I never remember afterward. You must try to remember. It's important."

Nalassa settled on her haunches, pleased at whatever opportunity gave her his attention. "They were strange words, my lord—frightening, too, some of them. But it's very hard to remember, since they meant nothing to me."

He took her hand and squeezed it gently. "What is your name?"

"I am Nalassa, daughter of the river god Asopos."

"Nalassa, please try."

She nodded slowly, staring at the ground in front of them. "You still have not told me *your* name."

"I am Proteus, son of Okeanos."

"Lord Proteus!" Her expression mixed surprise and befuddlement. "You are indeed an old one. Pardon, my lord—" She rose to her feet and bowed her head slightly toward him.

Proteus smiled despite himself.

"I'll tell you all I can, Lord Proteus."

He was grinning. "Good. Please do, but sit back down. You make me uncomfortable."

She stiffened at his mild rebuke, but after a moment she shrugged her slender shoulders and complied. Her brows drew together in concentration. "Change," she said slowly. "You used that word . . . *change follows change*—that was one of the things you said. And you said something about the Titans—not just them, but all the gods, I think."

"What about the Titans?"

"Titan against Titan," she said slowly. *"Titan against Titan, god against god.* And there was something about . . . about . . . I remember! *Change follows change—when god devours god."*

She looked up at him. "What does that mean?"

"I don't know. What else?"

"Power, force . . . *Power unleashed, force undreamt*—something like that."

"Please keep trying to remember."

"Something about birds—"

"What kind of birds?"

She frowned, seeking the exact words. *"The gull . . . the gull shall . . . weep."* She moistened her lips. *"The eagle . . . the eagle cease to soar . . . when . . . when . . .* This is it—*when the white mare rears her hooves and the broken willow pierces their hearts.* You said that many times. It's very odd."

Proteus seemed lost in thought for some moments. Finally he looked up. "What else, Nalassa?"

She shook her head abruptly. "That's all I remember. What does it mean?"

"I'm not sure."

She was staring at him. "Proteus," she said, almost to herself. "Lord Proteus, the Prophetic One. I've been trying to remember what I had heard of you. They say you know the future."

He rose to his feet and without looking at her climbed the steep cliff to look out across the plain. She rose to join him, but he climbed back down almost immediately.

"The goddesses have left, and it is time for me to go too."

"You didn't answer, my lord. Do you know the future? Those strange words, do they tell of what is to be?"

He shrugged. "I don't know the future any better than you."

"No, but you speak the future. That must be what they meant when they called you the Prophetic One. You fall down and begin to change shapes, and the words that come from your mouth tell what will be."

He had begun to walk down the valley. He paused and turned to look back at her. "The morning is growing late, and I have far to travel. If you want to continue talking, you'll have to walk with me."

She broke into a broad grin and began self-consciously arranging her disarrayed hair. "If my lord wishes, I will accompany him."

From the grotto she recovered her cloak. She threw it around her shoulders and trotted back toward him. They made their way down the narrow valley, bending aside the small trees and stepping over brush and bushes. A young deer scampered away at their approach, almost from under their feet.

"Tell me of Olympos, Nalassa."

She laughed. "You, one of the greater gods, know far more of Olympos than would a naiad. I spend most of my time with my sisters, or by myself in the forests. I seldom see anyone other than my family. Olympos! Why, I've only been there once, and that was years ago, with my father—and for only a brief visit."

"Come, Nalassa, you're not as provincial as that. You recognized the Muses. Rumor travels fast and far."

"I've heard rumors, that's true—but my mother always says that it is foolish to believe them. Still, the rumors are interesting, and it's interesting to hear of the doings of the Titans and the other gods. Just now everyone is talking about the marriage of Lord Crios to Lady Eurybie. They say it is to be held not on Olympos, but in the Kingdom of Lord Nereus, the sea god. Is that why you've come? To go to the wedding? They say it will be wonderfully fancy—"

"No," he replied, "but I know about the wedding. What else is said?"

She stopped walking and turned to look carefully at him. "I think you have something in mind, my lord. What do you want to know? Why not just ask, rather than waiting for me to stumble on it?"

"You're pouting. Such seriousness is unnatural to your features."

She turned suddenly and made a particularly grotesque face at him. "I'm not at all sure I like you," she said, and began walking ahead of him.

For some time she walked rapidly, without looking back. She wished that she had run harder and faster the night before, that she had taken her first opportunity this morning to slip away, perhaps to find her father and bring him back to punish the insolent ocean god. God of fishes, she thought.

Her feet were beginning to hurt and she found a large outcropping of rock to sit on. She rubbed her feet, glancing up every few seconds to watch as he approached. Part of her wanted to dislike him, if only because he gave her so little attention, but she found herself fascinated by the supple movements of his perfect body as he picked his way among the huge boulders that separated them. The naturalness of movement and perfect symmetry of the bronzed form drew her eyes to it again and again. As he came nearer, the sun picked out blue tints in his hair.

"Why are you tanned?" she asked as he reached her. "Why aren't you milky white, like a fish, from swimming around under the ocean?"

"Too many afternoon naps on the beach, I guess," he said, giving her a wry smile.

They continued walking but still without much conversation. Despite herself she kept going over in her mind the events of the night before. Her eyes kept wandering to his body, until she felt herself beginning to blush. Of course the gods often abandoned clothing of any sort, displaying their male bodies with an openness and naturalness unthinkable to a goddess. Still, Nalassa could not help feeling that she was staring overmuch.

At last they came to a wide gulf that opened into the Aegean through a narrow strait. She sat on a low hill, her toes in the sand.

"Well, Nalassa," he said, "I must leave you now."

"You're going to Olympos?"

He seemed not to want to answer, but finally nodded.

"Good-bye."

"Good-bye, Nalassa. I wish you well."

As she watched he ran toward the shore and dived far out into the glistening blue water. Without intending to, she rose and walked a few steps after him, watching for him to surface.

He came up out of the depths like a dolphin, white spray following him, then disappeared again. When he surfaced the second time he was much farther out. He waved at her, and she found herself waving back excitedly. She watched until he was out of sight, then returned to sit on the small hill, brushing her feet back and forth across the sand.

After a while she drew her knees up under her chin. The

same thoughts ran through her mind. He was thoughtless and arrogant, not really concerned with her at all. She should be glad to see him go back to his ugly fish. She should have run faster; she shouldn't have let him catch her. She had never let anyone else catch her. But she kept remembering the strength of his arms around her, the taste of his mouth on hers, the heat of his body and the rippling of his smooth, vibrant muscles.

Finally she stood up, threw her cloak over her shoulders and straightened her tunic. She began walking toward the north.

"Why shouldn't I visit Mount Olympos if I want to?" she asked herself out loud.

THREE

"I told you," Metis said as she adjusted makeshift clothing around the miniature, shivering god that the Muses called a man. "I found him near a stream, with many others of his kind."

Prometheus and Epimetheus gathered around her as she struggled to form the rectangle of cloth into a crude chiton. The man, recovered from his torpor but dazed by the events of the day, sat almost limply upon Metis's bed, allowing her huge fingers to manipulate him as necessary to make the clothing fit.

Metis had returned with the four goddesses to the palace of Kronos on Mount Olympos. Almost as soon as they reentered the massive walls, she made her way to her own room within the chambers of her sister Klymene.

Klymene was perhaps the loveliest of the many lovely daughters of the Titan Okeanos. If she lacked anything of beauty, she more than compensated for it through the charm of her manner and the sweetness of her disposition. She had married Iapetos, her Titan uncle, and gone to live with him in his brother's palace on Olympos, where she bore four children. Atlas, the eldest, was now fully grown and occupied an apartment of his own. Prometheus and Epimetheus were nearly the same age as Metis—physically and mentally if not chronologically, for the gods do not mature at a consistent rate—while Menoitios still suckled at his mother's breast.

Klymene had found herself longing for the companionship of her sisters and invited some of them to come to Olympos as her guests. Philyra, unmarried and unattached, accepted, and the youthful Metis begged to be allowed to go with her. The two Okeanids joined the household of Iapetos.

Prometheus and Epimetheus had been playing in the atrium, the spacious entrance hall and main room of the apartment. When Metis did not soon reappear from her room after returning from her outing, they followed her there. They found her drying the tiny god-creature after giving it a bath.

"You *will* keep your promise, won't you?" Metis continued as she finished adjusting the miniature chiton and prepared to stitch its edges. "You won't tell anyone about him? You promised."

"We won't tell," Prometheus assured her, leaning forward in his squatting position so that he could more clearly view the creature. "He does look like a god, all cleaned up and dressed. You can't see all the hair on his body. Why is he shivering so?"

The man had partially revived during his bath, trying vainly to escape from the bowl in which Metis had deposited him. Since then he had for the most part remained very still, clutching his arms across his chest. His skin was beginning to show almost a blue tint.

"I don't know. Maybe he's cold." Metis jumped up and ran across the room to one of the oaken chests in which garments of every sort were stored. She found what she was looking for and returned with an odd-shaped fur and a sharp knife. "This should be warm enough." Drawing the small dagger from its sheath, she fell to work cutting and shaping a tiny cloak from the fur.

"But why does he look like a god?" Prometheus asked as she worked.

"What do you want him to look like? A bird?" Epimetheus said, laughing. "Then he'd be a bird and not a tiny god."

"He's a *man*," Metis said. "Melpomene said that's what he is."

"But why does he look like a god?" Prometheus persisted. "Nobody's ever seen a god so tiny. . . ."

Metis fitted the little cloak around the creature and held him in her hands to warm him. "I don't have anything small enough to use as a clasp at the cloak's neck."

"You could sew it," Epimetheus suggested. "You'd have to leave the neck opening big enough for his head to slip through."

"I guess that's what I'll have to do." She lifted the fur back off the man and handed him to Prometheus. "Keep him warm while I finish this," she said.

Prometheus grinned as he took the man in his hands. Epimetheus scowled. "Let me hold him too."

"In a minute," his brother said, gently stroking the creature. "I can't help thinking it means something."

"What means something?" Epimetheus asked.

"That they look like us! What else have I been talking about?"

"I don't know. You're always talking about peculiar things. I'd never have time to think about anything myself if I always listened to you."

"Do you think Lord Kronos would let me keep him?" Metis interrupted, looking up from her sewing.

"I don't know why he shouldn't," Prometheus said.

"Lord Kronos might want to exterminate all of them," Epimetheus said. "Father says it was Lord Kronos who made the other gods hunt down and kill all the monsters."

"They're not all dead. Lord Hyperion still goes hunting for monsters to kill."

"He just likes to be away by himself," Epimetheus said. "He never finds any. They were all killed years ago."

"You don't know that. He may not have found the last of them yet."

"Nobody's found a monster in years. In ages. They're all dead," Epimetheus insisted.

"You don't know that. New ones could be born anytime, just like the men Metis saw."

"But what's this have to do with the men?" Metis asked. "Why should Lord Kronos want to kill them? They aren't monsters."

"Lord Kronos might consider them monsters," Epimetheus said. "He might kill them because they look so much like gods, but aren't gods."

"You don't know they aren't gods," Metis said firmly. "They may be *little* gods."

"Then why do they stay little? Why doesn't this one make himself big?"

"Maybe he doesn't know how. He's only a few days old."

Prometheus was still holding the man against his chest to warm him. "He's starting to look around a little," he said. "He's moving a lot more."

The man had indeed become more active. The bluish tint had left his skin and he was craning his head in every direction to observe the room and his enormous captors. He seemed to be trying to escape Prometheus's restraining fingers.

Metis had just finished stitching the little cloak together near the neck. She gently retrieved the creature, adjusted the cloak around it, and set it down on the floor. It took the man a few seconds to become steady enough to walk. The youthful gods watched quietly as he took a few hesitant steps. As his confidence increased, the man began cautiously to explore the room. At first the unfamiliar clothing impeded his progress, and two or three times he seemed to be in the process of ridding himself of the encumbrance, but each time Metis stopped him.

From outside Metis's room the children heard voices. Klymene and Philyra, who had been elsewhere in the apartment, were coming toward the room.

Metis swooped up the man and thrust him into her basket, which rested upon her bed. She turned to face the door, shielding the basket from view with her body.

A perfunctory knock was almost immediately followed by the door opening wide. Klymene stood in the doorway, Philyra just behind her.

"So here you are—" Klymene began, but her smile faded quickly to an expression of puzzlement as her eyes took in the room and its occupants. The room was exactly what one would fear from a child of Metis's age. Articles of every description lay scattered about it. Metis's herb collection, officially consigned to the ledge of the gallery just outside, had spread to every corner of the room.

Philyra, who felt especially responsible for overseeing her sister's conduct, let out a sigh of exasperation. Klymene, however, seemed more interested in the guilty expressions of the children. A look of suspicion, not unmixed with amusement, came over her face as she moved into the room.

"You left your toys scattered all over the atrium," she began. "I was going to tell you to pick them up before your father gets home. First, though, I'd like to know what you three have been up to.''

The children maintained stony silence˙ as she approached them. A quick glance disclosed the remnants of fur and cloth left lying on the floor near thè bed, along with the thread Metis had used in her sewing. She stopped directly in front of the young goddess.

''You seem strangely stationary for a child with your energetic temperament. Is there something behind you I shouldn't see?''

Metis began to shake her head but nodded instead. She stepped reluctantly aside. Klymene looked at the basket, then back at her young sister. Puzzled, she picked it up and flipped back the lid. As she looked inside she let out a gasp, almost dropping the basket.

''It's a *man*,'' Epimetheus said.

''Metis found it in the forest,'' Prometheus added.

Recovered from her surprise, Klymene peered into the basket again. Philyra joined her. Before long the man had again been freed and was attempting to walk upon the too-yielding surface of the bed.

Metis had to relate again the story of her morning adventure. ''Please don't tell anyone I have him,'' she begged in conclusion. ''Lord Kronos might not let me keep him.''

Philyra turned to Klymene. ''Is that true? Would Lord Kronos disapprove of this odd creature being kept here?''

Klymene shrugged. ''I don't know. I'll ask Iapetos. I don't see why there should be any problem, but he'll know for sure. In the meantime, Metis, keep him out of sight and trouble.''

''Isn't he cute?'' Metis asked, now holding the struggling creature against her breast.

''I suppose so,'' Philyra said without assurance in her voice.

''In a disturbing way,'' Klymene said.

''Why do you think he looks like us, Mother?'' Prometheus asked.

Klymene was stopped short by his question. His questions often had that effect on her. She stared into the handsome face and unknowable eyes of her son, reaching reflexively to brush back the locks of dark hair that covered his forehead.

"I don't know," she said. "But I do know that those toys are still waiting to be picked up."

Reluctantly Prometheus and Epime' :us began walking toward the atrium.

"Aren't you going to help them?" Philyra asked Metis.

"It's all right," Prometheus called back from the doorway. "It's our mess. She didn't even play with the toys today."

As soon as the others had left, Philyra took Metis by the hand and led her toward the bed. They sat side by side.

"Metis," she said, trying to make her voice as indulgent as possible, "I thought we had an understanding between us."

"You mean about the room?" Metis asked. "I'll clean it up."

"Yes, about the room, but also about this creature. While we're here, you're my responsibility. If you get into trouble, it's my fault. Mother was very clear that I should keep careful watch over you."

Metis's lips were pressed together and her eyes cast down.

"And your actions reflect not only on me, but on Klymene too."

"I'll stay out of trouble," Metis said softly, not looking up.

There were noises from the atrium, heavy knocks followed by a deep, masculine voice. Philyra rose and walked to the door to listen. After a moment she disappeared down the hall, only to reappear a few moments later.

"It's Lord Kronos!" she whispered emphatically.

FOUR

Kronos, Lord of the Titans and King of the Gods, stood just inside the doorway as Metis reached the atrium. She had paused only long enough to safely deposit the man within her basket, then followed Philyra back to the main room of the apartment.

He was the largest of all the gods, a giant among giants—tall and very broad-chested, with enormous shoulders and biceps which bulged even at rest. His only clothing was a golden rectangle of cloth wound about his waist and pinned by a simple gold fibula. Thick black hair hung like a mane nearly to his shoulders, merging in places with the curls of his full beard.

"Pardon, Lady Klymene," he was saying as Metis and Philyra edged slowly from the hall into the atrium. "I came in search of your husband, Lord Iapetos. Since he has not yet returned . . ." As he spoke his large, gray eyes relentlessly roamed the room, merely glancing over the divine inhabitants but scrutinizing the less visible corners and the closed and opened doors leading to other chambers. The look was not furtive; there was nothing fearful about it. It personified boldness and intense alertness—the instinctive response of a creature accustomed to finding enemies lurking nearby.

"He should be home soon," Klymene said. "I've been expecting him. I suppose he must still be in his workshop." Only the clutching together of her hands betrayed her nervousness.

"Probably so. That's where I was going," he said, his eyes suddenly returning to Philyra as he spoke. This time they did not flit away. "I thought I would stop on the way, in case he had returned early. . . . You and your sisters grow more lovely each day. The atmosphere of Olympos must be good for the daughters of my brother Okeanos."

Philyra became more and more flustered as he spoke, his eyes never leaving her.

Klymene acknowledged the compliment with a demure smile and slight inclination of her head. "Lord Kronos is too kind."

Metis had edged her way to one side and stood quietly with her back against the wall. Klymene's sons were nowhere in sight; she must have shooed them from the room.

Kronos smiled, and the smile, neither too broad nor too narrow, changed the entire aspect of his magnificent face. The craggy lines of stark majesty softened, now imbued with genuine interest and friendliness.

"Come closer, Philyra," he said. "You have no reason to be bashful about your beauty. Compliments are not to be feared."

Philyra hesitated, but finally managed to glance quickly up at him. "I do not fear them, my lord. I only mistrust them. They are often more kind than truthful."

Kronos turned toward Klymene. "Can she really not know how lovely she is?"

"I am too thin, my lord," Philyra said softly.

The Lord of the Titans carefully appraised her slender body. He shook his head slowly, talking still to Klymene. "She's refreshing. If only the other goddesses were a little less artful and a bit more natural, like your sister. Your father, Lord Okeanos, and your beautiful mother, Lady Tethys, breed fine children. This one, however, must never have looked at herself in a mirror. Too thin, indeed!"

He laughed, still shaking his head. "I seem never to have time to talk with the really interesting members of court—those who cluster and chatter around me take up all my time. I must put a stop to that. I will put a stop to it. . . . Philyra, how long have you been here on Olympos?"

Klymene answered for her. "She and Metis arrived nearly three months ago."

"Three months! I've seen them about the palace, of course—

many times, I suppose—but never really stopped to talk with them. You, child," he said, addressing Metis. "Have you found things to occupy you here?"

Metis nodded. "Yes, my lord, I—"

"Of course you have. You have Klymene's sons to play with, young . . ."

"Prometheus and Epimetheus," Klymene said.

"Yes, young Prometheus and Epimetheus. Fine, handsome boys." He turned back toward Philyra. "Three months, and I've barely had the opportunity to exchange more than a few words with you. This must change. I'm growing tired of the same faces around me all the time, with the same, tired conversation. You must come and dine with me tonight, Philyra—no, not tonight, for I have already promised to let myself be bored. You must breakfast with me tomorrow. I would like to hear about your parents and the briny realm they rule."

Philyra still could not bring herself to look up. "I fear I am a poor conversationalist; my lord."

"Nonsense. You would amuse me even if you never uttered a word, merely by your presence."

With the direct simplicity of a child Metis made her way to one of the ornate divans that lined the walls of the room. She sat down, feeling slighted by the way Kronos steadfastly ignored her. On the other hand, she was thankful not to be the subject of too intense scrutiny.

She fought against an almost overwhelming inclination to lie down as she continued following the conversation.

"It's settled, then," Kronos was saying. "You'll join me tomorrow morning, for breakfast. I'll be awaiting you."

Out of the corner of her eye Metis caught a movement near the opening into the hall. Sharp-eyed Kronos must have seen it too; he was now staring in that direction. A few moments later the movement was repeated, something scampering from behind the leg of a table toward a large amphora. Metis realized almost immediately that it was the man she had thought safely confined within the basket on her bed.

She moved quickly, springing from her seat. The little creature seemed intent upon avoiding capture. Nevertheless she managed after only a moment to scoop it up as it tried to dart from the amphora to the concealment of a number of thick cushions lying upon the floor. She clutched the man to her breast to keep him out of sight, and without a backward glance hurried straight toward the hall and her own room.

"Wait, child," Kronos called after her. "I would see the thing you are carrying. Bring it here."

"It's only one of my toys," she called back, intent on transporting the man out of the room as rapidly as possible.

"Bring it here, child," he repeated, not harshly, but with the self-assurance of one accustomed to instant obedience.

"Metis! "Klymene called after her, shocked that she would ignore the King of the Gods.

Metis hesitated in the doorway but did not turn to face them.

"Lord Kronos would see the creature you found," Klymene said. "Let him see it. Do as he asks!"

With unconcealed reluctance Metis turned and walked slowly toward the imposing figure of the Titan. As she reached him she held the man out in her hand.

An uneven smile touched the lips of the divine king. He took the creature from her with surprising gentleness, held it loosely in one of his enormous hands and studied it intently. Finally he looked up. "This is one of the creatures the Muses discovered. How did you come by it, child?"

"I was with them this morning."

"But they said they had brought none back."

Metis hung her head. "They didn't. I did."

It took him a moment to comprehend her statement. When he did he began to laugh. His laughter was deep, from the chest, with nothing forced or false about it. "They didn't know, then. You smuggled this creature back against their wishes."

Metis only nodded.

"Can it talk?" He held the man up in front of his face and shook it ever so slightly—for a god. The creature seemed to consider it a vigorous jostling, for as soon as the shaking stopped, it tried to free itself from the light grasp of the Titan.

Metis nervously shifted her weight from foot to foot.

"Has it any intelligence? The Muses said the creatures displayed curiosity."

"It would seem to be a bit intelligent," Klymene said, finally managing to edge Metis to one side so that she could take control of the situation before the child offended Kronos. "But we're not yet sure how bright the thing is."

"Very interesting," Kronos said. "Very interesting indeed."

As he began to hand the creature back to Metis, a knock sounded at the door. Responding to Klymene's imploring look, Philyra moved quickly to answer it.

The door opened to reveal the tall, black-mantled figure of Thanatos. With a slight bow he made his way into the room.

"Ah, good, you're here, Lord Kronos," he began in his rapid, intense manner, nearly oblivious to the others in the room. "I must speak with you. I recognized your voice from the corridor."

Kronos grimaced. "What is it? I'm occupied at the moment."

"A discovery, my lord. Something which will interest you greatly."

Frowning and sighing in resignation, Kronos said, "Well, you've tracked me down. Go ahead. What is it?"

Thanatos hesitated and began to stutter. "M-m-my lord, I m-m-must tell you in private. This is not—" He stopped abruptly, all his intense attention focused on a new object, the creature still struggling to escape from Kronos's hand.

The man had continued to try vainly to climb out of the restraining fingers of the god; now he became aware of the new face staring at him. All effort to escape stopped as he began to quiver.

Kronos looked down at him. "The little thing is terrified of you, Thanatos! It's shaking all over in fear."

Kronos started to hand the man back to Metis, but before the exchange could be completed, the long, pale fingers of Thanatos interceded hesitantly. The man began to shriek, his voice surprisingly loud and very shrill.

Kronos glared at Thanatos.

"Please, my lord," Thanatos said, "if—if I might . . . examine . . . this strange creature for a moment." His voice and entire manner were high-strung and his still extended fingers quivered as they drew back from the object of their sudden fascination.

Metis, however, did not hesitate. She plucked the man from Kronos's hand, hugged him to her and ran toward the door.

Kronos turned on Thanatos angrily. "What do you mean by acting like this?"

Thanatos fumbled unsuccessfully for words, his gaze twitching back and forth between Metis and the king.

"Answer me!"

Finally Thanatos recovered his composure enough to say, "My Lord Kronos knows what interest I take in peculiar life forms of every sort." He forced himself to speak slowly. "Please accept my—my abject apologies for my lack of courtesy, but—but I seem to lose control of myself when I encounter something that arouses my interest to the degree that this little creature has aroused it. I—I have never seen such a thing before. I would very much like to examine it."

Klymene had intercepted Metis before she could disappear from the room. The child was shaking her head as she faced Thanatos.

"No, he's mine. He's mine and I don't want you to touch him. You frighten him. He's afraid of you. He's still shaking."

Thanatos edged toward Kronos. "If I might speak with you about this privately for a moment. . . ."

Kronos frowned. "You always want to speak in private. Why must you be so secretive? It's very impolite."

Klymene was trying to take the man from Metis, determined that the creature must be handed over if Kronos so asked. Kronos held up his hand and waved her away. "Let the child be," he told her, his expression clearly showing his displeasure with the commotion Thanatos had caused.

Thanatos fidgeted, rubbing his hands together and doing his best to communicate without words to his master how imperative it was that they talk privately. At last he leaned toward Kronos and whispered in the god's ear. Kronos frowned still more deeply, then sighed.

He turned toward the sisters. "I've stayed too long already. Lady Klymene, if I should miss your husband, please tell him that I'm anxious to see him. Lady Philyra, I shall be looking forward to your sweet face across from me at breakfast tomorrow." His eyes moved to Metis. "Young lady, please keep me informed of your tiny ward. I'm interested in everything that happens on Mount Olympos."

He turned toward the door. Thanatos opened it for him and, without having directed a single word to the inhabitants of the apartment, followed his master out into the corridor.

FIVE

The Titan Iapetos had his workshop on one of the lower levels of the palace of Kronos, where most of the dark rooms were given over to storage. Here the cast-off possessions of the gods lay half forgotten alongside raw materials of every sort.

Piles of thick pelts and tanned hides reached nearly to the ceiling. Large lidded baskets, stacked one atop the other, were filled with wool, flax, or finest silk; huge wax-sealed amphorae held dyes and perfumes. Elsewhere row upon row of teak, cypress, and ebony, brought from vast distances, lay ready for some god to cut and shape. Elm and cedar trees, stripped of their branches, were neatly stacked for the kiln or hearth, while bins of copper ore awaited smelting. There were whole rooms of gold and silver and ivory. Other rooms overflowed with chests of precious stones.

It was to this level that Kronos made his way, the natural briskness of his pace forcing the lanky Thanatos into an uncomfortable trot at his side. They descended wide, spiraling staircases and traversed lengthy corridors. As they walked, Thanatos turned continually to reassure himself that they could not be overheard.

"The little godling can wait," Kronos said gruffly.

"Well, yes, Lord Kronos, but I think if you understood the possible importance—"

"But it *can* wait?"

"Well, yes, my lord, but—"

"Then, vulture-loving child of Nyx, *let* it wait!"

"But Lord Kronos, this could be an important piece of the puzzle. The sooner—"

"You should take a lesson from your less inquisitive brother," Kronos said, his tone now good-humored. He nodded down the corridor in front of them. "He never lets himself get unduly enthusiastic."

A shapeless mass covered a shadowed bench in an alcove just ahead. As they approached, the gray mass began to stir, rising up on the bench. Kronos slowed to a stop as a puffy face appeared from amid the wrinkled folds of a faded cloak. Bleary eyes blinked at them.

"Have the benches grown any softer, Momos?" Kronos asked without the suggestion of a smile.

Momos rubbed the sleep from his eyes, grumbling as he made vain gestures toward smoothing the cloak over his shoulders. "No, they haven't," he said. "The floors are too hard too. You should see to them. They make too much noise."

"Now the floors are making noise?" Kronos asked. "Has someone taught them to talk?"

"They make noise when anyone walks on them," Momos explained.

"Ah, I understand," Kronos said, chuckling. "The marble slaps too hard against bare feet."

"Against sandals too. You should make quiet marble."

Thanatos, who despised his brother, glared with unconcealed contempt at the paunchy, rumpled god. "If you'd sleep in your own bed, you fat fool, it wouldn't matter how much noise anyone made in the corridors. Why do you think you have your own quarters?"

Momos rose from his seat with what he must have considered great dignity. "That's another thing. This palace is too big. Every place is too far from every other place."

Kronos laughed with genuine amusement. "I shall remember that when we build a new palace."

Momos nodded. Grumbling to himself, he shambled off down the corridor in the opposite direction. Kronos watched almost until he was out of sight.

"I can't imagine why you even talk to that fool," Thanatos said.

Kronos shrugged. "He's the only one of the gods I can almost trust."

"Trust! You trust that doddering, fat . . . All he ever does is complain and criticize. He criticizes you more than anyone else."

"Not trust—*almost* trust. He never tries to hide what he thinks."

Thanatos shook his head in bewilderment. Kronos began walking again, and Thanatos hurried after him.

"The other thing I wanted to tell you," he said, "it's the most amazing discovery. . . ."

"Can it wait too?"

"Well, yes, I guess it can, but—"

They entered the stairway that led to the lower levels. Kronos took a torch from its sconce and gestured to Thanatos to do the same.

"But it is absolutely amazing. When I tell you—"

"But it *can* wait?"

"Yes, Lord Kronos."

"Very good, Thanatos. In two or three centuries you may acquire a modicum of patience. It's an important virtue, absolutely essential for the fulfillment of any ambitious project. I must give you a full dissertation upon its merits. You will remind me."

"Yes, Lord Kronos," Thanatos said glumly.

They had almost reached Kronos's destination. "I don't know why you've insisted on walking all this way with me," he told Thanatos, "but you can make yourself useful. Go through the storerooms and find the most beautiful mirror there, of gold. It should be full length, for a goddess to properly appreciate her own appearance, but I suppose we'll have to be satisfied with whatever you can find. Dust and polish it, then deliver it to Lady Philyra, the sister of Klymene."

"But my lord, that could take hours. The discovery I have made—"

"I will come to your chambers when I've finished," Kronos said with a finality tantamount to dismissal.

Turning his back on Thanatos, Kronos entered the workshop of Iapetos without announcing himself, carefully closing the door behind him. He paused by the forge, first placing his hand near it, then touching the side; the metal was barely warm. No detail escaped him as he moved through the apartment.

He found his brother in one of the rear rooms, hard at work. Nearly thirty seconds passed before Iapetos became aware of his presence. With a quick movement he threw a rag over something on his bench and turned to meet the intruder.

"Oh, it's you, brother," he said, swirling around on his stool and standing.

Kronos came toward the workbench and lifted the rag from the object it had hastily concealed. He nodded approvingly and took the object in his hands, almost with reverence. "It's finished?" he asked.

Iapetos nodded. "I haven't ornamented the hilt yet, but aside from that—"

"That doesn't matter. No one else has been here? No one knows of its existence?"

"No one but us," Iapetos said softly as Kronos searched his aquiline features for any trace of duplicity.

Kronos had ensconced his torch in the atrium of the workshop, and now he took the long, heavy weapon in both hands and held it near the oil lamp that burned upon the table. The bronze blade glistened.

"It still needs a bit more sharpening," Iapetos said.

Kronos shrugged. "You can do that later." He ran the edge of his thumb along the blade, then held the weapon extended from one hand as he tested the balance.

"This is what you had in mind?" Iapetos asked. "This one is satisfactory?"

"Yes, I think so. What have you done with the other?"

Iapetos made his way to a corner of the room. From behind a jumble of objects he withdrew a similar weapon, tall as a full-grown holly tree. The blade was straight, lacking the long, gradual curve of the newer one. Iapetos brought it to Kronos.

The Lord of the Titans held one in each hand, making slow, slashing movements with the swords. Then he lay the new, curved one on the workbench and took the other in both hands. Very deliberately he snapped its bronze blade across his knee.

"Melt the pieces down," he instructed, handing Iapetos the two halves. "Melt them down so that no one may ever look upon the bronze and guess what it once was."

Iapetos nodded in assent, his eyes peering into those of his brother. "When I began this task for you, I promised to abide by your wishes. The curved blade satisfies you more, but the straight one might have been of some use—if there is any use for a knife longer than a leg." As he spoke, Iapetos seated himself in front of his bench and began to hone the sword's edge with a stone.

"It's my wish, brother," Kronos said, "that only one of these long knives ever exist. The other must vanish as though it had never been made. And no one must ever know about this one."

"*I* know," Iapetos observed.

"What is known can be forgotten."

"Perhaps, in time," Iapetos said. "But for the present I can't help being curious. What is the purpose for such a blade? It would be of little use for the tasks normally performed by a knife. An ax would do better for chopping wood."

"There is no need for you to know its purpose, brother. I needed the skill of your hands, and you have given it to me admirably. I also need your silence. And loyalty. Do I have them?"

Iapetos continued sharpening the long, bronze blade, now moving the stone in light, polishing strokes. "Were the gradual curve of the blade not important," he continued, "you would have accepted my first effort. A curved blade would be excellent for slashing." He looked up. "For clearing away bushes and saplings, for instance."

Kronos did not answer.

Iapetos applied the final strokes of the stone, then held the sword upright by the hilt. "It would make a fearful weapon with which to attack a god, wouldn't it, brother?" He turned it around and handed it hilt first to Kronos. "Of course, you have no need of that."

Kronos studied him through half-lidded eyes. Finally he said, "I want you to pledge me your silence."

"I've already pledged it," Iapetos said. "You shall have it. No one shall learn of this through me."

"You will obliterate every trace of the first sword?"

Iapetos nodded.

"And your loyalty? Do I still have that?"

"As much as ever."

Kronos's face unclouded and he laid an affectionate hand on his brother's shoulder. "Good. I need you." He hefted the sword again. "I'm very satisfied. You've never done better work. I'll take it with me now."

"I can still embellish the handle."

"No, it's not necessary. This is fine. Do you have a cloak? I didn't bring one, and I need something to conceal this."

They walked together to one of the other rooms, where Iapetos lent him a long, dark mantle. Kronos wrapped it about the sword in such a way that none could determine what lay within.

Just before they reached the main door Kronos turned toward him again. "You will take care of the other one—soon?"

Iapetos nodded. "Today. Before I leave here."

"Good." Kronos clapped him on the shoulder again. "Good, brother, I know I can always count on you." He turned and left the room.

For a few minutes Iapetos stared vacantly at the closed door, then slowly made his way back to his workroom. From behind a mound of clutter he brought out a third sword, identical to the second. He carried it to his bench and began to sharpen it.

SIX

Just outside the door of Iapetos's workshop Kronos was accosted by Thanatos, who had been waiting for him to reappear.

"What are you doing here?"

"I've been waiting for you, Lord Kronos, to talk to you as you walk back."

Kronos glared at him in annoyance. "What about the mirror I asked you to find?"

"Here it is." Thanatos brought out an enormous mirror of polished gold from among the shadows. "I found it without much difficulty, and have been dusting and polishing it while I waited."

"Do as I told you," Kronos commanded, keeping the cloak-wrapped sword to one side, where Thanatos would not see it. "Bring it to Lady Philyra—now!"

"Y-y-yes, my lord."

Kronos stood watching as the god hefted the heavy mirror and stumbled down the corridor with it. He waited until Thanatos had had time to get all the way up the stairs, then proceeded hurriedly to his own chambers on the uppermost floor of the palace.

Passing quickly through innumerable outer rooms, he came at last to a small, nearly empty one. Laying the sword on a table, the Titan went to a cupboard and withdrew a large object draped in black. He carried it to another table, depos-

ited it there, and from an adjoining room brought a stool. He
worked with these until he was satisfied with their arrange-
ment. The stool stood atop the table and the draped thing atop
the stool, the whole reaching nearly to the height of the King
of the Gods.

He stood back a little and pulled the cloth free to reveal the
huge clay bust of a god, a god peculiarly free of facial
features. It had eyes and nose and mouth, but portrayed no
one.

From the other table he took the sword, unwrapping it and
holding it loosely at his side. He positioned himself in front
of the bust, the sword almost dangling from his hand. Twice
he reached forward and adjusted the bust so that it faced
exactly the direction he wished. He stared into the lifeless
clay eyes.

Suddenly the sword flew back to a position far behind his
head, then swept forward in a whirling arc. The clay head
rolled free, striking the floor with a thud. Part of the clay
shoulder followed it down.

For a few moments the Lord of the Titans stood staring at
the headless figure.

He lay the sword aside and picked up the moist clay.
His fingers trembled as he began to reshape it and work it back
onto the bust. When he had it firmly reattached he took up his
position again. Again the sword whirled and the clay head
thudded to the floor.

For nearly an hour he worked without stopping, reshaping
and decapitating the senseless clay until the bust ceased to
resemble anything divine.

He allowed himself to sit quietly in a thickly cushioned
chair for ten or fifteen minutes, his thoughts clustering fast
and thick. Finally, with a deep sigh, he rose and put away the
clay and the sword. He locked them both within the cupboard.

Thanatos was awaiting him in the hall, pacing nervously.

"There you are, my lord," he said as Kronos appeared
from one of the doors. "This way, my lord. . . ."

"Did you deliver the mirror?"

"Mirror? Oh, yes, as soon as I left you. This discovery
may be the most important yet. It's another—"

"Did she like it? Was she pleased?"

"Pleased? Who? Oh, you mean the Okeanid."

"Yes, the Okeanid Philyra," Kronos said crossly. "Does she like the mirror?"

"I suppose so, my lord." Thanatos looked at him with a puzzled expression.

"You suppose so!"

"Yes, my lord," Thanatos said, nodding. "It's an attractive piece of furniture, for those who care about such things."

"Didn't she say anything? Didn't you notice how she reacted when you gave it to her? Did her eyes light up? Did she smile?"

"She said it was lovely and that I should thank you. Yes, I think that's what she said. As to whether or not she smiled, I really didn't notice. But as I was saying, my lord, this discovery presents not only a new part to the puzzle, but one that we did not even suspect existed."

They had reached the entrance of the apartment in which Thanatos was allowed to live and work. Pushing open the enormous double doors, Thanatos stood to one side to allow Kronos to precede him.

"This discovery of yours," the Titan said, "it better be important. I'm growing weary of your pestering."

"It's very important." Thanatos followed his master through the open doors and pushed them closed.

The small apartment, one of the suites set aside for Kronos himself, was fitted and furnished in gold and ivory, ebony and teak. Now it was cluttered to overflowing and thick with dust and debris.

"Clean this place up," the Titan grumbled.

"Of course, my lord; as soon as I can find time."

They continued through the series of rooms to the bed-chamber, which testified even more forcefully, not to the laziness of the occupant, but to his singlemindedness. Precious moments could not be squandered on anything as insignificant as cleanliness.

A massive bronze door blocked their way at the rear of the bedchamber. Thanatos ran his fingers along a portion of the nearby wall in search of a hidden catch. A click sounded and the heavy door swung inward.

Kronos recoiled at the dark portal, the odor of decay billowing out from the opening.

"Can't you do something about this smell?" he demanded.

Thanatos seemed not to hear him. He was already busy

lighting the lamps that were set in niches all around the walls. At the noise of his movements something began to moan softly and make muffled, whispering sounds.

Kronos forced himself to look slowly around the room. It was crowded with brass tables and cages of living animals, birds and mammals of many kinds. One table held a long row of brass instruments; light glittered from their cutting edges. Most of the other tables were covered with neatly dissected animal corpses. Usually the removed organs lay neatly arranged along one side of the opened body. Many were in an advanced state of decay, with flesh now browned and desiccated.

Kronos stepped over an almost-filled bucket of congealed blood as he moved to pick up one of the oil lamps. The whispering sounds had continued, and he followed them back into a dark recess of the room, thrusting the lamp forward to dispel the darkness.

"Over here, my lord," Thanatos was saying.

"Can't you stop this noise?" Kronos said, distressed by the entire atmosphere of the room. As he spoke, the light fell upon the decapitated head of a god. It hung by the hair from a peg in the wall, a tiny, completely formed body dangling from its neck.

"It's only Oizys. Come see this, my lord."

Kronos drew back. "What does he want? He's trying to say something." He watched in horror as the flabby lips moved soundlessly.

Thanatos came to Kronos's side, intent upon leading him to the other side of the room. "He can't talk yet. His body hasn't regenerated fully enough. The lungs are too small to make words, so he makes little whispering or moaning sounds as best he can. He's probably hungry again."

"How long has it been since you've fed him?"

Thanatos shrugged. "A few days, I guess. I have to feed the others or they'll die, but sometimes I skip him."

Kronos's face hardened in indignation as Oizys ceased trying to speak and began to whimper. "Why don't you feed him, then?"

"I'll feed him later, my lord. Right now I want to show you—"

"Feed him now, Thanatos—feed all of these creatures—or I'll see to it that you don't eat yourself for a week."

Thanatos, who sometimes forgot to eat for days at a time, hurried to fulfill his master's command. He located the bag of grain that he kept for the animals and dumped a large quantity into a flat pan. He made a circuit of the room, tossing food into the cages. The birds began to flutter excitedly, the pigs to grunt. Finally he rejoined Kronos, placing the pan on the top of one of the tables.

"I can't understand how you can stand to be in this place," Kronos said, his eyes returning again and again to the oval face and flabby lips of the head.

"My lord found it interesting enough when I first showed him what happens when a god's head and body are severed."

An almost imperceptible shudder ran through the King of the Gods. "Feed Oizys quickly so you can show me this new thing that you think is so important. I want to get out of this dreadful room. I warn you, my patience is growing short."

Thanatos lifted the head of his brother down by the hair and lay it face down in the pan. Immediately Oizys began to grunt and crunch the grain in ravenous abandon.

Without a second glance at the creature, Thanatos led Kronos toward the far side of the room. The location and darkness had conspired until this moment to hide the thing upon the table from the Titan.

"Here it is, my lord," Thanatos said with a flourish of the lamp he held in his hand.

"What . . . ?" Kronos moved closer to peer down at what seemed to be a divine body. The eyes were open and staring blankly. The lips were drawn back in a humorless grin. One hand hung limply off the side of the table, but when he touched it, he discovered it was not limp at all. It was stiff and cold.

Kronos drew away, a terrible oath slipping from his lips. "What is it?" he asked, almost whispering.

"A nymph, my lord. Or at least it was. It's dead now."

Kronos was shaking his head. "No. No, that isn't a nymph. At least not like any I've ever seen. Look at the hair. It's white. And the skin is dried out and wrinkled."

Thanatos nodded. "Nevertheless it's a nymph. A dead nymph."

"That can't be," Kronos said. "Nymphs are not animals. They are goddesses—less powerful than other goddesses, perhaps, but still divine. They are immortal."

"That's what everyone has always thought. Until now."

"Maybe she's only asleep, unconscious."

"She isn't asleep," Thanatos assured him. "If you lean close to her you can already detect the odor of decay. Her body has begun to decompose." He grinned broadly. "She's dead, my lord."

"Detect the odor!" Kronos exclaimed in a suppressed voice. "How can anyone distinguish an individual smell here?"

"My nose is very acute. You can take my word for it, she's very dead." He was almost gloating over his discovery now.

Kronos stared down at the corpse. Finally he shook his head again. "There's some mistake. She was some kind of freak. The gods are immortal. They don't die like animals. They don't become meat for jackals."

"That could be true, my lord. Still, it is a very important piece of information, even if she was not a typical nymph. I think you're wrong, though."

"But why does she look like that?"

"Part of her appearance is due simply to her being dead. But the white hair and wrinkled skin—they're what make you doubt she was a normal nymph. Perhaps you've never noticed, but there is a similar thing that happens to animals when they live to be very old. Their bodies begin to wear out—somewhat as flowers wilt or trees die branch by branch. I think the same thing must have happened to her."

"But why hasn't it ever happened before?"

"There always has to be a first time. I think this is it. If I'm right, other nymphs—the oldest of them—will begin to wear out, just as this one must have. She needn't even be the first, for that matter. Living as they do—by themselves for the most part—a number may have withered and died without anyone being aware of it. I do know that she died from the inside—there are no external wounds."

Kronos only stared down at the once beautiful body.

"That, of course, leads to the next question," Thanatos continued. "If she could die, could she be killed?"

"Who was she?" Kronos asked suddenly.

Thanatos shrugged. "Just one of the thousands of nymphs who teem among the hills and valleys. I found her body in Aetolia, where my servants had discovered it."

"The vultures," Kronos said.

L.O.T.C.P.—3

Thanatos nodded. "No one else was around, not for a very long distance. No one but you and I know of this."

"Are you certain she isn't asleep?" Kronos asked.

"I'll prove it to you," Thanatos said, plucking from a nearby table a sharp, gleaming instrument. He ran the edge along the forearm of the corpse so that the flesh opened to a fair depth. "See, the ichor doesn't flow, even from a relatively deep wound. It only oozes out. . . ." He performed the same operation on his own forearm without the slightest hesitation, cutting not quite as deeply. "See, the ichor flows out immediately." He displayed his arm.

Kronos watched in shocked fascination as the thick, translucent substance that is the immortal blood of the gods welled from the long cut and began to run down Thanatos's arm.

Thanatos wrapped his arm in a makeshift bandage. "The questions raised by this discovery are fascinating, and it will take a long time and much more research to answer them. Can all nymphs die? Can they be killed, or only die of old age? If nymphs can die, can the other lesser gods? Are all of the gods mortal to some degree?" He stared into Kronos's face, a razor smile spreading over his lips. *"Can the gods be killed?"*

Kronos wanted to look away from this creature who spoke of death and decay so offhandedly.

Thanatos walked partway across the room, Kronos following him, glad to be away from the nymph's corpse. Thanatos stopped beside the headless body of Oizys.

"It's been two months now since I cut off Oizys's head, but his body remains imperishable. If I cut it, ichor flows, just as though it still had a head and were completely alive. After a day or two the wound heals completely. The heart continues to beat—very slowly. Yet it hasn't begun to regenerate a head. I suppose the head will grow back a completely new body and this body will remain just as it is, lying here and twitching occasionally—perhaps forever."

He spun around to face Kronos, his face and hands animated by intense interest. "The power of regeneration must be centered in the brain—but not completely so. See where I amputated his finger—it's coming along nicely and soon will be full size again." He rubbed his hands together. "There's so much to study. Scars, for instance. I had to inflict twenty-seven cuts on the body before I could get one to scar. That may mean that the regeneration response works imperfectly, that it sometimes makes a mistake. But many experiments still have to be performed to be certain.''

The head of Oizys had begun to make low noises again. Thanatos went to it, yanked it out of the pan of grain, and hung it back on the wall.

Kronos stood brooding over what he had seen and heard. At last he said, ''She died from living too long?''

''That's my first thought, but I must have time to make experiments. I want to see how the body decays. That could provide important clues. I've been unable to kill Oizys, even when I cut his skull in half. He just went into some kind of deep sleep until the two halves grew back together properly. . . . Still, if you give me time, it's very possible that I may find the secret of killing a god.''

''What an awful gift you dangle before me.''

''Gift, my lord?''

''Yes, with your studies, should they succeed.''

''I don't understand. You mean if I learn how a god may be killed? That would be a powerful weapon, and would repay you for allowing me to make my experiments here.''

''Why are the gods *gods*?'' Kronos went on. ''How do they differ from animals? Why are they deathless?''

''You said the knowledge might be useful to you. . . .''

''Indeed, it very well might be—why else would I put up with this carrion room of yours? The nature of life, of mortality and immortality—those are things fitting for the King of the Gods to know. The limits of immortality! I have many enemies, and such knowledge could be a potent weapon indeed. Cleave a divine head in half and the god is incapacitated until the halves heal back together. Decapitate him and his body flops to the floor, powerless against you. Not pretty things to consider, but potentially very useful.''

''But Lord Kronos, it would be ever so much more efficient if you could kill your enemy.''

Kronos shook his head sadly. ''You don't understand, do you? You tell me blithely that the gods may not be immortal after all. This one nymph has died for some reason or other, and perhaps you can find a way that even the great gods can be killed. But death is a double-edged dagger. If I can kill my enemies—my enemies can kill me! If they can die, then I too can die—you can die!''

Thanatos's pale, narrow face watched unblinkingly, polite but unperturbed.

"No, you really don't understand." Kronos shrugged. "I've seen enough. Keep me informed, but I don't want to have to come back here unless absolutely necessary. No one saw you bring the nymph?"

"No, my lord. I was very careful. I concealed both of us in dark clouds."

"Good. No one must learn of this." Kronos began to leave the room.

"A moment more, Lord Kronos," Thanatos said as he followed him.

In the bedchamber Kronos paused, listening impatiently.

"This new creature, the one Metis discovered . . ."

Kronos nodded. "What about it?"

"I must have it."

"Why?"

"To learn what it is. To dissect it and see how it differs from the nymph and Oizys, and from animals."

Kronos thought for a moment. At last he said, "Do what you must. But don't draw attention to yourself, and don't involve me in what you do. You're tolerated here because I need your work—the knowledge it promises. I make no pretense of liking it. You must be discreet."

"Yes, my lord, I will. One last thing. I must establish the mortality or immortality of nymphs, and to do that I must have another to experiment on."

Kronos shuddered, turning away and walking toward the front of the apartment. Thanatos followed directly behind him.

"Well, my lord? May I acquire the things I need to continue my work?"

In front of the main door Kronos paused. "Do what you think necessary, but let no one discover it. I don't even want to know about it."

He turned and left the apartment of Thanatos, a disconcerting, churning sensation deep within him.

SEVEN

Proteus, the shape changer, moved effortlessly through the blue depths of the Aegean. Slow, powerful strokes of his huge tail fins sent him skimming along just above the languidly waving growths of the sea-bottom plain. Silent, rainbow-colored fish frolicked about him or followed in his wake.

Coral-covered cairns of rock rose nearby like ghostly castles. An eel, startled at his approach, sought shelter within the crevices. A scarlet, spiked creature watched him from unblinking eyes.

Even his brief, overnight sojourn on land had left him longing for the magnificent solitude of the blue depths, where even sound seemed to move at a more leisurely pace. The enchanted vistas of sunken mountain and valley calmed him and quieted his apprehensions.

He traveled slowly, perhaps because of the mild uneasiness with which he looked forward to arriving on Mount Olympos. More than once he had to conceal himself when a golden-haired Nereid came within sight. Sometimes he lolled behind an outcropping of rock until she swam away; other times he metamorphosed himself into a dolphin or other sea denizen to escape her notice.

Although he intended to visit his brother-in-law Nereus, the king of the deep Aegean, he preferred to conceal his presence in the area until the time of that visit, after he had been to Olympos.

Tranquil hours slipped away as he swam, until at last he neared his destination. He came up from the water draped in seaweed and waded toward the shore of a shaded cove. A few hours remained until twilight. He located a cave, and drawing himself up into it, fell quickly asleep.

When he awakened, night had fallen. He came out of the cave and stood for a few minutes surveying his surroundings. The moon had risen, full and clear. Moonlight speckled the sea with silver.

Mount Olympos began almost at the beach and stretched more than twenty-five miles inland, its many peaks thrusting upward toward heaven like the fingers of a gigantic rock hand. An immense, ragged gorge faced him; beyond it precipitous limestone walls rose nearly two miles into the sky, disappearing among dark clouds.

With a deep sigh Proteus allowed himself a last, lingering look at the sea. Then he transformed himself into a gull and began the arduous ascent, flying just above the dark forests that clung to the mountain slopes. The powerful wings of the sea bird carried him both inland and upward, toward the home of the Titans.

Innumerable small streams cascaded downward, cutting deep channels. Whenever possible he followed these paths, skimming along above the water. As he rose, the dark forest growths thinned and finally vanished completely. It grew cold, and the air thinned. Clouds clustered around the mountain peaks.

Above the clouds began the precinct of the gods. The air grew pleasantly warm and thick again; sweet smelling, too, with the slightest suggestion of the odor of pansies. The sky above was completely clear, its velvet blackness studded with a million stars.

Now, more than ever, he flew close to the face of the cliff, hugging the shadows. Ahead of him stood the palace of Olympos, bathed yellow gold in the moonlight. It seemed to grow out of the mountain peak, tier upon tier partially carved from the rock summit, partially constructed from huge limestone blocks.

He settled amid the shadows and carefully observed the long, narrow galleries that ran along the outside of each floor of the palace. There, or within the rooms just beyond the galleries, he could discern moving figures, and so he was forced to move forward stealthily. He took on the form of a serpent and slithered closer, shielded by rocks and boulders.

When he was quite close he paused to more carefully observe the inhabitants of the apartments facing him. One of these apartments particularly drew his attention, and he began making his way in its direction. At the base of the palace wall he resumed the shape of a gull and flew almost straight upward. He lighted first upon the marble balustrade, then dropped to the gallery floor as he reassumed his natural shape. Silently he moved to a point from which he could observe the interior of the apartment.

A youthful goddess laughed gaily as she lay on her bed. A tiny creature shaped like a god was walking on her stomach, and she kept catching it as it started to fall. Proteus studied her features until he was certain of her identity, then stepped boldly into the room.

"You seem to have made a pet of that one."

The goddess sat up, sending the man on her stomach falling. She managed to catch him in midair and set him down quickly beside her as she turned to face the intruder.

"Who are—" As she spoke, her expression changed from surprise and indignation to puzzlement, then to recognition. "Proteus!" she exclaimed, leaping from the bed and running toward him.

She threw herself into his arms. He lifted her up and swung her around twice before setting her back on her feet and holding her at arm's distance to look at her.

"You've grown so much, I wasn't sure I recognized you," he said. "You'll be full grown before long."

"I recognized you right away—well, almost right away. How could I forget my favorite brother, even if this is only the third time I've seen him?"

"Is it only the third time?"

She nodded emphatically, managing to look reproachful at the same time. "I ought to scold you. Anyone would think you dislike your family. How are Mother and Father? Have you seen them?"

He nodded. "The same as always."

"You mean they're fighting every minute of the day and night. But why are you here? I can't imagine anything that could get you to Olympos. Wait till Philyra hears— What am I thinking of? She's in the next room. I'll get her."

But before she reached the door, his fingers closed around her wrist and held her back. "No, Metis. Don't call her. At least not yet."

"But she'll be delighted to see you. And so will Klymene."

He was shaking his head. "Not now. I don't want anyone else to know I'm here."

"I don't understand. Why don't you want to see them?"

He put his hands on her shoulders. "Metis, there's something peculiar going on here. At least I have reason to believe there is. Lord Okeanos has sent me to find his friend, the sea god Aigaion. Until I've had time to discover what the situation is, I want my presence to be kept a secret."

"Aigaion was here," Metis said. "I saw him when we first arrived, but he must have left. I haven't seen him since then."

"Neither has anyone else. That's why our father sent me."

Metis's eyes grew wide. "What do you think happened to him?"

Proteus shrugged. "It's said he displeased Kronos."

"You think Lord Kronos has done something to him? Imprisoned him? But wouldn't all Olympos be talking about it? Wouldn't I have heard?"

Proteus shrugged again.

"But why keep your presence a secret from Philyra and Klymene?"

"Metis, you're the first friendly face I've encountered. If not for that—and the bit of assistance I require—you might not know either."

She grinned back at him. "How can I help?"

"I need information and shelter. May I stay here tonight, after I've had a look around?"

"Certainly!"

"Good. I also need to know where the apartments of the Titans are located. Kronos is still on the uppermost level, I presume."

She nodded and proceeded as best she could to give him the information he required, often elaborating unnecessarily. He let her continue uninterrupted.

"Very good, Metis," he told her when she finished. "I should be able to find my way now."

While they had been talking, the creature called a man had managed to slip down the side of the bed to the floor. He was exploring the far corner of the room when Metis noticed him. She picked him up and held him against her breast.

Proteus walked back toward the gallery and Metis followed.

"You will come back here tonight?" she asked.

He nodded. "But don't wait up for me. I'm going now to see what can be learned among the shadows."

"Shadows?"

"That's a delicate way of saying I have a lot of snooping to do, a lot of listening at doorways. Before the night is over, I hope to know more about Olympos than the King of the Gods himself."

"Be careful," she said. "I think Lord Kronos could be very dangerous."

An expression of deadly seriousness flickered across his face. He stooped and kissed her lightly on the cheek. "You said the chambers of Crios are on this floor. Which way?"

She pointed to the left. "You could follow the gallery, except for the partitions."

As she watched, he transformed himself into a gull and flew in the direction she had indicated.

EIGHT

There were twelve Titans, children of Gaia and Ouranos—six male and six female—the most powerful of the gods, the lords of the world. Vast ages before, when the earth still teamed with primordial monsters, Okeanos, the eldest of the Titans, had withdrawn with Tethys, his wife and sister, to rule over their wide, watery domain. Kronos, succeeding his father as King of the Gods, led the other Titans to their new home in the palace on Olympos. With the exceptions of Mnemosyne, who had never married, and of Crios, who would soon wed the sea goddess Eurybie, Titan married Titaness—Kronos and Rhea, Hyperion and Thea, Koios and Phoibe, Iapetos and Themis; but eventually Iapetos put aside his first wife, who was barren, and took instead the Okeanid Klymene, his niece.

It was these ten, in particular, that Proteus wanted to locate among the inhabitants of the palace.

He darted away from Metis, flying along the balcony railing and swerving out around the partitions that separated the galleries into private sections. Around the far side of the building he located the chambers of Crios without difficulty. Still in the form of a gull, he perched outside the first lighted room he came to.

The Titan, however, lay stretched upon a divan, dozing lightly. Proteus allowed himself a few minutes to study Crios's face and form, then spreading his wings, dropped silently down to the floor below.

For nearly two hours he flitted from apartment to apartment, acquainting or reacquainting himself with many of the
occupants of the palace of Kronos upon Mount Olympos.
Koios sat distractedly with his wife Phoibe as she sewed and
tried to discuss domestic affairs with him. The nine Muses, in
groups of two or three, chattered incessantly, their conversations occasionally interspersed with short bursts of song.
Sometimes the rooms fronting on the gallery were vacant, and
more than once Proteus crept recklessly into an apartment to
listen at the door of an inner room.

After completing his initial circuit of the lower levels of the
palace, he turned his attention upward, intending now to
investigate the chambers of Hyperion. His route brought him
back near the apartment of Crios, and a strident voice led him
to perch again outside the large atrium.

Crios was awake now, and decidedly unhappy. Additional
lamps had been lit, and the Titan was sitting on a three-legged
stool, his elbows on his knees and his face in his hands as
Eurybie, sister of Nereus the sea god, paced the room in front
of him. Her full, golden hair flailed around her as she moved.

"Well," she demanded, her fists coming to rest on her
stately hips, "are you just going to sit there?"

He looked up at her slowly. "At least after we're married
I won't have to see you as much. I don't know why I ever let
myself get talked into this." His low voice was filled with
bitterness.

Eurybie was tall and very beautiful, with a robust figure
that seemed doubly voluptuous within the clinging folds of
the peplos she wore. "You really are a spineless wretch,"
she told him, only occasionally favoring him with a glance as
she paced the room. "You know very well why you're
marrying me. Because your brother told you to. And you dare
not disobey him."

Crios only glared sullenly.

"You don't think I'm pleased about having you for a husband,
do you? Would I have chosen you if I had any other choice . . . ?
Oh, I wish I had been born a god instead of a goddess!"

Crios looked up. He was of middle height and slender, with
a slight paunch. His shoulders slumped and he had the habit
of watching the floor when he walked. "That, my lady, is my
fondest wish also," he said softly. "But why do we have to
talk about all this? It was settled long ago."

"Yes, but your brothers want to talk some more." Eurybie's voice became patronizing. "They implore your attendance. I suppose they'll miss your sparkling wit. All that's required of you is your presence. I'll do all the talking for both of us. You won't have to stammer out more than *hello* and *good-bye*. . . ."

"Then just go without me. I'm weary of these continual machinations. If this keeps up, I'll find some cave to live in, far from all of you."

She laughed, a flighty, girlish laugh completely unsuited to both her personality and appearance. "You're welcome to your cave, once we're married and I'm safely a member of the family. Kronos may think he needs you, but you and I know better." She tapped her sandaled foot impatiently. "Are you going to come, or shall I make up some excuse for you? I have to get back soon, before the others start to arrive."

He glanced nervously around the room, as though seeking some plausible reason for absenting himself from the meeting.

"I could tell them you slipped on the stairs again. Or better yet, you could go and actually do it right now, so I won't have to lie."

"This is madness," he said. "Sheer madness, to let myself get involved in this."

She shook her head slowly, making little reproachful sounds with her mouth.

"Who's going to be there?"

"Koios and Iapetos, you and me."

"Not Kronos?"

She shook her head. "He doesn't even know about it. That's the idea. Koios wants to discuss things without Kronos evaluating every word." She retrieved her scarlet cloak from a chair and swirled it around her shoulders.

She turned and gave him a final, withering look. "Goodbye, then."

He sighed. "Wait a moment. I'm coming." He rose wearily.

"Sorry, can't wait. You *can* find your own way, can't you? You do know where your betrothed lives?"

The door closed behind her and Crios stood perfectly still, his head bowed, for what seemed like a long time. Finally he began to straighten his simple, unadorned chiton, disappeared into an adjoining room to return a minute later with a drab gray mantle wrapped around him, and made his way out of the apartment.

Proteus waited impatiently until Crios left, then came down onto the gallery, assuming first his own form, then after a few moments consideration, the semblance of the Titan Koios. Leaning out over the balcony, he drew up from below wisps of cloud and formed them around himself in the likeness of the tunic he had seen Koios wearing, and into a nondescript cloak.

He moved quickly to the door, cracked it open and peered out into the corridor. Crios was just disappearing around a far corner. At the other end of the corridor, however, a lanky, almost emaciated figure paced nervously back and forth near the entrance of another apartment.

As Proteus watched through the narrow opening, the agitated figure seemed to come to some resolution. Turning suddenly, the god stalked down the corridor toward him. Proteus pushed the door closed and pressed his ear to it, listening as the muffled footsteps passed by and continued in the direction that Crios had taken.

He had intended to follow Crios from a distance. Now that was no longer possible. His earlier explorations had not led him across the apartment of Eurybie. If he hoped to locate it—and the Titan meeting—he would have to turn again to Metis.

No sooner had he determined to return to Metis's room by way of the galleries, than he heard the sound of a door opening or closing in the corridor. He looked out again.

It was Metis. She was creeping down the wide hall, an apprehensive look upon her face and something clumsily concealed under her cloak. He waited until she had almost reached the doorway from which he watched, then stepped out into the hall and pulled her into the room with him, smothering her cry of alarm with his palm.

"Quiet, sister! It is I, Proteus."

"Oh, Proteus, I'm so glad to find you," she said, panting for breath as he let his body slip back into its natural form. In her excitement, even the facility with which he changed shapes did not astound her. "Thanatos sneaked into our apartment and tried to take the man from me. He tried to force me to tell him where he could find the others."

She seemed to remember the thing concealed under her cloak, and brought out the tiny, godlike creature. "I think I'll call him Alalkomeneus," she continued. The name meant

Guardian. "I've been trying to think of a name for him, and he certainly did his best to guard me from Thanatos. In our struggle we broke a vase, and little Alalkomeneus, who was on the floor, somehow picked up a piece of the vase and jabbed it into Thanatos's ankle. Oh, how brave you are, little Alalkomeneus!" she cried, hugging the creature to her. "Besides," she concluded. "it'll be amusing to have such a big name for such a little god."

"A wounded ankle wouldn't have stopped him for long."

"No, but it must have been quite painful"—she grinned— "judging from how loudly he yelled. Klymene came to see what was the matter. Thanatos didn't know what to say, and just gave her a little bow and walked out."

"But why are you smuggling Alalkomeneus down the hall?" Proteus asked.

"I'm afraid Thanatos might come back. Klymene is going to have Iapetos complain to Lord Kronos, but Thanatos is capable of anything. He might come back to steal Alalkomeneus while I'm out."

Proteus nodded. "I suspect your fears are well grounded. Just before you appeared, there was an odd-looking god pacing the corridor near your apartment—a tall, thin creature, quite nervous."

"That's him. That has to be him. You see, Alalkomeneus is not safe there. I was going to take him to Thalia, the Muse. I'm sure she'll take care of him for me."

"She was one of the goddesses with you when this creature was first discovered?"

"How did you know?"

"I saw you. I was there—nearby, anyway. Metis, I don't have time right now to talk. I need your help. Do you know where Eurybie's apartment is? Can you lead me there?"

"I think so. She has a small suite on the floor above, near Lord Hyperion."

"Good. Listen, Metis, don't take your pet to Thalia. Thanatos might decide to question her, too, and find him there. Leave him here, in one of the inner rooms without windows. Crios will be gone for some time—I can promise you that. You'll have time to lead me to Eurybie's chambers and then come back for him."

Metis seemed unsure. While she vacillated, Proteus moved quickly to look into the adjoining rooms.

"Here, this one will do. Turn him loose inside and pull the door closed."

Metis examined the room carefully and reluctantly agreed. She kissed the creature and set it on the floor. "I'll be back soon," she whispered to it, then closed the door.

Proteus had reassumed the semblance of the Titan Koios. The corridor was empty, and within moments they were on their way toward a massive circular staircase. The corridor twisted and turned, and as they rounded a corner a rumpled gray mass began to stir on a bench set back in a narrow alcove.

Grumbling under his breath, Momos sat up and rubbed his eyes. He rose slowly to his feet and began to walk away from them. Proteus pulled Metis to a halt and turned to watch the retreating figure.

"A better choice, don't you think?" he asked.

"What do you mean?"

He waited until Momos was out of sight, then transformed his body. He became much shorter and heavier, with a protruding belly. Deep furrows lined his face and his eyes became surrounded by puffy sacks of flesh. At the same time he reformed the phantom clothing he wore into a perfect imitation of Momos's faded garments.

Metis watched the metamorphosis in wonder. "I wish you could teach me to do that."

He smiled. "It's a talent; something you're born with, not taught."

"But how can you go from one to another so quickly and easily? Shape changing is exhausting! I could never do such a perfect imitation of another god—I don't think anyone else could. Just holding a different shape is hard. Doesn't it tire you?"

Proteus shook his head. "Now that I'm Momos, you'd best walk ahead of me. Not too fast, though."

"But why is Momos better than Koios?"

"Because we know where Momos is."

They reached the stairs and he let her get almost halfway up before mounting the first step. She climbed slowly, so that she would not get too far ahead, and had almost reached the landing of the next floor when she came face to face with Thanatos. The god stopped directly in front of her. He glared at her.

"Where are you going this time of night?" he asked, blocking her path. "I'm surprised you've deserted your precious little creature."

Proteus, still in the role of Momos, was coming slowly up the stairs toward them. He seemed to be watching the steps, but actually he was carefully observing everything taking place above him.

Metis tried to edge around Thanatos. He countered her move so that she could not pass. But then he stepped unexpectedly to one side. As she climbed past him his hands shot out to press against her body, nimbly searching her before she realized what he was doing.

Proteus, head bowed and lips mumbling, had almost reached them. Metis, once past Thanatos, bolted up the remaining steps. Thanatos continued downward, pointedly ignoring what he thought to be his brother.

Metis waited for Proteus a little way down the seventh-floor corridor. "Let's hurry," she said. "I want to get back to Alalkomeneus."

She led him rapidly through a maze of passages, finally pointing to a door just ahead.

"Thank you, sister," he told her. "Hurry back to your pet. I'll see you again as soon as I can."

She returned to Crios's chambers as quickly as she could without drawing attention to herself. Thanatos was nowhere in sight, and she went in immediately.

"I'm back, Alalkomeneus, my brave little Alalkomeneus," she called as she entered the inner room.

Nothing moved within the room.

"Alalkomeneus," she called, looking slowly around. A single lamp burned on a small table. She picked it up and used it to light the wall lamps. She went down on her knees and searched behind the furniture.

Alalkomeneus was gone.

NINE

The corridors of the palace of Olympos were lit by torches ensconced at regular intervals along the massive stone walls. The fitful illumination left long, dark stretches where light refused to reach. In a few places moonlight streamed in through high, broad windows set within deep alcoves.

As Metis left him, Proteus moved toward one of these windows, which opened upon an exterior gallery. By this route he hoped to gain access to the apartment of Eurybie. He paused long enough to resume his own form and to darken his cloak; then, with one hand on the windowsill, he vaulted through the opening and dropped to a crouching position on the narrow floor of the balcony.

A soft breeze was blowing, rustling his sable hair as he crept forward. From ahead of him, distant and muffled, came voices, among which he could distinguish the clear, unwavering tones of the sea goddess Eurybie. He hesitated directly outside a dark, open window; other windows lay ahead, leading into the same apartment. Many of them were lighted. After a few moments consideration he climbed silently over the stone sill into the blackness of the room.

He felt his way along, letting the distant voices guide him through what seemed a maze of pitch-black chambers until at last he came to a room lit only by the dim yellow light that entered through an open door. The voices had become clearly distinguishable now, and he moved to position himself opposite the door, where he could see clearly into the adjoining room. Pulling his black cloak almost completely around him, he settled himself on the floor amid deep shadows to watch and listen.

Eurybie had found time to ornament herself with gold and silver bracelets and to confine her luxuriant golden hair beneath a silver tiara upon which were mounted delicate, jade-petaled flowers. She and her three Titan guests sat in a tight circle near the middle of the room, small tripod tables drawn up beside each chair.

"Lord Koios," Eurybie was saying, "I wasn't aware that you had grown more cunning than your brother. If Lord Kronos says his plan will work, I'm much inclined to believe him."

Koios set aside his goblet of nectar. "That's one of the points I've been trying to make. But we haven't talked openly about this, and I think we must before we go any further. I know how I became involved, and I'm not pleased by it. Kronos simply took it for granted that I had agreed to my part in the plan. He left it to me to tell him otherwise. Of course, I never did. . . ."

Crios, sulking in his chair, nodded. "That's almost exactly what happened to me. Before I knew it, not only was I committed to helping him in this mad scheme, but I was engaged to marry *her*!" He sneered the final word.

Eurybie smiled benignly at him. "Do you really think I've the better part of the bargain, darling? The very thought of your weak, trembling hands on my body makes me decidedly ill."

"Who wants your body?" he demanded. "It's as icy as the far slopes of Olympos."

"Is it?" she asked, completely unruffled by his comments. "I didn't know you felt that way. You certainly didn't seem to the night you came whining and begging to touch it."

Koios held up his hand for silence while Crios, livid with embarrassment, sank even more deeply into his chair, muttering bitterly.

"Please," Koios said, "this is important. Let's not waste what little time we have. We may not have another opportunity to talk freely. Kronos has drawn us into this affair, and as far as I can see, he's smoothly manipulated things so that we haven't been able to talk among ourselves. I think it's important that each of us know how thoroughly committed the others are. I think it's important we each understand exactly how serious a step we're taking.''

He looked directly at Crios. ''Yes, as Kronos tells it, it'll be quite simple. Okeanos and Nereus have been plotting against him. During the celebration following your marriage, when the moment is right, Kronos and Iapetos and I will make prisoners of Okeanos and Nereus. Kronos will justify himself to the other gods by displaying proofs of treachery, and all will be fine.

''This sounds well enough, but can we indeed make prisoners of them? Nereus may not be much of a problem, except for his proficiency at changing his shape, but Okeanos is very strong. Then, even if we do succeed, will the proofs convince the other gods? More than that, will the numberless spawn of Okeanos accept them? Or will they plot against us?''

He turned slowly to look at each of his companions. ''I said before that there could be very serious ramifications, and I mean that—whether we succeed or fail. Our actions could cast the gods into a thousand years of strife. I wonder, has each of you considered this?''

Iapetos sat quietly, his face expressionless as he listened and watched the others. Crios looked frightened. ''I never wanted any part of this,'' he complained. ''All I want is to be left alone.''

Koios turned his attention to the sea goddess.

She smiled at him. ''My actions are guided by the same principles that guide yours—that guide each of us. I act out of respect and love of Lord Kronos. Whatever he asks of me, I'll do. I haven't sought this out, but I have no qualms.''

Koios smiled ironically. ''I admire your devotion to my brother,'' he said, ''but I can't help remembering something you seem to be overlooking.''

''What's that?'' she asked softly, her turquoise eyes staring at him with perfect ingenuousness.

''By selflessly serving Lord Kronos, you'll find yourself queen of the sea.'' He glanced toward Iapetos. ''And you, brother, will rule the deep-flowing ocean. Isn't it so?''

''Why shouldn't it be?'' Eurybie asked, answering for Iapetos. ''His wife Klymene is loyal to Lord Kronos. As a daughter of Okeanos she has a claim to the throne, and her husband with her. Both Iapetos and Crios will rule their domains wisely and loyally. The Titans will rule the entire world. You should approve of that—you should be joyous at the prospect.''

"Okeanos is also a Titan, and my brother. And as far as I can tell, Lord Nereus has never done us any harm.''

"You forget that they both plot against Lord Kronos," she replied, becoming more animated. "They invite their own overthrow.''

Koios shook his head somewhat sadly. "Kronos *says* they plot against him.''

"Do you doubt his word?" she asked.

He avoided her question. "Eurybie," he asked, "why do you hate your brother? Has Nereus done something to you to make your heart so cold to him?''

"I love my brother," she said. "But even love can't blind me to his actions. He opposes Lord Kronos; therefore I must oppose him.''

"And thereby become Queen Eurybie," he said, looking at her beautiful face and lovely, unflinching eyes. "The sad part is I half believe you. I don't think you hate him, but you don't love him either, Eurybie. I don't think you have any feelings for him at all, or for anyone else. You want to wear a crown, and the only one available happens to belong to your brother's wife. Its price is that you must help plunge your brother into the endless night of Tartaros.''

Eurybie, still smiling, only shrugged her shoulders.

"You do realize, of course, that in actuality you'll be no more a queen than you are now. Oh, Crios may be king, and certainly he'll do just as you tell him, but Lord Kronos's price remains to be paid. It'll be he who rules the sea in your name—or you'll surely follow your brother to Tartaros.''

"I'll have no reason to disagree with Lord Kronos," she said. "I'll be pleased to follow his advice.''

"His *advice*! Advice that comes prancing and bleating like a lamb. Beware, Queen Eurybie! At any moment that lamb can resume its natural shape, and its roar will shake you from your throne.''

For once the sea goddess remained silent.

Koios looked sadly at Crios. "And you, poor brother—there's a lion in your future too—a lioness, rather. You've got a lioness by the tail, pulling you down the trail behind her. At the end of the trail lies a crown, but the crown lies

within her den. Once she has the crown, she'll gobble you
whole."

Crios, more uncomfortable than ever, refilled his goblet
and drank rapidly.

"What of you, Iapetos?" Koios asked.

The Titan looked up slowly.

"I can't understand why you would sanction such a thing—
you, of all the gods. How can you lend yourself to a project
that would consign your brother, the father of your beautiful
wife, to the pitiful nether world? I can't believe Klymene
would approve of this. Certainly she wouldn't do it merely to
become queen of the ocean. Does she even know? Have you
told her?"

Iapetos shook his head.

"Lord Kronos wouldn't want her told," Eurybie said.

"What will she think when she learns?" Koios demanded.
He hesitated, studying his brother's stony face. "She won't
allow it. She'll leave you rather than stay with a husband who
betrayed her father."

"He's only doing what must be done," Eurybie said, growing tired of the conversation. "We're all doing what we must
do. Get to your point, Lord Koios, though I think I've
uncovered it."

He looked at her inquisitively.

"It's very simple, after all. Each of us has a reward
promised for his services—a kingdom. Each of us, except
you. You feel slighted, don't you? Your services must be
worth as much as ours." She laughed. "And you're quite
right. The only difficulty is that no kingdom remains for you
. . . unless you'd like to rule over Tartaros."

Koios was shaking his head sadly.

"I suppose a crown wouldn't make you more amenable to
the righteousness of Lord Kronos's cause?"

Koios sighed in frustration, turning to Iapetos and Crios.
"Can't I make you two understand? I'm trying to tell you that
we're courting disaster. The dreadful injustice to which we
are making ourselves parties could bring this palace tumbling
down around us. Kronos has always envied and distrusted
both Okeanos and Nereus. Maybe it's because they haven't
totally bowed to his rule, maybe there's some other reason.
He's finally determined to be done with them—at whatever
cost, even if it destroys all he's created, all the good he's

done. If you really love him, you'll think long and hard before you let him do this.''

Koios had become highly agitated and plunged on now, regardless of the consequences of saying too much. ''As for this evidence of his, all I've seen is poor Aigaion. Do you really believe what he said—or do you think he would have said anything Kronos told him to say? He was terrified. He could barely stand without help, he was so weak. The bruises all over his face showed that he had been beaten, probably for days. Is that convincing evidence?''

''What better?'' Eurybie asked. ''He is Nereus's own brother and mine, and a great friend of Okeanos. He admitted to sharing in their plot against Lord Kronos. Should Kronos deal tenderly with his enemies?''

''In his state he would have accused his own mother and father. If you'll be honest with yourselves, you'll admit that Kronos has become suspicious of everyone and everything. He sees plots everywhere, where none exist. He grows less reasonable each day. He's becoming—''

Koios stopped abruptly. A massive figure loomed in the doorway leading from one of the adjoining rooms. From beneath his broad, furrowed brow the King of the Gods surveyed them through smoldering, adamantine eyes.

TEN

Sheathed in darkness, wide-roaming Proteus, son of Okeanos, watched and listened intently as Kronos advanced slowly into the room. Silence had fallen over the assemblage at his sudden appearance, and the Lord of the Titans let his gaze move from one immobilized figure to the next.

Eurybie was the first to recover her wits. "Come in, come in, my lord," she said, jumping to her feet. "We'll make room for you to join us."

She went to fetch a chair while the Titans rose awkwardly to greet their brother. They began to fumble with their own chairs and small tripod tables, moving them backward to enlarge the circle.

"Please be seated, my lord," Eurybie said, escorting Kronos to the place she had prepared for him. "I'll bring you nectar to refresh yourself."

Without a word he took his seat. The other Titans were forced to follow his example. Eurybie set a full goblet near his hand, but he did not reach for it. Instead he continued to look slowly from one to the other of them, his face, except for the eyes, an impenetrable mask.

"Well, Lord Kronos," Eurybie said, still trying to break the silence, "to what do we owe the pleasure of your visit?"

Very slowly he ran his hand over his wide forehead and through his black hair. "I've begun to wonder, of late. . . .

I've begun to wonder if, perhaps, I haven't been letting my imagination run away with me.''

He paused to look inquiringly at each of them. ''It must be my imagination, after all. I keep imagining that the gods are conspiring against me, that there are plots all around me.'' His eyes settled on Koios. ''Here, for instance.''

''It may seem that way, Kronos—it may have sounded like that, but that wasn't my intent. We only wished—''

''*We? You* seemed to be doing most of the talking.''

''Y-yes, I suppose I was,'' Koios said, his face now very pale, and beads of sweat standing out on his forehead. ''I suppose I had the most questions to ask.''

Kronos smiled the barest tinge of a smile and sank back into the deep cushions of his chair. ''Yes, quite a few questions . . . about every aspect of this undertaking. How many of them, brother, relate at core to the merits of the project in which we're all mutually involved—and how many to the validity of my thought processes? That does seem to be what you were getting at.''

His gray eyes bored ruthlessly into the pale blue ones of Koios, so that Koios was forced to look away.

''My lord, I apologize if anything I said has offended you. I don't know how much of this conversation you heard—''

''More than enough, I should think.''

Since Kronos's arrival, Iapetos had maintained much the same attitude as he had displayed earlier. He looked up now. ''Lord Kronos,'' he said softly, ''I would say a few words.''

Kronos turned to face him. ''Say them, brother.''

''Koios has doubts about your plan, and he's expressed them openly before us. He's said that we should talk together, that since our success depends on how well each of us does his part, we should know just how thoroughly each of us is committed to the plan. What he says makes good sense.''

''Perhaps,'' Kronos said, ''but he also doubts the truth of what I've told him.''

''He thinks you haven't told us in enough detail how your plan is to succeed,'' Iapetos said.

''No!'' Kronos said, nearly losing control of himself for the first time. ''No, he doubts *me*. He doubts that Okeanos plots to depose me.''

Kronos half rose from his chair, glaring at them in suppressed fury. His huge hand reached out, pointing directly into Koios's face. "I tell you that our brother Okeanos has never had any love for me—that since the day I assumed leadership of the Titans he has resented and envied me, and plotted to destroy me. He has cursed my every success, cheered each little reversal I've encountered. There at the end of the world, in the sunken castle from which he rules his fishy domain, he has brooded and kept counsel with himself, always with the single goal of bringing about my downfall. He has fed himself on bitterness and hate. He has plotted against me time and again—sending lies out into the world to turn the other gods against me—and now, with the help of sly Nereus, he hopes finally to taste my defeat."

Kronos stood fully erect, his face twisted in anger. "It shall not be. I have endured his petty conspiracies and lies too long already. Now I'll be done with him—forever!"

He was quivering slightly as he spoke, his eyes flashing back and forth over the others. "He and interfering Nereus have finally overstepped the limits of my patience. I shall rid myself of them—with you, if you choose to help me, but without you if I must."

Koios, who had drawn away from Kronos, cast an astonished look at Iapetos. Iapetos, however, did not seem surprised at Kronos's claim that he could depose both gods without assistance.

"We all know the duplicity of Okeanos and Nereus," Eurybie said as soon as Kronos lapsed into silence. "Come, sit and calm yourself, my lord, that you may put to rest those little concerns of Koios."

Kronos slumped back into his chair, letting his head nod forward. For perhaps a full minute he was completely silent. Finally he looked up again, once more composed.

"Pardon me," he said, "but I have endured a great deal from both of them—more than any of you suspect." He looked directly at Koios again. "All right, you have doubts about my plan. I've told you all you need to know right now, all that concerns you. I don't intend to tell you any more, though I can assure you that I know exactly what I'm doing. We will succeed, and without much difficulty. The testimony of Aigaion, one of Nereus's own brothers, will prove the treachery of both Okeanos and Nereus to the satisfaction of anyone willing to hear the evidence without bias."

He was watching Koios carefully, perhaps gauging his

reactions. "I suppose there is the chance that the children of Okeanos may not want to believe the evidence, but that will be their decision. It will be their decision, too, if they wish to contest my actions. Perhaps it will mean a thousand years of strife. I doubt it, but I will not flinch from the prospect. This deed must be done."

Koiós listened uncomfortably.

"As I said, I'd like to have the help of each of you, but if you have reservations, if you prefer not to take part in this, you need only say so. Not just Koios, but any of you."

He looked at Eurybie.

"Oh, I'm most certainly with you, my lord," she said.

He turned to Crios.

"Yes, my lord. You have only to ask."

Iapetos looked up as Kronos turned toward him.

"And you, brother," Kronos said. "I already know that I can count on you, don't I?"

"I will serve you as loyally as I am capable," Iapetos said.

Kronos turned at last to Koios. "Only you remain. I tell you frankly, if you want to disassociate yourself from this project, do it now."

Koios looked quickly from one to the other around the room; each of them was watching him. Finally he nodded his head. "Yes, Lord Kronos," he said, "I'll work with you. I'll do as you ask me."

"Good," Kronos said, smiling slightly as he rose from his chair. He walked toward Koios and laid a hand upon his shoulder. "You've made the right decision, brother. You won't regret it."

Without another word he turned and left them. They sat in silence until they heard the door to the corridor close behind him.

Koios was wiping perspiration from his forehead. Crios, almost limp after the nervous strain he had undergone, moaned softly.

Iapetos rose.

"One moment," Koios said, rising also and stepping near him. "I'd like to talk to you for a few moments."

"I don't want to talk to anyone," Crios said, rising and walking toward the front of the apartment. Eurybie began to follow her betrothed, but stopped just within the room to turn back and listen.

"Iapetos," Koios said in a low voice, "I don't know why you're going along with this. I know it isn't out of fear. Whatever your reason, think carefully before it's too late. You heard our brother raving against Okeanos. He really believes Okeanos wants to depose him, and now he seems to actually believe he can overcome both Okeanos and Nereus—and all those who will defend them—by himself. Think what that really says about the person to whom we have bound ourselves."

"I have been thinking," Iapetos said. "And I'm beginning to suspect he might be able to do it."

"Still have doubts?" Eurybie asked from the doorway. "Oh, well, I don't guess it matters. You've agreed to do your parts, doubts or not."

Eurybie accompanied the gods to the door and let them out. As soon as they had gone, she leaned against the closed door, shoulders drooping and arms hanging limply at her sides. Her lassitude lasted for only a moment, however. Lifting her cloak from its wall peg, she draped herself in its long folds, adjusted her hair, then left the apartment herself.

Proteus, who had been about to make his own exit by the same route that had brought him here, now rose to his full height and quickly moved to the door through which Eurybie had just departed. Reassuming the form of Momos, he followed her out into the corridor.

ELEVEN

Even in the form of Momos, a denizen of the dark corridors, Proteus had difficulty following Eurybie without arousing her suspicion. She paused regularly to look behind or down intersecting corridors. Each time she turned in his direction, Proteus flattened himself against a shadowed area of the wall or disappeared into an alcove. He hung back until she rounded a corner, then came forward down the empty passageway like a sudden breeze.

She ascended a little-used circular staircase and made her way directly, if furtively, to the chambers of Kronos himself upon the topmost floor of the palace. Without hesitating she went to the looming bronze double doors and tapped softly. One section of the door opened and she disappeared within.

Once she was out of sight, Proteus moved quickly down the corridor and pressed his ear against the thick door. Unable to discern even the smallest sound within, he turned immediately to an adjacent door on the same side of the corridor, cracked it open long enough to glance within, then passed silently into the dimly lighted interior.

He hoped that this suite of rooms, which appeared from its furnishings to be part of the private chambers of the King of the Gods, would connect with the apartments into which Eurybie had been admitted; otherwise he would have to make his way to the exterior gallery and attempt to gain entrance to the neighboring suite by that route. Continuing to mimic the shambling gait of Momos, so that he would be mistaken for that god should he be observed within these rooms, he moved in absolute silence from chamber to chamber, pausing at each door, listening first, then cautiously opening it.

At last he found himself at an entrance bridging into a second series of rooms. Now he could hear low voices, one of which might very well be that of Kronos. The second he recognized instantly as the distinctive tones of the sea goddess.

The intervening rooms were dimly lighted, and he was now forced to move along the walls, carefully avoiding the furnishings placed there, which, were he to stumble over them, would quickly draw attention to his presence. He darted across open spaces where he might have been observed had he not carefully waited until both god and goddess were looking away. Finally he reached a point from which he could both see and hear. He settled himself behind the concealment of four huge amphorae and a stack of bulging skin flasks. Lying upon the floor behind them, he could peer into the next room.

Kronos was beginning to mix nectar and fresh spring water in a large, golden mixing bowl formed in the shape of a dragonlike monster. His hands were trembling, and Eurybie took the ewer from him before he spilled the contents. He relinquished his place before the side table and threw himself down on a high divan.

"Koios is a coward," he said, "a miserable, traitorous coward. . . ."

Eurybie shook her long golden hair, a hand moving to brush away the curls that clung to her cheek. "You came too soon. You should have waited until everything had been said before showing yourself."

"I lost my temper," he admitted somewhat ruefully. "But I heard enough. Enough to know just how little I can trust them."

She laughed softly, beginning to pour their drinks. "But now you'll never know what might have been said."

He frowned, taking a goblet from her. "I didn't need to hear any more. Koios can't be trusted, Iapetos is loyal but unenthusiastic, and Crios is a wimpering cur—but we both already knew that."

"I was afraid you'd thrash the lot of them. I've never seen you so angry. You were quivering with rage." She raised her goblet to salute him. "And they trembled, my Lord Kronos—trembled with fear as you trembled with anger!"

He smiled despite himself.

"Still, I think you squandered a wonderful opportunity to learn just what each of our comrades is thinking. It would have been better if you had restrained yourself a little longer. Crios I can tell you about—he'll do exactly as you say, no more and no less. But Koios and Iapetos . . . ?"

Kronos shrugged, sipping nectar. "And so will they. I know all I need to know."

She settled beside him on the edge of the divan. "And what's that?"

"That I must work a bit upon Koios."

She watched him closely, leaning toward him as she spoke. "And what do you mean by that?"

"He has doubts. We must help him overcome those doubts."

"Well, go on. I'm listening intently. You have my fullest attention."

He looked at her through half-closed eyes. "Not yet, Eurybie. I must have time to brood upon it. Koios, my dear brother, has grown plump and comfortable. He no longer has any initiative. If he were more insecure . . ."

"He seemed quite insecure this evening."

Kronos smiled. "Tonight he was as self-assured as a mountain by comparison with the way he will be."

"He'll serve you nonetheless, just as he is."

"Yes, I think you're right. He'll serve me—but not as I wish to be served." He stood up, restless.

"You mean he won't be trembling to please you."

Kronos's smile broadened. "Very good, Eurybie! Trembling in his attempt to please me, and pleasing me because he trembles." He began to walk back and forth in front of her. "It wasn't always this way, that I had to connive for their faith and loyalty. Once they gave it to me willingly."

His mood changed and he slumped down on the divan beside her, sitting in gloomy silence. Finally she rose and went to refill her goblet. When she returned she stood in front of him, watching him.

"What are you thinking?" The tinge of lightheartedness in her voice did not ring true.

"I could do it without them," he said, looking up slowly. "I *could*, you know. I can if I have to. I've been thinking that perhaps I should let them go, even Iapetos. His heart isn't in it.''

She shook her head. "You need them—"

He started to interrupt, but she continued talking.

"You need them even if they don't lift a finger. You need their complicity. Maybe you could somehow overcome both Okeanos and Nereus by getting them alone and secretly incarcerating them, but you can't afford to do it that way."

"Why not?"

"You mustn't seem too ambitious, my lord. Acting alone, you would seem ruthless, oppressive."

"I would prove the justice of my cause."

She shook her head. "All the proofs in the world would not be as useful as the passive support of Iapetos. With him at your side the other gods will believe without questioning, and accept. The support of Koios and Crios will have a similar, if not as great effect."

"Perhaps you're right."

"If you act alone, it won't be long before rumors begin to circulate against you. Soon the other gods, a few of them at least, will begin to scheme against you and—"

"They already scheme against me," he said sullenly. "Everyone schemes against me in one way or another."

An amused smile played upon her lips. "Everyone? Even I?"

"Even you."

"And how do I scheme against you?"

"By trying to bend me to your will."

"Oh!" She laughed. "But you like the way I do that, don't you?" Her hand rested on his thigh.

"At least I know what you're doing. You don't try to hide your motives from me."

"I hide nothing from you."

He smiled softly. "You want a crown. Since I plan to give it to you, we have no area of contention."

She took his goblet from him. "You look tired. Why not rest now?"

He stretched out on the divan and she stood beside him, gently stroking his hair and toying with the curls of his beard.

"I meant to ask, my lord, what of Aigaion? You do have him somewhere safe? He will be at the wedding to testify?"

"Oh, quite safe, I assure you. You need not fear for his

safety; he is under my personal protection. Everything is arranged. He will arrive with my entourage.''

"But is that wise?" she asked. "If he is allowed to talk to anyone before—"

"I told you, Eurybie, it's all arranged. He will say nothing until I call upon him to testify to the treachery of Okeanos and Nereus. Tell me, is there still no word from Okeanos?"

She shook her head.

"If he declines to attend your wedding, then the plan will not work. We'll have to begin again."

Eurybie frowned. "Could we not still act against Nereus?"

"Okeanos knows how I feel about him. Once he learned that Nereus had been deposed, he would know that I had finally decided to act. He would be doubly warned—doubly on guard. He might even move against me, rather than wait for me to act."

She dipped a finger in his goblet and let the nectar drip between his lips. "Everyone has a weak point," she said.

"What do you mean?"

"Your brother's pride is the flaw through which he can be influenced. Play properly upon his pride and you can lead him to do just as you want. Make him feel that it would be cowardly to avoid you—to avoid coming to the wedding, for instance—and he will undergo any danger to prove how fearless he is. You couldn't keep him from attending."

"You know him very well, Eurybie. He'd face any risk to gratify his pride. Perhaps we'll have to do something of that sort, if he declines your invitation. Eurybie, you'd make a dangerous adversary. I'm glad you're on my side."

She bowed slightly toward him. "Indeed I would, Lord Kronos."

He thought silently for a few moments. "What's my weak point, Eurybie? You said everyone has such a flaw in his character. Tell me where I'm weakest, that I may guard myself there."

She smiled down at him, leaned forward and brushed his lips in the lightest of kisses. "Why, my lord, that's no secret. Everyone knows your weakness. It's the ladies, of course!"

His low chuckle grew until his entire body shook with laughter. He stroked her cheek with the back of his hand. "Yes, I guess that's true enough. Isn't there another, one that might not be so obvious?"

"Not that I can think of."

He watched her carefully, pensively. "That's a fault you don't understand at all, isn't it?"

"Your lustful nature, you mean?"

"Yes, that's what I mean—its reciprocal side. You feel nothing, Eurybie. Don't deny it. It's true. You're incapable of feeling; you're cold to the core, and you use your body without emotion—because you have no emotions. I, on the other hand, am one who savors . . ."

"Thank you for enlightening me. I thought you were merely lustful."

He laughed, drawing her down toward him and kissing her. "One who savors his emotions, I was about to say."

She drew away, pouting.

"You're angry because I said you have no emotions?"

She shook her head. "No, I'm not angry. It's true. Everything we do is done for a reason, my lord. You, for pleasure; I, for advantage. When you like, I give you pleasure—for my advantage. I see no real difference."

"I have other motivations as well. Duty. Necessity. Justice."

"Necessity rules everyone. Duty is nothing but a perversion of pride, and justice is an illusion."

He pushed her away, sitting up again. "You really believe that, I think."

"Of course. Shall we debate it?"

"Some other time. Your talk of my weakness has reminded me of something. Do you know Philyra, the sister of Klymene?"

"The Okeanid?" She shook her head. "I've seen her, but I didn't really pay much attention to her." She cocked her head to one side, her eyes glittering. "Why, my lord? You wish to savor her?"

He smiled but did not answer.

"I suppose she's attractive. All Okeanids are attractive. If you like, I'll see what I can learn about her, though I can't imagine why you would bother just now. In a couple of weeks I'll let you take your pick of golden Nereids!"

"She has a certain charm. Yes, let me know what you can learn of her."

"All the goddesses have a certain charm to you. To me they're only so much—"

A knock sounded at the door, and as they turned toward it,

the door opened to admit a chestnut-haired goddess of medium height and full figure. Rhea, wife of Kronos and Queen of the Gods, halted as she saw Eurybie. Her features, already drawn, stiffened perceptibly.

"I didn't intend to interrupt," she said. "I'll return to talk with you later."

Eurybie had sprung to her feet. "Oh, you haven't interrupted, my lady. I was just going." She yawned beneath an only partly concealing palm.

Eurybie edged to one side to pass her on the way to the door. "Good night, all," she said, pulling the door closed behind her.

TWELVE

Kronos had risen as his wife entered. Now he recovered his golden goblet from the floor beside the divan where Eurybie had left it and drained its contents of sparkling red nectar as he resumed his seat upon the edge of the divan.

Rhea came slowly deeper into the room until she stood almost directly in front of him. He watched her through weary eyes, admiring despite himself the way the sheer material of her purple peplos draped her stately figure. Her long rich hair was arranged atop her head in a simple but attractive coiffeur and held in place by a narrow tiara of electrum studded with jade. Finally, when he had finished his drink and set its container aside, she looked directly at him and began to speak.

"Lord Kronos, my husband, I have a right to know what you are plotting."

He stared at her in mild amazement. "I've always admired your directness. It's a quality most of the gods lack—or suppress. What are you referring to this time?"

"Something is going on and you're trying very hard to be secretive about it. You ought to know by now that you can't keep such things from me."

"That's apparent. I'll ask again, though. To what do you refer?"

"There was a meeting tonight. Koios and Iapetos were there, and you must have been too."

"How do you know that?"

"Because neither of them were at home. I saw both Phoibe and Klymene, and Phoibe had seen Iapetos and Koios talking earlier. I know you weren't here."

"And on that basis you decided we must all be together."

She nodded slowly, refusing to drop her eyes. "Yes, with Crios and that—" She thought better of saying the word. "With Crios and Eurybie."

"And how do you know *that*?"

"I know where to look for you when you're not to be found any other place. When I got to Eurybie's apartment, the others were just leaving. I must have missed you somehow."

Kronos listened quietly, wearily. "Go on. You undoubtedly have more to say."

"I certainly do. I want to know what's happening. For months now you've had something in mind and—"

"Haven't I still the right, madam, to entertain thoughts of my own? You may be my wife, but my thoughts are still my own. At least I've been under that impression. Inform me if I'm wrong."

She held her body rigid before his scornful gaze. "I control neither your mind nor your heart, I know that. You've become a stranger to me, a husband only in name. Nevertheless I remain your wife—in name, at least—and as your wife I have a right to some consideration. I've long since accommodated myself to the fact that you are incapable of limiting your affections to a single goddess—a marvelous irony in the high-minded King of the Gods who first imposed marriage upon the world. . . ."

"The world must have order, and it is the obligation of the gods to impose order upon the shambles of nature. Before my rule we were little better than immortal beasts."

"Yes, but the laws you promulgate are for others, not for yourself."

He shrugged. "Some laws work better than others. Why must we talk of this? Eurybie was only here to discuss the meeting you went to such pains to uncover. You interrupted nothing, if that's what you think."

"Only because I arrived too soon," she said. "But Eurybie and her kind are insignificant. I've resigned myself to your nature. If I can't approve, I can look the other way—when you let me. Toy with her as you like, but don't cut me out of your life. *That* I will not tolerate!"

Tears huddled at the corners of her eyes. "You've drawn away from me, husband, and soon you'll no longer deserve to be called by that name. Ever since you brought that hideous creature Thanatos here, I haven't even been welcome in your chambers. He seems always to be fluttering about you, or creeping around the passages up here. I despise him—I can't imagine how you can abide his presence here, in your personal quarters. You should send him away. . . ."

Kronos listened resolutely until she lapsed into silence. He rose and went to the small table against one wall, refilled his own goblet and poured a second for her. When she refused it, he set them both aside. He slipped an arm around the mature fullness of her body and drew her toward him.

"Rhea," he said in his most soothing tone, "be calm, lovely Rhea. Sip nectar with me and compose yourself, then we'll talk as long as you like."

"I mean nothing to you," she complained bitterly. "I, who have dedicated my life to you. Haven't I loved you—do you realize how fully I've loved you?"

He pressed her to him, so that her face nestled against his enormous chest. As he ran his fingers through the thickness of her hair, the tiara she wore tumbled to the floor. Her hair unfurled under his caress. He led her to the divan and almost draped her upon it. As he kissed her, her arms moved slowly to encircle his massive neck. Her body grew soft and yielding beneath his muscular firmness and the supple touch of his powerful but gentle fingers.

He drew back from her abruptly, his face clouded. She tried to sit up but he held her down on the divan with one hand while the other moved across her lower abdomen, exploring the unexpected firmness he had found there.

At last she managed to pull free, or perhaps he loosened his grip. As she stood up, her foot struck one of the goblets sitting on the floor, and a pool of red nectar spread across the shining marble flagstones.

"Stand still," he warned. "You are with child." It was an accusation.

She gave in to his firmer will and overpowering strength. He reached out and held her jaw in one hand, forcing her to look at him.

"Answer me. Are you with child?"

"I think so." Her words were barely audible. He turned

away in rage, and she covered her face with her hands and began to sob.

"How long before it is born?" he demanded. Her divine body might display no more noticeable indication of pregnancy. She could be within months or hours of delivery.

"I don't know."

His rage drained away. After a few minutes he said, "You know it must be the same—just as before."

She shook her head vehemently.

"You must bring the child to me as soon as it is born."

She let out a cry of anguish and threw herself upon him, slipping down to his knees and clutching them fiercely. "No, Kronos—you can't demand this of me again. I want this child. You must let me keep this child!"

He took her arms and lifted her up. Her body twisted frantically from side to side, trying to break free from him.

"You must bring it to me," he repeated.

"No!" she shrieked, beginning to pound on his chest. "What have you done with my babies? Where are they? Give them back to me!" She scratched and shoved violently in her effort to free herself.

He let her struggle and weep until she had exhausted herself. Finally he said, "Rhea, you know what must be."

She looked up at him, calmer now, wiping the tears from her eyes. At last she said, "Tell me what you have done with the others."

"You don't need to know that."

"How can you say that? I—their mother—need not know what has become of them? You're a monster, to be so devoid of feeling."

"I only do what I must."

"Oh, that evil prophecy," she shrieked, "that lying, evil prophecy! I would give my life that those words had never been uttered, or that I had never married you. What do I care to be a queen when I can have no children?"

"I'm sorry, Rhea—more sorry than you can know. Remember that. I'm not heartless. I'm not a monster. I have tender feelings too. But I will not—I *cannot*—let the work of millenia be destroyed. All that I've built, all I've accomplished—it must not be destroyed. I'll do anything that is necessary to uphold it."

Her eyes gleamed behind the light film of tears. "No

good—no lasting good—can ever come from such evil, husband. Monstrous evil can only beget monstrous evil, and this unspeakable crime of yours—ripping my babies from my milk-swollen breasts—this unspeakable evil that you hide from every eye and ear, it cries out for vengeance. It calls vengeance down upon you!"

She stood tall and rigid, her body swaying slightly and her entire countenance ennobled by the depth of the emotions surging within her. "Oh, shameful god, the evil of that far-gone day will haunt you forever. You'll never be free of it. *Child, beware thy child. As you have overthrown your father, so shall you be overthrown!*"

He recoiled from her, repressed horror spreading over his face as the words fell from her lips. "Silence," he commanded.

"I've earned the right to say what I please. I've earned the right to curse you—paid for the privilege, paid in my own flesh. Listen well. I've obeyed you and I obey you still. But I want this child. Take it from me and I'll pine for the day on which the prophecy of Gaia and Ouranos is fulfilled. I'll bless that day. . . ."

Kronos had stepped back from her. "Nereus spoke the prophecy too," he said almost vacantly. "The wretched sea god pronounced the selfsame words. And never once had I breathed them to another, save only you."

"You needed no prophecy. The evil you did that day has haunted you ever since, and you won't free yourself of it by taking my babies from me."

"Still your tongue." His voice shook with anger now. "Had I not struck that blow, the world would still be as it was. Is that what you want? The gods would still be little more than savage beasts, forever fighting among themselves. Have you forgotten? I haven't accomplished all this through weakness and indecision. Nothing would have changed were it not for me—my strength and intelligence—yes, and cruelty. I've done what must be done, even when I found the act abhorrent."

His voice faltered, and he paused before continuing. "Rhea, you know me better than anyone. If I do evil, I do it only because I must. *Must*, a terrible word, even for the King of the Gods. . . . I've never done evil for its own sake, but only through necessity—another terrible, awesome word, before which even I must bow—before which everything that exists, god and animal, earth and sky and sea must bow. Look at what I have achieved. If you must remember my faults, remember my achievements also.''

She did not answer. Finally he said, "What are you thinking?"

"The same thoughts your brothers and sisters would think, if they but knew the depths of your devotion to duty."

"And what does that mean?" he demanded.

"That they would detest you as I detest you. That they would shrink from you as I do, if they knew how completely ambition has eaten away all that was once good and wonderful in you. . . . Tell me, is this heartache of mine reserved for wives, or do you deal in the same manner with your playthings when they become similarly discomfited?"

"Rhea, I warn you," he said slowly, his hands gripping hers more forcefully. "Dare not speak of this to anyone, or I swear by the earth itself that you've seen the light of the sun for the last time. Tartaros will embrace you as its own. I love you, but you must not contend against me, or I shall rid myself of you."

"Just as you rid yourself of our undesirable brothers," she said softly. "And, I suppose, of troublesome lovers."

"Just as I rid the earth of everything that causes turmoil and strife. Yes, even our monstrous brothers. I swear you'll join them in eternal darkness unless you obey me."

"I don't doubt it," she said, a small, mirthless smile trembling on her pale lips.

"Maintain silence and bring the child to me as soon as it is born—or you will leave me no choice."

"Of course," she said, "it will be *necessary*." She rose as she spoke, absently straightening the flowing folds of her peplos. She looked up at him a final time. "I obey you, my husband. I obey you—*and I curse you!*"

The door closed behind her, leaving him standing in the middle of the room. He sat upon the divan, letting his head sink into his hands. A minute or two passed, and then the door opened again. He looked up to find Eurybie coming toward him.

"I thought you were going to bed," he said wearily.

"Rhea thought that, too, I hope."

"What do you want? Where have you been all this time?"

"Waiting for her to leave." She sat beside him, smiling and adjusting the cascading tresses of her golden hair.

He became more tense as he watched her. "What did you hear?"

She looked at him innocently. "You mean, was I listening at the door?" She laughed. "I'm certainly not above such a thing, but I'm afraid it never occurred to me. Did I miss something good? I never for a moment thought your wife might have something interesting to say. Well, I'm forewarned—I certainly won't let such an opportunity slip away next time!"

His face was furrowed in a deep scowl. "I'm not joking, Eurybie. What did you hear?"

Her smile grew smaller but did not vanish completely. "I told you, I heard nothing. I started to return to my own quarters when I left here, but changed my mind before I reached them. I waited below till I heard Rhea descending; then I came back up. I thought you might want company, something a bit more relaxing than a wife. . . . You're very tense, my lord."

His enormous hand encircled her pearl-white throat. "Eurybie, lie to me now and I promise you'll regret that lie for a thousand years."

"I'm not lying," she said, her eyes meeting his without flinching—without humor, but also without fear. "I heard nothing."

His hand fell from her and for a few minutes he seemed lost in thought. Finally he said, "Would you betray me?"

"Only if you force me to, my love."

He watched her closely, scrutinizing the mocking half smile that so seldom left her.

"But you would never do that," she said. "Come, my lord, I'll put you to bed."

Taking him by the hand, she began to lead him toward his bedroom. "You're so tense," she said. "That's not good. You'll have trouble sleeping. You're lucky I decided to come back."

Proteus, still hidden in the next room, retreated to a more secure hiding place as they came in his direction.

THIRTEEN

Even though she had carefully searched the room, Metis refused to admit that Alalkomeneus could be gone. She had failed to uncover any exit through which he might have escaped during her brief absence, and had continued to search time and again over the same limited area, even inspecting the closed chests that lined the walls and two empty amphorae into which, just possibly, he might have clambered.

She called out as she moved about the room, trying to coax him to her. "Alalkomeneus, my little god, where have you gone? You mustn't hide from me. You know I'm your friend, and I'm worried about you. . . ."

Once again she fell to her knees and crawled about to look under furniture. The task became more hopeless with each passing moment. There were no windows through which he might have climbed, no crack under or around the door through which he might have squirmed.

"Oh, come out, Alalkomeneus—please come out!" she begged in desperation. "You know I won't hurt you. I love you, Alalkomeneus. I want to protect you from being hurt. . . ."

She stopped still. Thanatos—he had passed her on the stairway, coming in this direction as she led Proteus to the chambers of Eurybie. A cold dread grew within her. Logic told her that he could not have known Alalkomeneus was hidden here in Crios's apartment. But Alalkomeneus was gone, inexplicably gone, and Thanatos had been nearby. The thought played upon her mind. She stood in the middle of the room, her eyes vacantly scanning the crowded chamber for the hundredth time.

Finally, growing more and more convinced that Thanatos must be behind this mysterious disappearance, she left the room. She was angry, and frightened too. The thought of her little friend in the hands of that god made her quail, but what could she do? She walked slowly, by turns dejected and furious, back toward her own room. Thoughts of vengeance began to occupy her.

No, she thought after a moment or two, this was not the time to plan revenge. Her first concern should be to try as hard as she could to find and rescue Alalkomeneus. Vengeance would have to wait until later. If Thanatos had stolen the little god-creature, she would steal him back. Only then would she allow herself the time to properly evolve a plan that would amply repay the trouble and heartache she was suffering.

She had almost reached the chambers of Iapetos when Philyra met her in the corridor. "So there you are, child," her sister said, obviously exasperated. "I've been searching all over for you. It's long past your bedtime. Just what do you think you're doing, traipsing about out here? Metis, if this keeps up, I'm not going to have any choice. I'll have to send you back—"

Philyra stopped short, staring down at her sister's tear-streaked face. Her indignation slipped away and she took the sobbing child in her arms.

Metis spilled out to her all that had happened, from the intrusion of Thanatos into her room through her discovery that Alalkomeneus had disappeared. During the recital, which was interrupted a number of times while she tried to regain her breath, Metis omitted all reference to their brother Proteus, whose presence on Olympos was still unknown to Philyra. She had hidden Alalkomeneus in Crios's room in an attempt to avoid Thanatos, who had been haunting the corridors; there was no need to give every detail.

Outraged at the conduct of the god, Philyra nevertheless realized that Thanatos stood in special favor with Kronos. Gently she led Metis back toward her room, trying to comfort and calm her. The child clung to her.

The entrance hall of the chambers of Iapetos was now lit by a single small lamp; except for Iapetos himself, who had not yet returned home, the members of the family had retired for the night. Once in Metis's own room, Philyra helped her sister undress and then tucked her into bed. She sat beside her for a short while, at first talking softly to quiet her and then simply keeping her company until she fell asleep. Finally, walking on tiptoes, she let herself out of the room.

But Metis was not asleep. She lay very still, listening to the distant sounds her sister made as she prepared to retire herself. When the sounds ceased completely, the child swung out of bed and went quickly to the wall peg where her short white chiton hung. She slipped into it, wrapping and fastening it about herself with practiced, effortless skill. She moved as quietly as she could out of her own room and toward the entrance hall, where she paused to listen for almost a full minute. She heard only the small, unidentifiable noises that any building makes, even the palace of the gods.

She crossed the atrium and made her way down a short, narrow corridor. Opening a door slowly, she inspected the dark room behind and then stepped completely inside.

"Prometheus!" she whispered, feeling her way forward in the pale light that streamed in through the window. "Wake up, Prometheus!"

"What?" a sleepy voice answered. A barely visible figure sat upright.

"Who's there?" another voice asked from the opposite side of the room. Epimetheus was awake too.

"Shh!" she warned. "Please be quiet. I have to talk to you, and need your help."

"Mine too?" Epimetheus asked.

The boys slipped out of their beds and joined her. Soon the three were squatting close together on the floor in a patch of moonlight.

"Yes, you too." She told them much the same story she had told Philyra.

"But you don't *know* that Thanatos took him," Prometheus said when she had finished.

"What else could have happened?"

"You shouldn't have left him alone," Epimetheus said.

"It's a little late to worry about that," Prometheus observed.

"She could have brought him to us. We wouldn't have let Thanatos take him."

"Maybe you're right, but that didn't seem practical at the time," she said. "Thanatos might have come in here. I did the best I could, and now I need your help."

"You know I'll do anything I can for you," Prometheus said.

Epimetheus snickered loudly, and Prometheus glared at him.

"Just what's that supposed to mean?" Prometheus demanded.

"Oh, nothing, nothing at all," Epimetheus said, smiling slyly.

After a moment Prometheus ignored him, turning back to Metis. "What do you want us to do?"

"Come with me. If Thanatos took him, then Alalkomeneus is probably in one of Thanatos's rooms. I want to search for him and steal him back."

"I don't know," Epimetheus said. "None of us is supposed to go to the private chambers of Lord Kronos. Even our father doesn't go there without first being invited. It's not proper . . . proper . . . "

"*Etiquette,*" Prometheus said, supplying the word for his brother.

"It's also not proper etiquette for Thanatos to do any of the things he's done tonight," Metis said.

"I think Metis is right," Prometheus said after a few moments. "But there are things to talk about first. We should plan in advance what we're going to do. Do any of us know which rooms belong to Thanatos? I've never been to Kronos's floor."

The others shook their heads.

"Then how are we going to find his rooms?"

Metis and Epimetheus had no answer.

"And what if we're caught? Either by Thanatos or by Lord Kronos? What will we do then?"

Epimetheus shrugged. "I'd rather worry about it later, if it happens."

"That's not a very good way to approach a problem."

"But it may be the only way, this time," Metis said. "We don't have much time. We can't make plans for everything that might happen. I'm afraid we'll have to take things as they occur. Are you going to come or not?"

"All right. But I'd feel a lot better if we had more information," Prometheus said.

"So would I," Metis admitted.

Prometheus jumped up and went to get cloaks. He threw one to his brother and wrapped the other about his own lithe, bare body. Within moments the three of them made their way out of the silent apartment and set out at once for the stairway, chattering back and forth in excited whispers once they were in the corridor.

They had nearly reached Kronos's floor when Prometheus silenced them. "There's somebody below us, coming up!" he whispered. "I'm sure of it—we have to hide." He led them up the last few steps to the topmost floor of Olympos.

"I didn't hear anything," Epimetheus said.

"You weren't listening. Quick, let's get inside one of these rooms."

He pushed open the nearest door, and the others followed him inside. He left the door open just enough to look out, and a moment later a female figure came into view.

"It's Rhea," Prometheus said. As he watched, she entered a door not far down the hall from them. He turned toward the others, invisible in the darkness of the room. "Is everybody here? I can't see you."

"We're here," both Metis and Epimetheus assured him.

"Good. Rhea almost certainly was going to see Lord Kronos, so we probably know which room he's in. That'll make it easier to search the rest of the rooms, and less dangerous."

He turned back to the door and began to open it. Almost immediately he pushed it closed again, bumping into his companions as he recoiled into the room.

"What's the matter?" Epimetheus whispered.

"It's Eurybie, coming out of the room Rhea just went into!"

"That's interesting," Epimetheus said.

"Quiet." He pressed his ear to the door, trying to hear her departing footsteps. He opened the door stealthily again, made sure the corridor was clear, then led them out.

"All right," he said, pointing, "that's Kronos's room. Now all we have to do is find Thanatos's."

"You take this side of the corridor," Metis said, "and I'll take the other. Listen at each of the doors. If you hear anything inside, it's probably Thanatos."

"And what am I supposed to do?" Epimetheus asked.

Metis considered for a moment, then said, "Well, why don't you start down at the far end and work toward me. When we finish this side, we'll help Prometheus."

Separating, they proceeded to listen at each door. Long minutes passed, until finally they came together to whisper excitedly.

"What now?" Prometheus asked. "As far as we can tell, they're all empty."

Metis grimaced. "Then we'll have to search. Quietly open each door and look inside. We can do it the same way as before, Prometheus on one side, Epimetheus and I working on the other."

"But just what are we looking for?" Epimetheus asked.

"Anything that doesn't look like it belongs to Lord Kronos."

They split up again and proceeded as Metis had suggested. Epimetheus began at the far end of the corridor, and almost immediately signaled excitedly to them.

"Look in here!" he said as they reached him, swinging in one of the large double doors to expose a cluttered interior that could only have belonged to Thanatos.

"And I thought your room was bad," Epimetheus told Metis.

She scowled at him, but did not answer.

"It certainly isn't Lord Kronos's room," Prometheus agreed. "Well, I guess we'd better start searching—but be careful. Thanatos could be asleep."

They carefully closed the doors behind them. Within minutes they had explored the connected rooms. Thanatos was nowhere to be found. Nor was Alalkomeneus. They gathered together in one of the rooms to talk.

Metis, on edge from the excitement of their nocturnal adventure, was looking hopelessly about the room. "We'll have to search more carefully, look inside everything— anywhere that he might be hidden."

Prometheus shook his head. "Thanatos wouldn't keep him out here, not when he could be locked in that last room. We have to find a way to open that door."

They followed him to the rearmost room of the apartment, where he fell once more to examining the huge brass door, attempting to discover the secret of its lock.

"Be careful," Epimetheus warned. "What if Thanatos is inside there?"

Prometheus turned back toward them, frowning. "It doesn't matter. We aren't going to be able to open this. I can't find anything that even looks like a lock."

Metis, heartbroken at the failure of her efforts, sat down in a nearby chair.

"Well, what do we do now?" Epimetheus asked.

"We might as well search as carefully as we can, so we're certain Alalkomeneus isn't out here. Then, in the morning, we can talk to our father and get him to talk to Lord Kronos. Maybe Lord Kronos will make Thanatos give the man back."

Metis shook her head. "Thanatos will only deny knowing anything about him."

"Maybe so, but—" He stopped suddenly, listening. "What's that noise? Let's go!"

From the gallery directly outside the room in which they were talking came the sound of huge, flapping wings. Through one of the windows Metis caught a glimpse of something dark settling upon the balcony. A metallic clang sounded loudly as they ran back through the connecting rooms toward the corridor.

"Was it Thanatos?" Epimetheus asked as they closed the outer door behind them. "Did he see us?"

"I don't know, but we'd better get out of here," Prometheus said.

Hearts pounding, the divine children traversed the corridor as silently as they could in their agitated condition. They had almost reached the stairway when the door to Kronos's room opened. Prometheus led them into a nearby chamber, closing the door as Lady Rhea exited into the corridor.

"Oh, we're going to get caught," Epimetheus whined.

"Quiet," Prometheus warned him, watching from the door. "She didn't see us. She's going to the stairs."

"What about Thanatos?" Epimetheus said.

"He must not have seen us either. He hasn't come out of his room."

"Is she out of sight yet? I want to get back to our room."

Prometheus turned toward them. "Calm down. No one's seen us. We're all right."

"Look at this," Metis whispered. She was standing next to Prometheus, looking through the narrow opening. He turned to look again, then whistled softly.

"Eurybie," he said, "coming back to Kronos's room. I wonder what that means! Isn't anybody going to sleep tonight?"

"I don't care what it means," Epimetheus said. "Let's go home—now, right away."

They waited until Eurybie had entered the private chambers of the King of the Gods, then rushed for the stairs and descended as quickly as possible.

FOURTEEN

Nalassa of the slender shoulders and fluttering eyes had been walking since morning, with only occasional stops to rest her complaining feet or to eat a few handfuls of apples or other fruit plucked from the trees that grew along the path she followed. A number of times during the day she had started to abandon her journey, especially when an invigorating mountain stream or restful bower offered itself for her comfort; but always she stopped for only a few minutes, dangling her feet in the caressing silver water or lolling beneath the shade of towering cypress trees, then once again taking up her path toward the north and Mount Olympos.

The holiday spirit in which she had begun her journey rapidly dissipated, and she soon began to question the wisdom of her decision and to draw up objections of every sort. Her parents and sisters would wonder where she was, and she should have gone back to tell them she planned to visit Olympos. She had avoided doing that because she didn't want to have to explain her actions; still, they would be concerned about her, and their curiosity would have to be satisfied when she did return.

A central objection lay behind all the others. Lord Proteus had piqued her pride—a crime she might have overlooked with only minor difficulty. But he had also awakened the first glimmers of love within her. The combination of the two was inexcusable, particularly since she refused to admit the latter.

She had as much right to visit Olympos as the ocean god. There was no reason she shouldn't take advantage of the open invitation of the Titans. She wasn't following Proteus. That he was going there simply suggested the possibility of her own trip, that was all. Yet a part of her realized that her motivations were more complicated, that she wanted more than a holiday among the gods or the chance to take some little revenge on Proteus.

She told herself the many ways in which she would rebuff him when he once again decided to pay attention to her. He did find her attractive; she had little. doubt of that—though that little added still another small eddy to the turmoil of her emotions. On Olympos, among the gods and Titans, he would have to win her with delicacy and consideration, not by swiftness and strength.

But on Olympos there were many goddesses, some more beautiful than she, and some, undoubtedly, less concerned about the niceties of etiquette and courtship. The god who had shown so little personal interest in her this morning might show even less when surrounded by divine femininity. He might not even notice her among such an assemblage.

She threw up her head, straightened her shoulders, and threw out her chest at such thoughts. What did she care about the ocean god? She could ignore him just as easily as he could ignore her—and there were many gods on Olympos, as many gods as goddesses. Not all of them could be thoughtless and indifferent to her charms.

Yet he had been very tender when it mattered most, no more forceful than necessary to overcome her resistance. She was still unsure exactly why she had let him catch her—certainly she had not intended to. What perverse whim led her to reveal herself by bolting across his path as he came toward her in the moonlight? She had been well concealed among the rocks and bushes, watching his approach. He would have passed close to her without ever being aware of her presence if she had merely continued to lie perfectly still and remained quiet.

Instead she had jumped up and run across a wide, open area, an action that, in retrospect, seemed designed to tempt him into chasing her. Of course, she expected to have little trouble eluding him among the stark cliffs that had been her playground since childhood, where—to be completely honest—

he was rather awkward. Instead of easily outdistancing him, she hung back, toying with him—the thought made her blush— and letting him almost reach her before she scrambled away, just out of his grasp. As the chase continued, she delayed her reactions still more, so that each time he came closer and closer to catching her, and at last his outstretched hand, instead of slipping ineffectually from her slender wrist, held fast, yanking her back. Powerful arms encircled her, pinning her helplessly against him.

Still, she thought somewhat wistfully, he was very handsome, and the tenderness in his eyes and hands had served at least partially to quiet the helpless, trembling creature she had become. If, indeed, the time had come for her to be caught, she could have fared far worse. Perhaps, like fruit ripened and ready to fall, her season had finally arrived. Perhaps her long-standing inner equilibrium, delicately balanced between the growing needs of her body and her apprehensions concerning a final step into full adulthood, had at last been tilted a trifle too far by the vision of divine Proteus as he strode toward her in the moonlight.

Despite such thoughts she continued walking toward Olympos. Night began to fall, and now, far from home, she wished that she had traveled faster, or that she had not undertaken the journey at all. She walked a little more briskly, a cool breeze brushing through her long hair. The majestic might of Olympos was just becoming visible, thrusting upward from among the innumerable smaller mountains and hills in the distance. The final, weak rays of daylight fled and the moon began to rise, large and full.

The distance gave way beneath her divine stride. Stepping across a river, she detoured around a high bluff. As she drew nearer to Olympos, she began to dread the ascent that lay before her. Her pace slowed and she considered resting for the night. She had not remembered how steep the slopes were, or how high towered the jagged peaks of the mountain. The climb would be difficult beyond anything she had imagined, and she began to wonder if it were not beyond her capabilities. Her father, of course, would merely have metamorphosed himself into a flying creature; or, as when he had taken her to Olympos with him, he would have caused huge wings to grow from his shoulder blades, that he might carry her upward. Like many naiads and forest nymphs, she had never mastered the ability to change forms. At most she could cause a sort of blurring of her features, but then after an instant she invariably returned to her natural state.

She was getting quite close to her goal now, and her pace had slackened considerably. Nearby was a low, rounded hill, and she used it as a stool to sit upon while she contemplated her situation. In amazement she noticed the condition of her short tunic. Even in the moonlight she could see that it had grown very dirty during the day's journey—almost gray with dirt—and her legs bore a number of nasty scratches from the times she had been careless in pushing her way through thickets of trees.

The sea lay at some distance to her right; nearer, glinting in the moonlight, a number of small mountain brooks twisted and babbled their ways downward. It took her only a few moments to discard the idea of bathing tonight; she was far too tired. Instead she would rest for a few minutes, then find some comfortable place to sleep. In the morning she would bathe and wash her tunic, then lie in the sun while it dried. There would be time enough to worry about how she would reach the summit of Olympos; she was too tired to think clearly about it now.

She was about to force herself to rise and begin looking for a place to sleep, when a clanging noise attracted her attention. Not far away a dark, winged form was settling upon a rocky crest. Large, gangly birds followed it down, most of them perching on the rocks around the feet of the winged god, but two or three attempting to settle upon the god's shoulders, only to have him brush them away.

As soon as Nalassa saw these intruders upon her serenity, she rolled silently to the far side of the hill upon which she had been sitting. She pressed herself against the cool surface and watched in absolute silence as the god, tall and slender and beardless, folded his vulture wings against his back and turned his attention briefly to the large brass cage he had set upon the rocks at his feet. His vulture companions, of which there were nearly a dozen, had settled all about him, though some still stretched and fluttered their wings. One perched atop the cage, peering down at the creatures within and occasionally making short, pecking motions toward them.

She was reasonably sure the god had not seen her, and so her safest course lay in remaining perfectly still until he left.

He was looking around, first out toward the sea, then inland. He checked the cage, apparently to make sure the door was securely closed. Spreading his huge wings in a languid motion, he rose into the air and flew inland, soon disappearing among the peaks of a small group of mountains.

Nalassa watched until he was out of sight, then rose and crept forward to more carefully inspect the cage. The vultures had remained, as though to guard it, and so she did not approach any closer than necessary to see that within the brass enclosure were nearly two dozen of the small godlike creatures that Proteus had pointed out to her that morning. A few of them were examining the glinting brass that kept them prisoners. The bars were loosely set in their sockets and rattled when touched.

The vultures had not seemed to notice her approach; but now, as she turned to retreat to her hiding place, one of them began to screech and flap its wings. Rising into the air, it darted toward her, and the others followed its lead. Even though it was only a bird, not even as big as her fist, its sharp beak and raking talons could cause severe pain and even blind her. She swatted at them, backing away and trying to protect her face. One clung to her, sinking its claws into the soft flesh of her bare arm and pecking at her breasts.

A black shadow swooped downward. The winged god had deceived her, flying away only to circle back. A rock slid from beneath her foot and she stumbled just as he landed beside her, reaching out with an emaciated arm that, nevertheless, contained great strength.

As he lunged for her, she rolled away along the gravel surface, barely managing to elude his grasp. Nimbly she regained her feet and ran between two boulders, then darted into the greater darkness among overhanging rocks. There were no trees here, and little foliage in the barren area where she had chosen to rest. She had to find concealment among the boulders and shadows near a precipicelike hill. Panting for breath, she found an ink-black recess and hid herself, fighting to quiet her heavy breathing. From not far away she could hear the crunching sounds of small rocks being ground together beneath the god's feet as he walked. She pressed herself deeper into the recess. The crunching sound seemed to be coming closer.

She was trembling with almost uncontrolled fear, with a

stark terror that the still-rational portion of her mind found surprising. Her mouth was very dry, parched. She tried to listen, but now could not hear him. Far off a mountain brook still gurgled, and the pounding of her own heart seemed very loud.

Had he left? Or was he waiting for her to move, to show herself? If he had left, she should have heard the flapping of his wings.

No—she heard something now, the sound of creeping footsteps, of a god moving forward over the rough ground one step at a time. She held her breath, ready to bolt from her hiding place should she be discovered. Her muscles tensed in anticipation, ready to carry her scampering over the rocky ground. Very slowly the footsteps came closer, and now she could just barely see the god; moonlight glinted from his pale white face. His long black cloak was wrapped completely around his lean body, and his face turned slowly from side to side as he advanced, his dull eyes searching the black shadows.

Now his gaze turned directly toward her. Her muscles trembled as she forced herself to remain completely still. Did he see her? He seemed to be looking directly at her, but she thought—*hoped*—the darkness hid her from him.

He continued walking. She waited until he was out of sight, having turned a corner in the ravine, then crept from the shadows of her hiding place and moved quickly in the opposite direction.

She had taken only a few steps, though, when a vulture began to shriek loudly from high above her. Within moments the sky was filled with the birds, each screeching fiercely as it darted downward, swooping at her head and face with raking talons. She ran, holding her hands to her face. The ravine twisted first one way, then another, but the vultures followed above her, refusing to let her escape. At the mouth of the ravine she came face to face with the god.

This time she did not try to avoid him; she ran straight toward him, and as his arms reached out for her, she threw herself against him, knocking him to one side. Her ploy was only partially successful. His fingers closed upon her arm and swung her back. She struck at his face and chest with her clenched fists and tried to kick with her bare feet.

For a few moments he dodged her blows, which seemed more to annoy him than to hurt, but then he struck her across the mouth with the back of his hand. She staggered, the strength gone out of her, and sank slowly to the ground at his feet.

Dimly, as though observed from a distance, she was aware of his actions. Crouching beside her, he drew a dagger from within his cloak. With it he cut long strips of cloth from her tunic, then proceeded to bind her hands and feet and finally to gag her. Throwing her over one shoulder, he carried her back to where he had left the brass cage. He grasped its handle with one hand, then spread his wings.

Accompanied by his entourage of vultures, Thanatos began the long ascent to Olympos, the barely concious naiad over one shoulder and the brass cage clanging in his hand.

FIFTEEN

Once Kronos and Eurybie passed him on their way to the king's bedroom, Proteus slipped from his hiding place and moved quickly through an open doorway toward another series of rooms. It was his intention to search the personal chambers of Kronos for Aigaion, the missing sea god.

He moved swiftly, even in the form of Momos, returning to the outer gallery to gain entry to other suites and venturing out into the main corridor to procure a torch when he needed light. Only the bedroom of the king and the chambers of Thanatos avoided his inspection. The sound of Thanatos fluttering about his apartment warned Proteus away before he could be detected.

Finally, unable to locate the cell in which Aigaion was imprisoned or any clue to the god's whereabouts, Proteus returned to the outer gallery. Transforming himself into a gull, he swooped downward through the night air, flying completely around the palace. Only a few apartments still showed signs of wakefulness, and he flew past each of these. One drew his attention particularly, so that he perched outside to observe the inhabitants.

It was the apartment of Themis, the former wife of Iapetos. Iapetos was with her, standing near the door, apparently about to depart. As Proteus watched, the Titan turned suddenly and took the goddess in his arms. She seemed not to respond to his impassioned kiss at first, but gradually her arms slipped around him. When their lips finally parted, she was clinging to him. A moment later he left her. As the door closed, Themis threw herself upon the nearby couch and began to cry.

Proteus continued back to Metis's room. He found her there, but not alone. Her sister Philyra sat beside her, her expression very serious as she lectured the child. She had caught her trying to sneak back to her room after the unsuccessful attempt to find Alalkomeneus in the chambers of Thanatos.

Assuming his own form, Proteus stepped into the room. "Not long ago," he told Philyra, "Klymene would have been preaching to you, not you to Metis."

Philyra leaped up from the bed at his sudden appearance, a startled cry on her lips. The cry became an exclamation of delight as she recognized him.

"Brother!" She ran toward him, threw her arms around him as warmly as Metis had. "Oh, it's been so long since I've seen you."

Metis had jumped out of bed as well, and was now standing beside them. "Proteus, you won't believe what happened—"

He drew back from them. "Quiet, both of you. You'll wake the others."

"What's this?" Philyra asked, turning toward Metis. "You knew he was here?"

Metis nodded. "He didn't want me to tell you."

She looked back at her brother, more puzzled than hurt.

Proteus nodded. "I'll explain it all to you in a few minutes. I wanted to have the opportunity to look around before anyone knew I was here. Even now it's still important—at least until I decide just what has to be done—that my presence be known only to you two."

"You mean you don't want Klymene to know?" Philyra asked.

He nodded. "No one but the three of us. Not Klymene, nor Iapetos, nor anyone else, until I tell you otherwise."

"If that's what you wish, brother," Philyra said, "but Klymene will certainly be disappointed. She loves you very dearly and speaks of you often to her husband and children."

Metis interrupted. "I have to tell you what happened. Thanatos stole Alalkomeneus from—"

"Quiet child," he warned her. "Keep your voice low. I want to hear what you have to say, but speak softly."

She did as he bid her, quickly relating the entire story. As she reached the end of it, Philyra said, "And I had gone to look in on her, and found her gone. The child is becoming incorrigible." She laughed. "Not that she didn't have provocation, but I was dreadfully worried about her and didn't know what to do, since Lord Iapetos was still not home. . . ."

"*I* am going to take care of Thanatos," Metis said.

Proteus looked down at Metis. "I'm sorry," he said simply. "I know you were very attached to the little creature, and it certainly was my fault that you left him in Crios's room."

"No," Metis said. "It's not your fault. Thanatos wanted him and would have kept trying until he got him."

"Possibly so. It's still possible that you may be able to get him back. Perhaps tomorrow I'll be able to help you. I want to learn more about Thanatos anyway—but I must tell you, there are far more serious things going on here on Olympos, and I'm afraid most of my time—much of your time as well, both of you—will have to be devoted to them."

"What are you talking about?" Philyra asked.

"Okeanos has sent me here. His friend Aigaion, a brother of Lord Nereus, has disappeared—apparently while visiting Olympos. Can you tell me anything about him, Philyra?"

She shook her head. "I saw him here once or twice. I never even stopped to think about it when I didn't see him again."

"From what I heard tonight, I believe Kronos has made him a prisoner—here on Olympos, I think. It seems that Kronos forced him to admit to being part of a conspiracy by Okeanos and Nereus to overthrow Kronos."

"But that's impossible," Philyra exclaimed. "Father would never do such a thing."

"Nor would Nereus," Proteus said. "Father sent me here to help Aigaion, but I've found something of greater concern to us. Kronos plans to use this imaginary plot as an excuse to depose our father and Lord Nereus. At the wedding of Eurybie, when both of them are together and off guard, Kronos will take them prisoner. Probably he plans to send them to Tartaros. A number of Titans are conspiring with Kronos. If his plan succeeds, Crios and Eurybie will be the new rulers of the sea."

"And our poor sister . . . ?" Philyra said.

Proteus nodded. "Queen Doris will accompany her husband, I suppose." He hesitated. "And the ocean will be ruled by Iapetos and Klymene."

"That can't be true," Philyra said. "I don't believe it."

He shrugged. "It's true, though Klymene is unaware of the role she is to play. Iapetos hasn't told her yet."

Metis was shaking her head vehemently. "You must be wrong, brother. The first thing you should do is tell Klymene. Things can't be as they seem."

"I hope you're right, but no, I don't want Klymene to know any of this. Not until I've had time to learn all I can and to think all of this through."

"But certainly there's no danger now," Philyra said. "Not now that we know about it and will warn our father and King Nereus."

"There's more danger than ever."

"But if they're warned, they can simply avoid the wedding," she protested.

"You forget our father. It would be cowardice to avoid danger, or at least that's how he'll feel. As to Nereus, he won't flee either. No, they'll both walk right into the danger."

"But they'll defend themselves. Certainly our father will."

He nodded. "Indeed he will, and—"

"And that would mean open hostility among the gods," Metis said.

"Yes," he continued, "and the world as you know it would cease to exist. The gods would take sides, and the order which has made possible all that has been built will crumble. And in the end both Nereus and Okeanos might be overthrown anyway."

"What can we do?" Philyra asked.

Proteus ran his fingers through his dark hair. "Warn Okeanos and Nereus, of course, to put them on their guard. More importantly than that, I think, we must try to do what we can here. Perhaps there is a way we can break up this conspiracy before things have gone too far. If I can find Aigaion and free him, it might weaken Kronos's position. I don't think he would abandon his plan just because his witness is gone, but the other Titans might be discouraged. From what I overheard Kronos saying, I think Aigaion must still be here on Olympos. At the very least he can't be far away. Kronos plans to take him to the wedding in his own entourage.''

He paused for a moment, then continued. ''Tonight the moon is full. We have until the new moon, when the wedding will be held. It won't be easy. Kronos is not only powerful, but extremely clever. His cunning must not be underestimated. . . .''

''Could we do to him as he would do to our father?'' Metis asked.

''No. Not only because we probably aren't capable of such a thing, but because the end result would be the same. Some of the gods would continue to support Kronos. They would fight against us. Our only course right now is to learn all we can so we can be ready to twist any opportunity to our advantage—and to try to find Aigaion.''

''I still can't believe Iapetos would have anything to do with this,'' Philyra said.

''I saw him with my own eyes. I heard him discuss this plot with his fellow conspirators.''

''Perhaps he, too, plans to work against Kronos. Perhaps he's only pretending,'' Metis said.

''Brother,'' Philyra said, ''here is something that might be of use to us, though I don't like to say so. Lord Kronos has taken a sudden interest in me. He's sent me a valuable gift and invited me to breakfast tomorrow morning. I've been upset over it all day, but Klymene says I can't tactfully decline his present or his invitation.''

''What are you suggesting?'' Proteus asked.

An embarrassed flush spread across her face. ''I was thinking that someone . . . someone in that position might be able to learn things we couldn't otherwise learn.''

He laughed. ''Philyra, are you volunteering to give yourself to him to gain his confidence?''

Her embarrassment became extreme. ''No! You know I couldn't do that. I—I was only thinking that if I—if I *toyed* with him for a few days, keeping him at a distance but—''

Proteus shook his head. ''That's very noble of you, but it wouldn't work. He isn't someone to toy with, and I doubt you could hide your true feelings.''

''I suppose you're right,'' she said softly.

''There's something I should tell both of you,'' Proteus said. ''Metis, I mentioned earlier that I had seen you and the

Muses when you found Alalkomeneus and the other men. I was across the plain from you, in a valley. I fell into a prophetic trance. There was a young water nymph with me, and afterward she told me what I had said."

"What was it?" both sisters asked, leaning forward.

"I'm going to tell you. It would seem to apply to what is happening here on Olympos. You know that when I speak of the future, it is often in riddles and difficult or impossible to interpret. I want to remind you of that."

"Go on," Metis said. "What was it?"

"This is what I said, as best the nymph could remember it: 'Change follows change when god devours god. Titan against Titan, god against god . . . power unleashed, force undreamt. . . . The gull shall weep, the eagle cease to soar, when the white mare rears her hooves and the broken willow pierces their hearts.' "

" 'The gull shall weep . . .' " Philyra said. "The gull must be our father—he often takes that shape."

"And the eagle would be Kronos," Metis said.

"Our father shall weep and Lord Kronos shall cease to soar—does that mean that he will cease to rule? Oh, what does it mean, brother?"

He shrugged. "Perhaps that is it. It seems likely."

"Then we are doomed to failure," Philyra said, "for whatever we do, our father shall lose."

"Not necessarily," he said, seeming suddenly very weary. "Our father would weep if he were forced to harm his own brother. The prophecy could be read that way."

"But Titan will fight Titan—and that's just what you're trying to avoid. 'Titan against Titan, god against god'—with terrible new forces unleashed. Doesn't that mean that we will fail if we try to prevent all this from happening? Change will follow change and god will devour god—isn't that what you said? Doesn't that mean that the gods will fight against each other, whatever we do?"

He shook his head. "Change follows change *when* god devours god. If we can keep the gods from fighting each other, none of that need happen."

" 'The gull shall weep, the eagle cease to soar, when . . .' What was the last part of it?" Philyra asked.

" '. . . when the white mare rears her hooves and the broken willow pierces their hearts,' " Proteus repeated.

"Who's the white mare?" Philyra demanded. "What's the broken willow?"

Proteus shrugged. "The interpretation lies hidden in the future."

"Proteus," Metis said, "couldn't the gull refer to you as well as to our father?"

"That has occurred to me. I don't think we can learn very much from this prophecy now. Too much is in doubt, but I felt I should tell you about it."

He looked wearily around the room. "It's late and I'm growing tired. Philyra, may I sleep here in Metis's room?"

"Her bed's small. I'll bring blankets for matting."

"Yes, please. I'll be quite comfortable on the floor."

While Metis prepared for bed and Philyra went to procure blankets, Proteus returned to the gallery and leaned over the railing to draw up shreds of cloud from far below. When enough of the nebulous material had collected in the palms of his hands, he stared down fixedly at it. The wisps began to form themselves into the shape of a living creature, coalescing and darkening. It turned deep green, and except for its eyes and mouth, was shaped like a fish; but now Proteus commanded hawk wings to grow from its back. The creature heaved rhythmically at first, then began to twist and wriggle. He stroked it until it started to make soft, almost mewing sounds.

He raised the creature so that its deep eyes, embued with intelligence, looked into his own. "I send you to Lord Okeanos, King of Ocean Depths. Fly swiftly with your wings, swim as rapidly as your fish tail can propel you through the blue depths, and say to Lord Okeanos—'From Proteus, your son: Greetings, keen-sighted Titan whose ears are as sharp as his eyes. The hunter does not turn back when the spoor is old, the trail long and treacherous. Beware—the eagle hunts the gull beneath the new moon.' Say these things to Lord Okeanos and to none other."

The creature purred as he spoke.

"Repeat the message," he commanded.

The creature obeyed, speaking in an odd, whispering voice.

"Good." Proteus threw the phantom messenger far out into the night. He stood there watching as it spread its wings and began to fly in the direction of the palace of Okeanos.

Philyra had just entered with blankets for him. With her help he spread them on the floor and then lay down.

As Proteus drifted toward sleep, elsewhere in the palace another god stirred toward consciousness. He had been sleeping for a very long time. While he slept he did not have to think or remember, and wakefulness inevitably led to one or the other of those painful occupations.

In his still groggy state he started to stretch the stiffness out of his body. His body refused to stretch, refused to move at all. He tried to open his eyes and look around, but everything was blackness. He could not even be sure if his eyes were open, because he could not move his eyelids. Then he started to remember. He was pinned down somehow, held fast, and no amount of exertion would serve to move an arm or leg or finger or toe.

He was not even sure now whether he was lying down or standing up. His muscles had been locked in the same position for so long that he could no longer determine their state with accuracy. He wondered how long he had been like this, just what had happened. The memory eluded him, and he turned his mind instead to his more immediate problem.

He would make one last attempt to move some part of his body. He would flex the index finger of his right hand—not actually move it, but flex it ever so slightly. For a few moments he gathered his strength in preparation, but then he realized suddenly that he could not even find his finger. He could no longer sense where it was located.

What had happened? Why could he not remember?

Aigaion, the sea god, wondered if his mind was becoming frozen too.

SIXTEEN

For Alalkomeneus the day had been no more extraordinary than the three that had preceeded it, since he had battered his way out of the dark warmth of the mud womb in which he had developed.

Lacking both language and experience, he perceived rather than thought—and all the world seemed to be his to perceive. When the wind blew across the plain, it swaddled him in the lush, sweet smell of tall grass. The crackling of dried leaves beneath his feet provided exquisite sensual delight.

Soon there were others of his kind, but he paid them little notice. He accepted them as he accepted the earth and the sky, the gentle caress of the breeze and the soft murmuring of the stream. He had an overwhelming need to learn the taste of everything, and when an acorn cracked beneath his strong teeth, he discovered the sweet kernel within. When he ate many of them, the discomfort within him went away, replaced by a warm satiety that made him want to lie for a long time in the soft grass.

The second day there were more creatures like himself, and still more on the third. One tried to push him away from the thick pile of acorns he had gathered, but he pushed back. The man fell down and made loud, peculiar sounds with his mouth.

One of the men learned to throw rocks, making them splash in the stream, and before long Alalkomeneus and most of the others joined him. There were small, winged creatures—not the insects that buzzed and fluttered about constantly, but other, larger creatures which settled in the ash and oak trees and made lovely warbling sounds. Occasionally these flying things settled upon the ground, pecking among the grass, and some of the men found amusement in throwing rocks at them. Alalkomeneus threw, too, even though he liked the sounds they made and did not want them to fly away.

The birds always flew off . . . all but one. Its wings would not flap properly. The men kept throwing stones at it. Alalkomeneus wished that it would go away, because now it made harsh, squawking sounds, not the pretty ones he liked. Finally it grew quiet, and Alalkomeneus wandered off to find other diversions.

He came upon the bird later, as evening was approaching, and was surprised to see that it was still there, partly covered by jagged rocks. It was even more colorful than before, with a red wetness over much of its body. He nudged it, but it refused to move by itself. He cleared away the rocks and picked it up. The head hung limply to one side and the wet redness transferred itself to his fingers and hands. No matter how hard he shook the creature, it refused to sing or even to make the harsh sounds he disliked. He did not like the way the red wetness felt on his hands, and he dropped the bird so that he could wipe them on the grass.

Thus passed his days, in dimly perceived needs, in simple sensual delights and instinctive fears. The fears came upon him most often at night, when the world became dark around him and the haunting cries of hunter and hunted spoke directly to his nervous system. The distant cough of a lion always made him shudder.

And then Metis and the other goddesses intruded upon his three-day-old world, snatching him from his peers. Once he recovered from the paralysis that had overwhelmed him, he accepted Olympos as he had accepted the world below. The walls of the palace loomed around him, so high that he was not really aware that he was within an enclosure. The very atmosphere of Olympos made his skin tingle with life and well-being. When Metis held him against her breast, the perfume of her body—infinitely delicate, yet full and rich—intoxicated his senses, lulling him into drowsy comfort beyond anything he had experienced. Her warmth crept into his bones and quieted every fear and emotion, so that he wanted nothing more than to have her go on holding him.

As the gods talked—Metis, Prometheus and Epimetheus, Philyra and Klymene—the divine music of their voices danced and twirled within his brain. He watched their every movement with wonder, overwhelmed by the perfect grace of their slightest gestures. The sight and sound of them, even the most awkward of them, made his senses spark and tingle, so that whenever he was away from them he sought to regain the enchanted vision denied him.

Then there was Thanatos, whose mere presence unleashed waves of terror—a mindless, gibbering, instinctive fear that ignited every molecule of his being. Such a fear could not be overcome, but it could be momentarily forgotten. When he saw Metis, his goddess, wince and cry out from the god's blows, he rushed forward to pound upon Thanatos's foot. The god seemed not even to feel his attack, and Alalkomeneus fell backward next to an enormous shard from a broken vase. The shard was as large as a boulder, though not nearly as heavy. Lifting it above his head, he ran forward to throw it. Instead he stumbled, and the jagged point came down against the god's ankle.

He was content after that, cuddled against her, bathed in the perfume of her skin and the music of her voice. He was content until she left him closed up, alone, in the room of the Titan Crios. Almost immediately loneliness and loss overwhelmed him. He began to search for a way out of the room, that he might once again drench himself in the warmth of the goddess.

Along the base of each wall ran a frieze of red and black silhouettes depicting forest and plain, antelope, boar, and bison. The landscape was nearly life-size. Alalkomeneus, innocent of pictorial representations, approached it as soon as he discovered he could not follow Metis through the door. The flat surface puzzled him, and he felt his way along it, searching for a point at which he could enter the peculiar vista. In the course of his exploration he discovered a crevice. Almost completely hidden by the black silhouette of which it was a part, it was further camouflaged by the shadows that obscured that portion of the room.

He pulled at the opening and a few pieces of a rocklike substance crumbled away. Soon the ragged fissure was large enough for him to squirm through. Inside, the opening flared into a tunnel-like passage, worn smooth and almost completely circular. The smell of age hung heavily in the air, and within a few steps of the entrance the darkness became so intense that he could distinguish nothing. The man stopped near the mouth of the passage, hesitating as he became more and more uneasy. The smooth walls and hoary odor made his scalp prickle. He turned to climb back out into the room, but slipped on one of the rock fragments. Before he could catch himself, he rolled down the steeply inclined surface. His head struck heavily against the smooth stone floor, and he tumbled downward into the utter blackness.

When he regained consciousness he was lying in a nearly horizontal section of the passage. His head and limbs ached, but the thick clothing in which Metis had dressed him—which he had found so annoying earlier—had saved most of his body from other damage. In both directions the tunnel sloped upward, and so he could not tell from which direction he had come. After a few minutes he rose and began walking. When the incline became extreme he crawled forward on his hands and knees.

Tired and uneasy, his mind filled with images of Metis and the other gods, he followed the twists and turns of the passage. A number of times the tunnel veered into a dead end and he was forced to return to the main passage. From behind the wall at one of these dead ends he could clearly hear the distant voices of gods. He pounded against the rocky surface until his hands stung, and yelled in his small, human voice, but no one seemed to hear him.

The tunnel remained more or less horizontal for some distance, then turned upward. His only awareness of time was in how tired and hungry he was becoming, but a number of hours must have elapsed. He stopped to rest more and more often. Each time images of the gods and the gnawing of hunger made him resume his journey. The path continued upward, assuming an inclination that made walking even more difficult and tiring.

At last a light came into view, dim and far away. He rushed forward, panting for breath. As he neared it, the light increased in size until he could see that the entire area of the passage was open at that point. A foul smell, at first faint, grew in intensity.

He stopped at the edge of the passageway, where it opened into a room of the palace. Unlike the entrance in Crios's room, which was almost at floor level, this exit was high on the wall, just below the ceiling. From the edge of this precipice he looked down upon a chamber lit by wall lamps. Almost immediately he recognized the dark-mantled figure that moved about among the many tables. At the sight of him Alalkomeneus recoiled, stumbling back into the dark passage.

Fear gripped him, but so did curiosity. Behind him lay only the endless tunnel. Slowly, stealthily, he crawled back toward the lip of the passage. Lying at full length, he positioned himself so that only his eyes and the topmost portion of his head protruded into the room. In fearful fascination he watched the actions of the god.

Thanatos had returned to the room only a short time before. Nalassa, bound with strips cut from her tunic, lay huddled near a wall. She was still gagged. On a broad table the god had set his brass cage; inside it Alalkomeneus could recognize other creatures like himself.

The god was moving quickly back and forth, occupied with his work. He spoke aloud, perhaps to the naiad, perhaps to himself. Suddenly he went to the cage, pulled open a door on its top and thrust in his hand. He brought out a squirming, shrieking man.

Thanatos carried the man to the table he had prepared. Laying him on it face up, he held the squirming body in place with one hand while the other reached for a small brass blade. With a single deft motion the god pulled the gleaming instrument across the man's neck. The head popped away from the body and blood gushed from the neck in pulsing spurts. The body twitched for a few seconds, then lay still.

Watching in mingled horror and fascination from his high vantage point, Alalkomeneus had seen all that had happened. He saw the red wetness spout from the body and remembered the bird that refused to sing or fly away. He did not understand what had taken place, but suddenly he felt very bad inside. Edging back from the opening, he rose to his feet and ran back down the passageway. He ran until the light was no longer visible behind him, then collapsed upon the floor.

The two images—the limp, red-smeared bird and the creature so like himself, but with head and body separated and red, sticky wetness gushing out—kept rising within his brain. Mentally he kept hearing the shrill shrieks of the man and the hoarse squawking of the bird as it tried to flap its broken wings.

He started running again, trying to escape the images and sounds, but they followed him, stayed within his mind. He ran until his legs refused to run anymore. Collapsing on the floor, he moaned softly for a minute or two, then slept. He dreamed red and haunting dreams.

SEVENTEEN

Sleep had come upon the palace of Olympos. One by one the gods and goddesses had yawned and stretched and finally retired for the night. Stillness settled upon the palace, and in sleep's train followed capricious dreams.

Kronos, King of the Gods, slept fitfully. Eurybie slumbered beside him, untroubled, her head pillowed upon his massive biceps. In his dream the slight weight of the goddess's head against his arm, and the light pressure of the furs that covered him, seemed confining—seemed to grow more confining with each moment. In his dream he struggled to escape the growing, smothering imprisonment—not of these insignificant weights, but of the cramped cavern within the earth in which Ouranos, his father, was planning to put him.

Dimly, in some half-awake portion of his mind, he realized that the old dream of his youth had come again to torment him; the realization served to reassure him for only a moment. The small, still aware part of his mind was swept under by sleep, and again his towering father stalked the world, the ground trembling beneath his feet.

Terror-stricken, mud-streaked, the Kronos of old ran to hide himself among the hills and tall trees. In the distance he spied Gaia, his mother, and now he ran toward her, threw himself into her arms, sobbing in fear.

From behind her back she brought forth a huge sickle,

toothed with jagged pieces of adamant, and thrust it toward his trembling hand.

Beads of translucent ichor hung suspended from the teeth of the weapon, glinting in the moonlight. Now he noticed that in her other hand his mother held a severed head, the head of Nereus. Wide eyes glared at Kronos as the mouth opened and closed, like that of a fish. Words drifted from the mouth, rather than being spoken, coming toward him in slow waves.

"Father, beware thy child . . . Father, beware thy child . . . beware thy child . . . thy child . . . thy child . . ."

Now he realized that his mother no longer held the sickle; instead it was the sword made for him by Iapetos, with which he planned to decapitate Nereus. Clear droplets of ichor dangled from it. His mother was speaking too. The words came like the low voice of the wind, and he struggled to listen and comprehend.

"Child, beware thy child . . . thy child . . . thy child . . ."

Divine blood dripped from the ragged neck of Nereus and from the gleaming edge of the sword, bubbling as it touched the ground. From it began to grow goddesses. Within moments they were full-size, three goddesses draped in black night, their hair bristling with serpents. Gaia was gone, replaced by the centermost of them, who held the bronze sword in one hand and the head of Nereus in the other. The goddess on her right held an upraised torch; the one on her left, a long, cruel whip. They had continued, unbroken, the chanting of Gaia and Nereus, their voices filling him with dread.

"Father, beware thy child . . . child, beware thy child . . ."

The head of Nereus transformed itself, so that now the middle goddess held an infant by its feet, ichor dripping from its decapitated neck. As she proffered the body to him . . .

Kronos awakened, sitting upright in bed. Eurybie stirred at his side.

"What's wrong?" she asked, yawning lazily.

Shivering in the dim light of a single small lamp, he sat hugging himself and pulling the covers up around his chest and shoulders. "Light more lamps. By the earth and sky, Eurybie," he cried, "light more lamps!"

She jumped out of bed and did as he requested. When she had finished she said, "There, there, my lord, all the lamps are lit and everything's all right."

Wiping the sweat from his brow, he turned upon her savagely. "Be quiet, will you!"

She tried to put her arm around his shoulder. He shook it away.

"My, it must have been a *very* bad dream."

"Just leave me alone," he said. "Go away."

Drawing herself up haughtily, she dressed and left the room without speaking another word. He heard the outer door of the apartment close behind her.

Kronos remained sitting on the side of the bed, still shivering and hugging himself. He kept pressing his eyes shut, as though to keep out the dream and the memories it stirred. Finally he took a heavy cloak from one of the wall pegs and carried it out onto the gallery of the apartment. He caused enormous eagle wings to grow from his shoulders, then flew down from the palace, not toward the earth below but to a distant peak of Mount Olympos.

Reabsorbing his wings, he wrapped himself in the cloak and began to walk among the craggy rocks. Here the air was cold. Snow lay upon the rough path he followed.

Below him lay the sea of clouds, reflecting upward the diminishing light of the moon. Where the clouds parted he could look down upon vast stretches of hill and mountain and forest. He walked slowly, sunk in deep and troubled thought.

His mind turned automatically to the long years of his childhood, when his father and mother walked the hills and forests in the form of immortal gods. He and his brothers and sisters had lived in squalor and ignorance, worse even than the wild animals. Having no thick fur to shield them from the cold, they plastered their skins with mud to keep themselves warm. They devoured raw cattle and deer plucked up from the vast herds that swarmed upon the grasslands. They fought each other continually, for scraps of food or for a cavern large enough to serve as shelter.

From time to time he would visit his enormous mother, receiving joyously the thoughtless kisses and caresses she bestowed. He would sit and watch her for hours. She was a vision of loveliness, lying upon her back in fields of flowers and thinking her unknowable thoughts. He yearned for her caresses and soft words whenever he was away from her.

And he despised the brutality of his brothers. As the youngest of the Titans, he had spent his earliest years hiding from them in their wrath, yearning for the day of his maturity, when they would tremble at his advance—when they would hide from *his* fury.

All of them feared their father, mighty Ouranos, who dealt blows to insolent mouths and was not at all sure he should ever have fathered this Titan brood. Gaia, their mother, had also borne six monstrous children, creatures of ugliness and violence, and these had taxed Ouranos's patience beyond endurance; monstrously misshapen, they were overbearing and presumptuous as well. He thrust them into a cavern within the earth and kept them confined there. In time he began to think that perhaps he should deal with all his offspring in this manner.

Gaia wept for her unlucky children and grew tired of the tyranny of her husband. She began to wish to be free of his dominance, but all the Titans feared him. None wanted to risk his blows and imprisonment.

But Kronos, fearful as the others, thought a great deal about what she said. He imagined himself overthrowing their father and replacing him as foremost of the gods. Visions of all he might accomplish competed with terrifying fears of punishment if he should fail. Gaia encouraged him, until finally hope of success outweighed fear.

She gave him the enormous sickle toothed with jagged pieces of adamant, and showed him where to hide. Night came, and then Ouranos. In the darkness Kronos crept from his place of concealment, reaching out his shameful hand and then swinging the great sickle, lopping off the first thing that came within his grasp.

Ouranos rolled upon the ground in agony while Kronos, covered with ichor, was horrified to discover that he had castrated his father. Throwing the quivering flesh as far as he could, he ran to hide himself in fear and shame. Ouranos, crippled by pain, shook off his divine form and returned to dwell in the firmament, nevermore to come among them.

These memories seemed very distant and dreamlike now, as Kronos came to a rock throne carved by nature in the side of one of the peaks of Olympos. Seating himself there, he leaned forward, his head supported by one hand, and stared out across the broad earth below.

Even in his pain Ouranos had cursed him and prophesied evil. *"Child, beware thy child. As you have overthrown your father, so shall you be overthrown!"* That act—those words—never left him. They hung always in the background, behind each thing he did or said. He could not escape them. He had gone to Gaia to be reassured, but she confirmed instead of denying: *"Child, beware thy child. As you have overthrown your father, so shall you be overthrown!"*

He grew to be the largest and strongest of them, the cleverest and most daring, and in the fullness of time he came naturally to assume the place vacated by his father. He became the leader of the Titans, the King of the Gods. Slowly, uncertainly, he began the eon-long process that was to lead the gods out of the quagmire of ignorance and bestiality into which they had been born, toward Olympos.

His monstrous brothers, of course, could not be allowed to roam freely upon the face of the world. The havoc they wrought proved that; and finally he defied his mother's wishes and confined them in dark Tartaros, beneath the earth. Gaia, saddened by his action, withdrew from the gods, abandoning her divine form and no longer walking among them.

His great project, as finally symbolized by the palace of Olympos, had taken vast ages to accomplish—how long no one could say, for the years had slipped by uncounted. Envious Okeanos remained in his own realm rather than bow to Kronos's rule, but most of the great gods and many of the lesser ones had gradually gravitated toward the palace high in the sky. Olympos became a new sun, bathing the broad earth below in the new ideas of culture and cooperation and enlightenment that radiated from it. All that was good and productive he encouraged; all that was destructive he sought to crush. Kronos had reason to be proud of his achievements; more than anyone else, it was he who had made them *gods*.

Yet always the prophecy haunted him. There were methods of avoiding offspring—irksome and unreliable—but for most of their marriage Rhea had seemed barren, incapable of conceiving. He had almost come to believe that he had nothing to fear as long as he was careful in his dalliances. And then Rhea bore their first child. He had no choice but to dispose of it.

"As you have overthrown your father, so shall you be overthrown!"

The memories depressed him. Sighing deeply, Kronos rose and returned to the palace. Extinguishing most of the lamps, he lay down and tried to sleep. He twisted and turned. Memories haunted him. Finally he arose, wrapped himself again in his cloak, and went out into the hall and down the stairs.

He came to a room on the floor below and let himself in. Rhea lay soundly asleep, her body curled up with her knees drawn toward her bosom as she lay on her side. He crawled into bed beside her. She sighed softly but did not awaken as he molded his body against hers.

Somehow the familiar curves of her body soothed him, driving away troublesome thoughts. In a few minutes he was asleep.

On all Olympos only one other god remained awake. He, too, was restless, his mind recalling the very scenes that made sleep most elusive.

How foolish he had been, how stupid, how silly. He could almost hear the senseless braggadocio with which he thought to impress Kronos and the other gods over supper. Lord Okeanos was such a good friend of his. Lord Nereus prized his counsel. He was a welcome guest in both their palaces.

It had seemed such innocent conversation. How was he to know that at least one of his listeners would find a perverse significance in his self-serving jabber? How was he to know that his invitation to a private audience with the King of the Gods was not the high honor he had sought, but a prelude to torment—and betrayal?

He could not rid his mind of the towering bulk of Kronos as the Titan stood over him, demanding the truth, raining blows upon his cringing body at each attempted explanation. "Okeanos is no traitor, my lord. Nereus is loyal to you. I'm not a traitor, Lord Kronos!" But it did no good. After a while the blows had a way of making him less certain what the truth really was.

He had never been particularly brave, but he never thought he would betray his friends either. He was weak, and the blows refused to cease. Kronos put the words in his mouth; he only had to utter them. "They want to destroy you, Lord

Kronos. They plot against you. They hate you, Lord Kronos! Yes, it's just as you say. I've heard them say that many times, Lord Kronos. . . .''

The memories shamed him and he sought to push them from his mind, to remember instead where he was and how he had gotten in this state. But his mind was growing sluggish again. . . . Soon he too slept.

EIGHTEEN

Lachesis awakened, neither abruptly nor by slow degrees. She had been soundly asleep and dreaming; then her eyes opened and she sat up in bed. Atropos, her sister, was already awake, rubbing her eyes. Klotho sat up a few moments later. The three sisters exchanged questioning looks.

"I'll light more lamps," Atropos said.

"Yes, please," Klotho said. "Oh, I'm chilly." She pulled a heavy fur blanket around her shoulders.

Atropos lit a taper from the agate lamp they had left burning and used it to light other lamps around the room. Soon the flickering yellow light illuminated much of the bedchamber. Returning to where Lachesis sat on the edge of her bed, Atropos rubbed her arms to warm them. Lachesis held out a blanket to her, and she quickly wrapped it around her bare body.

"It was a very peculiar dream," Atropos said.

"Very peculiar," Lachesis agreed.

Klotho nodded in agreement as the others looked at her.

"I hadn't envisioned the little creatures very well from your description of them," Atropos continued. "They're cute in a way. Not all that ugly, really."

"I like them too," Klotho said, yawning.

"And they're not gods at all," Atropos said. "That was clear from the dream."

"Perhaps not," Klotho said, "but they must be important. Don't you think they're important?"

"I don't know," said Lachesis. "I've had the most peculiar feeling all day, since I saw them. . . ."

They lapsed into silence. Finally Klotho rose and went to look in her mirror. She brushed her hair into place with her fingers.

"I think we'd better go now," Atropos announced.

Klotho turned away from the mirror. "Yes, I think so."

Lachesis rose from her bed and the three of them went to the small doors that led out onto the gallery. They stepped outside, into the cool night air, and stood side by side next to the railing.

"Are you sure we should do this?" Klotho asked, looking down at Atropos, who was the eldest but shortest of the sisters. "I'm a little apprehensive. . . ."

Atropos held her hand and nodded. "Yes, I think so."

Now the three held hands, letting the blankets with which they had wrapped themselves slip to the stone flagging of the gallery. They began to transform themselves.

They came down from Mount Olympos as three crows, gliding downward through the clouds on the cool night air. They flew first east, then north, over towering forests and jutting mountains, over tangled glens where wild boar grunted in their sleep and across wide plains of nodding antelope, mammoth, and woolly rhinoceros. At last they came to a small clearing hidden deep within a thick forest. A wooden hut waited for them in the moonlight. Clothing themselves in gowns of dusky night, they joined hands and hesitantly approached the aged building.

"I'm afraid it isn't Olympos," Lachesis said softly.

"No, but it's ours," Atropos answered.

The door creaked on its wooden hinges as they entered. A small lamp burned upon a table.

"There's a hearth," Klotho said. "I'll kindle a fire."

Lachesis and Atropos stood near the center of the small room as their sister worked; they looked slowly about the dark, shadowed interior. There was but a single table with a few small chairs.

"We'll have to make our own beds," Lachesis said.

"There are more than enough leaves in the forest," Atropos told her.

Within a few minutes Klotho had the fire roaring, and the sisters gathered about it to warm themselves. The bright flames revealed the stark bareness all around them.

"Shall we start to work, cleaning and making our beds, or shall we wait?" Klotho asked.

"I think we'd better wait."

They waited for nearly five minutes, the door of the cabin left open wide.

Darkness came down a hillside and moved through the tall pines toward the door of the small cabin. It came in utter silence. The darkness crossed the short open space and entered the room. Klotho moved to close the door behind it while Atropos, greeting their brother, pulled out a chair from the table. The darkness pulsed, and the flickering light from the fireplace seemed momentarily to outline first one area, then another of a godlike form.

"You have decided," the darkness that was their brother both asked and stated.

The three sisters, now huddled together near the hearth, nodded in agreement.

"You have considered fully."

"Yes," Atropos said, speaking for all of them. "Yes, brother, we have considered and decided. We are pleased that you have selected us."

"Oh, yes," Lachesis said. "We're so tired of Olympos, of not having anything important and interesting to do." She started to laugh nervously, but the laughter died off abruptly, sounding distant and fragile.

The shadow moved, flowing into a corner of the room near the fireplace. It thickened, growing jet black. When it moved away, it left behind a golden spinning wheel.

Next the darkness drifted across the floor, occupying a portion of the room near the far wall. Once again it grew thick and impenetrable, then drew away to reveal an enormous loom with a golden shuttle.

Finally, from its position near the middle of the room, a dark tendril curled forth to cover a portion of the table. It retreated to leave behind small golden shears.

The sisters watched tensely, excited but perplexed. Their eyes moved back and forth between these new additions to the room and the shifting, shadowy shape of their brother.

"A new creature has come into the world," it said, "a pitiful, wretched thing that will dream proud dreams but become the food of worms. You three shall alot the fate of man."

The sisters listened intently, barely daring to breathe.

The darkness seemed to flow a little toward them. "Lovely Klotho," it said, "you shall spin the thread of life, strong or weak, perfect or faulty. As is your thread, so shall be the man. Demure Lachesis, you shall weave upon the loom, bringing together the lives of men so that they meet, run together for a little while, and then part. Your mistakes shall be their misfortunes; your fortuitous errors, their fortunes. When you miss a stitch, chance—for good or ill—shall play upon them. And you, proud Atropos, when you clip the thread with your shears of gold, a life will end."

Clutching each other's hands tightly, they watched the darkness.

"Are you satisfied? Will you accept this task?"

Hesitantly Klotho asked, "These creatures—man—will he be important?"

"Only as the pebble that tumbles down the side of a mountain."

"But such a pebble, in its fall," she said, "would strike other pebbles, and could cause an avalanche. . . ."

The swirling darkness did not answer.

"It will not be pleasant work," it continued after a few moments. "Your eyes will grow weak, your fingers will stiffen and swell. Your young faces will become haggard from the tears that will flow down your cheeks, and your backs will grow bent from the labor. Do you still accept?"

They consulted only briefly, then nodded their agreement.

"Then it is time to begin."

Each of the sisters went to her place—Klotho to the wheel, Lachesis to the loom. Atropos picked up the golden shears.

"Oh, look," Lachesis cried out. "The tapestry is already begun. There's already the beginning of a pattern. Here's a thread that's wandered astray from the others. I shall have to attend to him right away. And look—one of the threads has broken!"

She looked around to find her brother, but already he had left. Silently dark Moros, the spirit of Destiny and most dreaded of gods, returned into the night.

NINETEEN

The dreams of Alalkomeneus vacillated between red, squirming horror and luxurious bliss. Endless, twisting corridors tormented him with loneliness and darkness, always leading, at last, to a precipice overlooking the charnel room of Thanatos. The huge brass cage, glinting in the lamplight, dominated the room, its contents of creatures like himself visible only as dim shapes within. One by one huge bony-fingered hands drew out squirming, shrieking men and held them down upon the brass table. Alalkomeneus turned to run each time he saw the enormous, gleaming blade move across one of the necks—and found himself suddenly in the protecting arms of the young goddess Metis.

He awakened, cold and shivering, to find himself still shrouded in utter darkness. His body was bathed in a light film of sweat, and the stagnant, suffocating air of the passage made it difficult to breathe. His limbs were stiff and sore as he stood up. Probably he had not slept long; he was very tired. Nevertheless he was possessed by an overwhelming desire to find his way out of the darkness of the passage and into the fragrant presence of Metis.

Feeling his way slowly along the smooth, curved walls of the corridor, he walked slowly, haunted by the image of Thanatos and the sights he had seen. For some distance the path led gradually downward, often connecting with short side passages. He always followed these until they ended inevitably in a smooth stone wall that blocked farther progress and forced him to retrace his steps to the main corridor.

Even though he lacked any real conception of time, he knew that he had been walking for a long while. The mazelike tunnels, with their sharp or gradual inclines and numerous connecting passages, were something he simply accepted; it never occurred to him that they might have been built upon a plan and that he might figure out their design. Such a rationalism was completely beyond his experience. Instead he followed every possible avenue in hope that one might lead him out of the utter darkness.

For a long time everything around him had been completely quiet, except for the small noises he himself made. Now he became aware of distant, unrecognizable sounds. They excited him, renewing his hope and energy, so that he increased his pace as much as he could in the blackness. Time and again he dipped into offshoot passages, hoping to find light and freedom when he came to its end. Sometimes the noises became slightly more audible, but each time he was forced to turn back when the passage ended abruptly at another stone wall.

Finally, his feet aching, he sat down upon the floor, his mind automatically conjuring up images of the sweet-smelling forest. He missed Metis, but the forest had been pleasant, too, in its own way. He remembered the feel of the soft grass under his feet, wet with morning dew. For a little while he gave himself up to such memories, only to be drawn out of his reverie by the distinct, if distant, voices of gods.

He sat up straight, listening intently. Yes, it was voices, and one of the voices . . . ! He listened, all other thoughts banished from his mind. It sounded like his goddess, like Metis! Instantly he was on his feet, trying to follow the sound through the baffling passages, going a little way down a short tunnel, only to turn around immediately when the sounds decreased in volume. He began to run, trembling with anticipation.

The voices grew nearer, until at last a passage brought him to a stone wall behind which, he was sure, two gods were talking. He knew neither by name, but the images of Metis and Proteus filled his mind. Pressing his ear against the wall so hard that it began to hurt, he listened breathlessly. A cry of joy sprang to his mouth, and he began to shriek loudly. He yelled until his throat, already quite dry, became raw, and he pounded his hands against the wall until they grew numb.

Metis had awakened with the dawn, not quite half an hour earlier. For some time she leaned over the edge of her bed, looking down at her brother, waiting for him to show signs of wakefulness. Perhaps she sensed her eyes on him, or heard the small noises she made; his eyes soon opened and he sat up. She immediately launched into an almost nonstop conversation. Overjoyed at the presence of her brother, her youthful nature refused to be suppressed by the serious concerns of his visit.

"Oh, Proteus," she continued. "It's terrible of you to go off for such long periods of time, without seeing any of us."

Proteus smiled indulgently, and in the silence that followed— the first in some minutes—a peculiar, muffled noise became audible. Proteus leaned forward, listening.

"And now, when we finally do get to see you, it's only because a friend of our father is in danger," Metis continued.

Proteus leaned toward her, placing a hand upon her arm. "Quiet," he whispered, still listening carefully.

Both of them rose and began to walk softly in the direction from which the sound seemed to come. Proteus approached the wall, and with a single swift motion lifted a huge ebony chest and swung it out into the room. Behind it lay bare limestone. Throwing back the lid of the chest, he searched inside, finding only carelessly folded clothing.

Now they examined the wall, for the first time noticing the hair-thin fissure which described a nearly perfect circle upon the smooth stone surface.

Metis traced the line with her finger. "There's some kind of opening here, sealed up long ago. Listen—it's becoming louder, more frantic." She leaned closer, pressing her ear against the wall. Suddenly she jumped back, swinging around to face her brother.

"It's Alalkomeneus!" she exclaimed, her expression a mixture of incredulity and joy. "Oh, Proteus—it's my little Alalkomeneus! I recognize his voice!"

She had darted past him and was already returning, dagger in hand. Kneeling, she began to pry at the fissure lines with the point. "Oh, it's not working," she complained after two or three minutes of hectic effort.

Proteus knelt beside her and took the knife. She relinquished her position reluctantly.

"Do try to hurry. Listen to him—he knows we're trying to get to him. I can tell from his voice. Be patient, Alalkomeneus. Just a little longer, little Alalkomeneus. . . ."

Patiently and methodically Proteus worked his way around the circle, inserting the tip of the blade and prying outward, so that before long a large stone plug edged out of the wall toward them. He continued prying until enough of the stone had been exposed that he could grasp it with his fingers. He gave it a sudden twist and the flat limestone plate came free, revealing a dark, circular cavity behind it.

A shriek of joy came from within the darkness, and Alalkomeneus ran out of the opening, leaping the short distance to the floor of the room. Metis swooped him up into her arms and hugged him to her breast. Rising to her feet, she began to laugh and twirl about.

"I knew you'd come back to me," she cried. She lifted him in her hands and rained kisses upon his miniature face, nearly smothering him with affection as she danced about the room.

Proteus brought a lamp from across the room and proceeded to examine the aperture they had uncovered. When the light failed to reveal all he wanted to know, he ran his arm into the opening.

"Oh, I'm so happy to see you," Metis told the man, still holding him in her hands. "But how did you get there?" She swung around to Proteus. "What *is* that opening? How could he have gotten inside?"

Having finished his examination, Proteus returned the lamp to the table from which he had taken it and sat upon the bed. "I'm not certain, of course. But I can make a guess."

"That's more than I can do," she said, coming toward him. Alalkomeneus, nestled to her bosom, seemed to have found contentment. Eyes closed, he lay perfectly limp against her.

"Do you know the history of the palace? It wasn't built by Kronos. At least the original palace wasn't—it's been enlarged and altered since its original construction."

"If Kronos didn't build it, then who did?"

The ocean god frowned, running the fingers of one hand

through his thick, dark hair. "A very long time ago—when Ouranos still ruled the world—a goddess lived here upon Olympos. Her name was Eurynome, and she built this palace for herself and her consort, the snake god Ophion. I suppose she intended to populate the palace with her own race of gods— her descendants—but as far as I know, she never had any. Instead she and Ophion were the sole inhabitants of these thousand rooms. They lived alone for what must have been vast ages, until Kronos took the palace from them."

"How do you know this?" Metis asked.

He smiled. "I'm only telling you what I've heard. I'm not that old, young sister. Haven't you heard this before?"

"No. I'd remember if I had."

He nodded. "Probably Kronos would just as soon have it forgotten. He flung Eurynome from a cliff and threw her lover after her. Thus Kronos became Lord of Olympos."

"But what does this have to do with the hole in the wall?"

"If you examine it, you'll notice that it's almost perfectly circular. It seems to be a passage, not simply a hollow. The inside is extremely smooth, as though the rock has been polished by eons of wear. Every portion has been worn smooth. . . ."

She was watching his face, her own expression showing that she did not understand what he was getting at.

"I would guess that this passage was made by the snake god Ophion as a means of passing from room to room and level to level. Probably such tunnels traverse the entire palace. Kronos, when he took possession, must have had the openings sealed up."

"But how could Alalkomeneus get inside?"

He shrugged. "He must have found an opening in Crios's room, where you left him. Once inside, it would be very easy for him to become lost."

"But he found his way here, to me," Metis said, hugging the man against her cheek.

Proteus stared at the dark hole. "These passages could prove useful to us. It would be worthwhile to investigate them and find out where they lead. I doubt I'll have time, but you might do it, Metis."

"You mean we could travel through them, the way Alalkomeneus must have? We could make ourselves small, like him. I hadn't thought of that.'' She frowned. ''But what if I lost control? I'd return to normal size inside there. I'd be crushed!''

''All it takes is concentration.''

''I don't know. . . .'' She looked down at Alalkomeneus and smiled. ''The poor thing, alone all night long, with no one to care for him. Why, he must be starving by now. I must get him something to eat.''

She set the man on the bed near Proteus and rushed from the room, returning a few minutes later with an already mixed goblet of nectar and a bowl of fruit and nuts. From near the wall she pulled a small table toward the bed, set the food on it, then placed Alalkomeneus beside the food. The man seemed to regain his energy as he drank from the goblet, using his hands to carry the liquid to his mouth. The young goddess began cracking the nuts and dicing the fruit. Grown in the nectar-irrigated gardens of Olympos, they were far too large for him to handle effectively.

After he had eaten, Alalkomeneus curled himself into a comfortable position in Metis's lap. He snuggled contentedly against the warmth of her divine flesh and soon would have been asleep, except that disturbing images kept crowding his mind. Red wetness intruded upon him even here, in the lap of the goddess. He saw again in his mind the others of his kind, locked within the metal cage, and he saw also the frightened goddess struggling to free herself.

The images disturbed him, so that he kept opening his eyes to make them go away. He looked up into Metis's face, watched her mouth as it made sounds, peered into the enormous green pools of her eyes. As she moved her head, the thick dark ringlets of her hair danced like the branches of a tree in a strong wind.

Slowly the images in his head began to merge, so that now the bound and struggling goddess was Metis and he was the man in Thanatos's hand. He blinked his eyes rapidly, trying to make the thought-picture go away. Metis would not let that happen; she would not let Thanatos loose the red wetness that must be inside him.

But again he saw the others of his kind, confined in the gleaming brass cage. Why did the goddess not take them away from Thanatos? She must not have seen them in the

horrible room—if she had, then certainly she would have
brought them here, to keep them safe. All that was necessary
was for her to see them.

The wordless ideas flitted through his mind, impossible to
hold and examine; nevertheless he had arrived at an important
thought. He envisioned himself leading Metis through the
rock corridors, pointing downward into the foul-smelling room.
That she was far too large to accompany him by that route
was a conclusion he did not reach. She was a goddess.
Whatever her limitations might be, he was unaware of them.

He slipped down her thigh to the bed, then down the
sloping blanket to the floor. Metis always followed him when
he went somewhere by himself, so he expected her to follow
him now. He ran toward the entrance to the passage, making
loud noises to attract her attention. Before he had traveled
half the distance, the goddess picked him up and carried him
back to the bed.

Metis and Proteus were making mouth noises at each other.
He waited until she relaxed her fingers, then slipped out
between them. Once again he was nearly halfway to the
opening before she caught him.

"What is he trying to do?" Metis asked. She held the man
up in front of her face. "What's wrong, my little friend? Oh,
I wish you could talk to me."

"Why shouldn't he be able to talk?" Proteus asked.

"I don't guess there's any reason. But he doesn't."

"He's capable of making sounds. The hideous noises he
emits prove that. All that's necessary is for him to form them
into words."

"You're right. I must try to teach him to speak. But how
should I go about that? Or maybe he'll learn on his own, from
listening to us."

"There might be a faster way."

"How? Tell me!"

"A phantom messenger, formed of cloud, can be made to
speak. I've endowed both birds and fish with speech, though
they aren't smart enough to do more than repeat what they've
been commanded to say."

"Then you think . . . ? Please try. Please try, Proteus!"

The ocean god took the man from her. For a few moments
he seemed very agitated, but as Proteus stared down at him he
grew calm, at last lying passively in the god's cupped hands.

Proteus leaned over him, concentrating. The eyes of the god peered into those of the man.

Finally Proteus leaned still closer. "You can speak now," he said.

The words seemed to shoot through Alalkomeneus like thunder claps. His mouth gaped open. His eyes bulged and his body jerked convulsively.

Metis was beside Proteus, leaning over the man. "Can you understand, Alalkomeneus? Speak to me, little Alalkomeneus."

The man's eyes grew even larger. The music of Metis's voice tinkled and danced through his brain cells. His mouth opened. "Sp-eak," he said slowly, "sp-eak . . . to . . . me. . . ."

Metis threw her arms around her brother and kissed him. "You were right. It was possible—and you did it!"

"Pos-si-ble," Alalkomeneus repeated, drawing out the word. The magnificence of the sounds coming from his own mouth overwhelmed him. His mind was alive with sounds.

Metis picked him up. "Talk to us, Alalkomeneus. You can talk now."

"Talk . . . to . . . you," he said. "I . . . can . . . talk . . . to . . . you. . . ." He mouthed the words as he spoke, drawing them out so that he could feel them on his lips and tongue. He traced their course all the way from deep within his chest and tried to follow the lightning patterns they made as they sparked and crackled through his brain.

"Yes, Alalkomeneus," Metis continued, "you can talk now. Talk to me. Are you all right? How did you get in that dark hole? Was it Thanatos? Did he have something to do with it?" She held him near her face as she spoke.

"Give him time," Proteus advised. "It'll take a few minutes for him to accustom himself."

Images rose up in the man's mind as they spoke. Before, sounds and images had been completely separate things; now they were linked somehow—different aspects of the same thing. He tried to remember the image-thoughts that had vanished with the coming of language, then sought to interpret them into this new medium. He had to speak slowly to answer her, searching out each word.

"Thaan-ah-tos," he began, and dark, swirling shapes sprang up within his head at the sounds; "Thaan-ahh-tos . . . his room . . . his evil room where he lets out the . . . the red wetness inside, the . . . the blood, the red blood. . . .''

Metis exchanged questioning glances with her brother. "Lets out blood? What do you mean, Alalkomeneus? Lets out what blood? The blood of what creature?"

"Men like me, and . . . and there is a goddess, a goddess who . . . who can't move when she tries to move.''

"What's he talking about?" Metis asked Proteus.

"It sounds as though he saw something while he was in the tunnel." He turned toward the man. "Is that it, Alalkomeneus? Did the tunnel lead you to this room of Thanatos's? Is that what you're trying to tell us?"

"I went through the darkness," the man said, "through the long, still darkness of cold stone. At the end of the darkness I found the room, the room of . . .'' He hesitated, dreading to pronounce the sounds which, in his mind, were Thanatos.

"And there is a goddess there?" Proteus asked. "In this room at the end of the cold passage?"

"Yes, Proteus . . . Lord Proteus . . . Lord Proteus," the man said, becoming lost in the sound of the god's name, feeling the supple, flowing strength of the name and the god.

"A goddess who tries to move but cannot?" Proteus continued. "A goddess who is bound? Is that what you mean?"

The man only nodded. His mind was reeling. With language had come self-awareness and introspection. He barely heard them.

"What can he be talking about?" Metis asked.

Proteus shrugged. "I don't know. But I think we'd better try to find out. He won't be able to lead us to the room, but with our knowledge of the palace, and the footprints he left in the dust inside the passage, we should be able to find it. I hate to take the time, but this is worth following up."

"We're going to go through that little tunnel?" Metis asked apprehensively.

"You can wait here, if you'd rather. I'll go and return as quickly as possible."

She shook her head. "No, I'll come too. You might need my help." She smiled. "Besides, I'm not going to miss out on an adventure like this."

Proteus was staring at the opening in the wall. "We'll need a source of light. Is there a torch somewhere in the apartment?"

She shook her head. "The nearest one is out in the corridor."

Proteus stood up. Going to the table, he took her knife and cut two slivers of wood from the edge. "Take these and wrap the ends in pitch from one of the torches in the corridor."

"What are . . . ? Oh, little man-size torches for us to use." She took the slivers and hastened to do as he had instructed. When she returned, she handed them to him. "No one saw me."

He lit them from the night lamp, then handed them back to her. As she watched, his form began to blur and shrink. Within moments he was only a little larger than Alalkomeneus.

"Now hand me the torches," he told her. "It's your turn."

She frowned.

"Just concentrate."

Metis concentrated. Her body began to blur and shrink, but only for a moment. As she let the thought slip away, she returned to her normal size. "Wait," she pleaded. "I can do it."

She began again. This time the process continued until she was almost a third smaller than usual. Her concentration failed as she realized that her clothes were beginning to slip off. She caught herself before the metamorphosis was completely undone and spent nearly half a minute consolidating her gains.

"Oh, Proteus, just give me another minute or two," she said. "I can do it. All I have to do is keep thinking about my size while I think about whatever else, like talking! You didn't warn me my clothes would fall off. . . ."

He smiled. "This isn't a time for modesty, sister. Finish becoming small, then wrap yourself in illusion—like all females."

The process continued in spurts and relapses, until at last she stood beside him. "Oh, look the other way," she begged. "Give me a chance to get accustomed to this before worrying about decency!"

She had set Alalkomeneus on the floor near Proteus before beginning her own transformation. His mind was too overwhelmed with the words inside it to pay careful attention to what was happening. His lips moved in a continual mumble, repeating endlessly the words that happened into his head.

Two or three minutes passed. Finally Metis said, "I think I've just about got it. If you promise not to stare at me, I think I'll go like this. I don't have any extra concentration left, to make phantom clothing.''

Proteus handed her one of the torches, then led the way into the opening in the wall. Metis directed Alalkomeneus in after him, then brought up the rear herself. The man turned to look at her, his face beaming with admiration, gratitude, and love. He was aware of her metamorphosis, but paid little attention to it. A single thought possessed him: She and Proteus had given him language. They had made him like a god.

TWENTY

Proteus held the torch high above his head as he led the way down the short side passage and into the main corridor. Alalkomeneus followed a little behind him, carrying on a continuous monologue while Metis hastened him along.

They came to a halt just inside the main corridor. "I don't like this place," Metis said, shivering. "I wouldn't be surprised if we ran head-on into Ophion, the snake god."

"He came from this direction," Proteus said, pointing along the floor at the footprints Alalkomeneus had left in the thick dust. "The passage slopes upward too. That's a good sign." He began walking, and Metis followed, all her mental energy concentrated upon maintaining her tiny size.

"Ophion the snake god," Alalkomeneus was mumbling.

The passage led gradually upward, until it reached a place where it forked. It soon became apparent that the footprints would not prove a reliable guide; in the darkness the man had doubled and redoubled back upon himself. Both paths led upward. They followed one a short way, only to retrace their path when the footprints of Alalkomeneus turned back on themselves.

Most of an hour was consumed in their slow progress, until a spot of light became visible ahead. Alalkomeneus became excited and refused to continue walking.

"The room of blood," he said, his voice quaking.

Metis took his hand. "Don't be afraid, my brave little friend. I'm here with you. I won't let Thanatos hurt you."

"He won't hurt me," he said. "Metis won't let him hurt me."

"No, I won't," she said, "but you must be quiet. We don't want Thanatos to hear us. You mustn't talk out loud."

They moved forward, coming at last to the opening through which light entered the tunnel. The frightened man continued to hang back as the two gods stood at the edge of the precipice overlooking the dim chamber. A single small lamp had been left burning, its feeble rays illuminating only a small portion of the room.

Metis looked at her brother. A peculiar expression flickered over his features. "Is something wrong?" she asked.

He shook his head. "No. I suppose not. I just had the sudden impression that I have looked upon this awful place before." He shook his head again. "The smell is dreadful. Can you see the men or the goddess that Alalkomeneus mentioned?"

She peered downward again. "I think there's something over there, among the shadows. It could be the goddess. How do we get down from here?"

"That'll be easy enough. But why is this entrance to Ophion's tunnel open? Thanatos must have removed the plug that sealed it."

"So he knows about the little corridors," she said.

He nodded. "As far as I can tell, there's only one door to the room, and it's closed. Thanatos may very well be in the next room, so we'll have to be careful not to make any noise. Probably we'd better leave Alalkomeneus here. We'll have to leave the torches too. Let him hold them till we come back. Perhaps you'd better explain to him how to do it without burning himself."

As she attended to those details he turned and dived out into the room, transmuting himself in midair into a bird. As he landed upon the floor he reassumed his natural form, then lifted down Metis. Once safely upon the floor, she, too, reassumed her normal size.

The shape that had been only dimly visible before began to stir. Proteus approached it, smothering an exclamation of surprise as he recognized the naiad Nalassa. Despite the gag in her mouth, she tried to cry out. With a gesture he warned her to silence.

"Bring the lamp," Proteus whispered to Metis.

The young goddess hastened to do as he asked. She set it on the floor beside him, then searched for another to light for her own use. She found it in a wall niche.

"Try to find the men," he told her.

Most of the men were still inside the brass cage atop a large table. At the additional light in the room and the stealthy movements of the gods, some of them had awakened and begun to stir. As she approached them the light from her lamp fell upon a neighboring table. She froze, staring down at the decapitated corpse of one of the men.

She gasped, unable to turn her eyes from the hideous parody of life. The head lay nearby, eyes staring and mouth drawn into a mirthless grin. Dark dried blood stained the table. She set down the lamp to keep herself from dropping it.

Proteus had freed Nalassa's hands, and now she removed the gag from her mouth. "Oh, Lord Proteus," she whispered. "How can I thank you? How did you know I was here?"

"Quiet. You aren't out of danger yet." He finished loosing the bonds from her ankles. As he stood up she threw herself into his arms.

"Proteus," Metis called in a whisper. "Brother, please come see."

Disentangling himself from the naiad's embrace, the ocean god went to Metis's side. She pointed to the corpse on the table.

He frowned. "I'm afraid your little friends are mortal after all," he said softly. "Have you found the others?"

She nodded, gesturing to the brass cage.

"Good. Leave them till we've examined the rest of this room. Take your lamp and go that way. I'll go this way. Nalassa, stay here until we finish."

Metis took her lamp and began walking between the tables, the fetid smell making her gag for breath. Toward the rear of the room she came upon the corpse of the nymph. She fought back the nausea that threatened to make her faint, and forced herself to carefully examine the body. She prodded it to make sure it was dead, and noticed the glazed, staring eyes. The long cut on one forearm attracted her attention—it seemed to be the only wound on the dried and wrinkled body—and she

leaned closer to look at the pink-tinted ichor that had welled
into the slash.

Proteus hissed to attract her attention. "I've found something," he whispered.

"So have I."

She crossed the room to join him where he stood next to
the headless body of a god. She was trembling, and Proteus
put his arm around her.

"This is horrible beyond words," she said. "I found a
dead nymph over there."

"Dead? Are you sure? This god still lives, even without his
head."

"Yes, I'm certain. I think you should look at it."

A thrashing sound drew her attention as they crossed the
room. Proteus moved directly toward the rear of the chamber,
slipping his arm around her again as they neared the wall. He
thrust the light forward, revealing the head of a god, hanging
from a peg by its hair. From the healed-over neck depended
a miniature body, its arms and legs flailing in every direction.

"By Earth and starry Heaven!" Proteus exclaimed, taking
a full step back from the apparition. "It is the god whose
body lies upon the table. . . ."

The mouth of Oizys formed silent words while the body
floundered impotently.

"Who is it?" Metis asked.

"I don't know. Whoever he is, he's an ample demonstration of what Thanatos—and therefore Kronos—is capable
of." Proteus looked quickly around the dim room. "Quick.
Show me the nymph. We must not be found here."

He examined the dead nymph carefully, then shook his
head. "Let's go. We'll talk back in your room."

"What about the god—the head of the god?" Metis asked.
"We can't just leave him here, for Thanatos. . . ."

Proteus frowned. "No, I suppose not." He returned to the
wall and lifted down the head, holding it by the long hair.
The thing's thin lips continued to flap noiselessly, the little
body to wriggle.

"But how are we going to get it back?" Metis asked,
suddenly becoming aware of the potential difficulty. "Can it
still change sizes? I don't think the head can fit in the tunnel,
and even if it could, we'd have to drag it along."

Nalassa had edged her way across the room, closer to

them. "Change sizes?" she asked, coming directly toward them now. "What does she mean, my lord?"

"We came here through a small tunnel that runs through the walls of the palace," Proteus explained. "In order to return, we will have to make ourselves as small as the creatures in the cage."

"I can't change size, my lord," Nalassa said quickly. "I am only a lesser goddess—a naiad, a river nymph."

"Are you sure you can't," Metis asked. "I didn't think I could either, until—"

Nalassa shook her head again. "No, my lady. It's a power I don't possess."

"Then we'll alter our plans," Proteus said. He paused to think, then continued, "Metis, you and Alalkomeneus and the other men will go back through Ophion's tunnel. If I can get this god without a body to change his size, you can carry him with you. Otherwise Nalassa and I will take him. We'll make our way out as best we can."

"But there's a good chance Thanatos will see you," Metis objected. "I think that door must lead to Thanatos's apartment."

"We'll manage. If necessary I'll find a means of distracting him while Nalassa sneaks out."

"But brother—"

"Be quiet now. I can do whatever has to be done. Right now I want to get you and your friends to safety." He lifted the head of the god and held it so that he could peer into the creature's pain-dulled eyes. "If you can understand me," he told it, "and if you're still capable of metamorphosis, we need you to make yourself very small. We're here to help you, but we need you to do this so we can take you away from here."

The three of them waited, watching the head. Its mouth flapped and its body writhed, but it did not change size.

"Well, that's our answer," Proteus said after nearly a minute. He walked toward the front of the room. "Metis, you and I will deposit the men in the tunnel. Instruct Alalkomeneus to keep them together and away from the ledge. You and he will have quite a job herding them back to your room. Here, Nalassa, hold our unfortunate friend."

The naiad grimaced as he held the god out to her, but she forced herself to grasp the long hair. Proteus and Metis began transporting the mortals from the cage to the mouth of the

tunnel. When the cage was empty, Metis made herself small
again and Proteus lifted her up to join them.

"Take care, little sister," he told her. "We'll meet in your
room."

Nalassa was still holding the head of Oizys at arm's length.
He took it from her and turned his attention to the door. The
locking mechanism that had proven so difficult to Prometheus
the night before presented no problem whatsoever from the
inside. Proteus slipped the bolt back and the door started to
swing inward. He pushed it closed and held it as he transformed himself into a perfect replica of Kronos, King of the
Gods.

Nalassa's eyes widened. "My lord, you look—"

"This should make things simpler if we are seen," he said.
"Kronos has come to take you away."

She smiled broadly. "You *are* clever."

He let the door swing in, revealing a bedchamber. Upon
the bed was stretched, still dressed in a dark chiton and
without sheet or blanket, a limp, angular form that seemed to
be composed primarily of arms and legs.

Leaving Nalassa in the doorway, he crept across the room
toward a window. His phantom clothing had been abandoned
long ago, in another metamorphosis. He drew up cloud and
formed it around himself, so that now he was dressed as
Kronos had been. Returning to the naiad, he took her by the
elbow and led her across the room. He carried Oizys against
his side, away from the sleeping god. They had almost reached
the middle of the room when Thanatos began to stir.

Proteus pushed Nalassa gently forward, toward the next
room. Thanatos twisted first to the right, then to the left, and
finally turned on his side, facing away from them.

Crossing the remainder of the room, Proteus rejoined the
water nymph. Together they made their way toward the outer
corridor.

TWENTY-ONE

As they neared the chambers of Iapetos and his family, Proteus pressed Nalassa into the darkness of an alcove and once again forced the head of Oizys into her unwilling hand. Holding it by its dirty, matted hair, she looked up to find that it was no longer the King of the Gods who stood before her; instead she beheld the bent, paunchy form of Momos.

Small, plump hands settled upon her shoulders, gently pressing her back farther into the shadows. "Wait until I signal you," the god said.

As she watched he continued down the hall toward the entrance to the apartment, the regal, confident movements of the Titan king replaced by the tottering gait and absentminded demeanor of the divinity he now impersonated. His head was bent forward and he mumbled to himself.

He entered the apartment and moved slowly across the main room. Staring at the floor and mumbling softly, he seemed completely preoccupied. The atrium was deserted, and he walked in the direction of Metis's room. Just as he was about to turn down the narrow corridor, he came face to face with Philyra.

Rubbing her sleepy eyes, she almost collided with him before becoming aware of his presence. She stepped back with a start. "Who— Oh, it's . . ."

The false Momos stepped close to her. A plump hand closed over her mouth with startling suddenness and an arm encircled her waist. Before she fully comprehended what was happening and began to struggle, she found herself being carried back down the hall.

"Quiet," the god admonished her, carrying her through a doorway and into Metis's room. He set her down and immediately resumed his own form.

"Proteus!" she gasped. "What's going on? You terrified me!"

With a quick glance around the room he assured himself that Metis had not yet returned. He turned back to face Philyra. "Who's already awake?" he asked.

She stared at him, trying to understand the question. "You mean in the whole apartment? Metis isn't here, as you can see—"

"I mean Iapetos and Klymene, and their children."

"Iapetos has gone to hunt. I heard him leaving some time ago. Klymene is probably dressing. I don't know about the others."

He led her back toward the door. "I have someone outside, in the corridor, that I want to bring here without anyone seeing her. I want you to stand watch and signal if anyone starts to come toward the atrium."

"I'll try," she said. "But what's going on? Where have you been? Where's Metis?"

"I'll tell you later. There's no time now." As he spoke he reassumed the form of Momos and pushed her ahead of him out into the short hall, following as soon as she signaled that no one was in sight.

Proteus returned to the front door while she took up a position from which she could observe the bedchambers of her sister and nephews. Opening the door, Proteus gestured to Nalassa, who ran toward him. He directed her across the atrium and down the short inner corridor, so that within moments the three of them stood in Metis's room, the door closed behind them.

Metis had still not returned. Proteus settled into a chair.

"What happened to you, you poor thing?" Philyra asked the naiad, who was trying to cover herself with the remnants of her tunic. "How did you get—" Philyra stopped mid-sentence, for the first time noticing the head of Oizys hanging by its hair from Nalassa's right hand. She recoiled in horror from the thing.

"I'd introduce our fourth member," Proteus said, "but I don't know his name . . . and he's in no condition to tell us."

Philyra had turned away and closed her eyes. After a few moments she said, "I know him. That is Oizys, one of the sons of Nyx. What has happened to him?"

"Of Nyx," Proteus said slowly. "Then he is the brother of Thanatos."

Philyra nodded. "Won't you please tell me what this is all about? Who is this nymph? What has happened to Oizys?"

Proteus told his sister of the return of Alalkomeneus and the expedition through the tunnel of Ophion to the secret room of Thanatos.

"But shouldn't Metis be back by now?" she asked when he had finished. "Perhaps you should go after her, to be sure nothing has happened."

"She's probably safer than we are. If she hasn't returned in a little while, I'll go look for her. In the meantime why don't you see to Nalassa. She's probably very hungry."

Philyra turned to the naiad. "Oh, yes, I'm so sorry. Are you hungry? What would you like?"

"I'm afraid I can't even think about food right now," Nalassa said softly. "If I could clean up . . . if you could find something for me to wear . . ."

"Of course, I should have thought of that immediately. I'll see to it that you have a bath. Come with me."

"Not that way," Proteus said. "No one must know she's here."

Philyra considered for a moment, then said, "We can go along the gallery."

Nalassa held out Oizys to Proteus, then followed Philyra. They had to step over the innumerable boxes and vases of Metis's herb garden. As they left, Proteus pulled a cushioned chair up close to the one in which he sat and tried to position Oizys in it. He had to arrange cushions around the head to keep it from rolling over.

Settling back in his own chair, he stared thoughtfully at the bleary eyes and soundless mouth of his companion. "The brother of Thanatos," he said softly, as much to himself as to Oizys. "You should be able to tell a pretty story some day."

The head's dull eyes gave no indication of the thoughts that might be passing through Oizys's brain.

Proteus put his feet on a foot stool and leaned back in his chair. "I'm afraid my conversation won't be very interesting just now," he continued. "I have much to occupy my mind. Your brother will soon discover that he is missing several important things."

Meanwhile Nalassa and Philyra made their way along the exterior gallery, stopping to cautiously peer in open doors and windows before continuing past them. They walked only a short distance before coming to a large open hearth built upon the stone floor of the gallery. A doorway led into the medium-size room that served as the bath chamber of Klymene and her sisters.

The room was sparsely but luxuriously decorated. A life-size lion's head, made of gold, protruded from one of the walls. A fountain, fed by a crystal-clear spring at the very peak of Mount Olympos, issued from its roaring mouth and fell into a large sunken basin of marble. The continually circulating water was drained off through a number of small openings just below the upper lip of the basin, or could be rerouted through a spigot into a nearby marble tub.

Philyra kindled a fire on the gallery hearth and set water to heat, then returned to the room and opened a spigot to let cold water into the tub. It took a number of minutes for the water to heat sufficiently, but at last the bath was ready and Philyra helped steady Nalassa as she stepped down into it.

Philyra sat on the stone steps beside the tub, talking as she scrubbed the naiad's back. The conversation began with Nalassa's ordeal of the night before, but inevitably led to Proteus. Philyra learned with interest that this was the nymph who had been with him during his prophetic seizure. The exact details of their relationship interested her, but her sense of propriety kept her from inquiring too closely.

"I owe him very much," Nalassa said. "I'm very grateful to him."

Something in her voice made Philyra scrutinize her face. Sensing that she had more than a casual interest in her brother, Philyra determined to caution her tactfully.

"My brother is very special," she began off-handedly. "I love him very much, of course—we all do—but it isn't easy to understand him. He is the eldest child of my father, and I am one of the youngest, so I suppose our ages have something to do with it. He's seen and experienced so much in his life, more than you or I can possibly imagine. Sometimes when I look at him, all I can do is wonder what strange thoughts he must think—how silly my own concerns must appear to him.''

Nalassa hung on each word the Okeanid spoke; at the same time she strove to conceal her intense interest. ''He does seem distant, much of the time.''

Philyra laughed softly. ''Indeed he does. I think that his ability to look into the future must contribute to it. It's not a light burden to bear.''

''But he doesn't really see into the future. He told me that he never remembers after . . .''

Philyra looked upward toward the high ceiling, closing her eyes as she sought out a memory. ''I've heard it said that he was not always so—that long ago, long before I was born, he was as lighthearted as anyone. In those days he lived with my parents in their palace at the edge of the world, surrounded by his brothers and sisters. They say that in those days he was the most clear-sighted of prophets, that he never spoke in riddles and always spoke truly. It was only much later, when his visions came to him only in those terrible seizures of his, that he drew away from his family and began to roam the lonely ocean.''

The Okeanid smiled, shaking off the gloomy thought. ''I've always thought that he should marry, that perhaps that would cure him of whatever it is that makes him love solitude so much. But I doubt that will ever happen.''

Nalassa trembled to know why, but dared not ask.

''Oh, he's had many an opportunity,'' Philyra continued lightly. ''He has an eye for beauty, and the number of nymphs and goddesses who have caught his eye must be innumerable—but none has ever kept his interest. Many have fallen in love with him, only to be burned by their own passions.''

''Has he never loved, then?'' the naiad managed to ask.

''I don't know. Perhaps, perhaps not. It wouldn't matter in the end. The ocean depths would call him back. He wouldn't purposely hurt her, you understand. Probably he wouldn't even realize he was hurting her.''

Philyra stared at Nalassa. The grime had been washed away, revealing her lovely complexion. She was very beauti-

ful, the Okeanid realized; and probably already half in love
with Proteus.

"It's just not in his nature to love, I guess," she concluded, a note of sadness in her voice.

She helped Nalassa out of the tub, dried her, and brought
her a loose robe. She started to lead her back out to the
gallery, but changed her mind.

"This is silly. Wait here." She disappeared through another door, returning a few moments later. "There's no one
about. Come this way."

By a circuitous route she led her to her own room, which,
though small, was neat and tastefully decorated. Selecting a
delicately woven pink fabric, she brought it to the naiad.

"I think this will do just fine," she said, beginning to help
her adjust the peplos into the most fashionable folds. "There.
Now sit here and I'll do your hair."

Before doing as she was directed, Nalassa paused to admire
herself in the full-length mirror that stood against one wall.
"The splendor of Olympos is almost overwhelming," she
said as she turned from side to side. "I've never seen such a
wonderful mirror. To be able to see yourself all at one time is
itself a joy, but the workmanship is—"

They were startled as the door to the room opened. It was
Metis. "Proteus sent me to hurry you along," the child said.

One of the brooches that fastened Nalassa's peplos had
come loose and she was trying to refasten it. "Oh, I've stuck
myself," she cried, holding up her wounded finger. Ichor
oozed from a small gouge. Metis came close to her and
leaned down to examine the wound.

Philyra handed the naiad a small white kerchief to wrap
about her finger. "We're almost done. I only have to arrange
her hair," Philyra told her sister. "Sit down, Nalassa, and I'll
soon have you coiffured for the occasion."

Philyra stood behind her, and Metis to one side. After a
minute or two Metis said, "It's odd you can't change shapes.
Why is that?"

"I don't know," Nalassa answered easily. "None of my
sisters can. Most naiads can't."

"Does it affect you in other ways?" the child continued,
trying to make the question seem like idle curiosity. "If you
hurt yourself—if a rock crushed your foot, for instance—
would your foot just grow back as it had been?"

"I've never been so unfortunate as to have such a serious accident, but I'm certain it would."

"All done," Philyra announced. "Come look at yourself in the mirror."

The naiad laid aside her kerchief as she rose to follow Philyra. Metis picked it up and examined it hurriedly. A light pink stain discolored the material.

"I look lovely!" Nalassa exclaimed as she stared at her reflection.

The child glanced across the room at Nalassa, then back at the kerchief. Pulling a fibula free from her chiton, she deliberately punctured her own finger with its sharp point and squeezed out a single drop of clear, honey-thick fluid. A shiver ran through her. Her own ichor was completely transparent, without a hint of color; that of the dead nymph in the laboratory of Thanatos had been pink—like Nalassa's, though darker in shade.

"You certainly are lovely," Philyra was saying. "But we'd better hasten back to my brother now. Come on, Metis." She left them momentarily to be certain no one would see them if they took the route she intended, then led them back to Metis's room.

The child goddess followed slowly, sunk in thought. That tinge of color—so suggestive of the red blood of mortal animals—was it an indication of mortality?

"You took long enough," Proteus said gruffly as they entered.

"Perhaps so," Philyra answered, "but don't you think it was worth it? Look at Nalassa."

He barely glanced in the naiad's direction. "Please come here. Things have become even more pressing than before."

As Philyra approached she became aware of the nearly two dozen men who crowded around the entrance to the small hole in the wall. Alalkomeneus stood just outside the opening, directing them as they came out of the tunnel to procure nuts or slices of fruit, then returned to the tunnel to eat.

"Has everyone else left the apartment?" Proteus asked.

"They seem to have all gone down to breakfast."

"Good. We have to decide some things very quickly; if we don't, events will decide for us."

"What about her?" Metis asked, gesturing toward Nalassa.

"She knows I'm here, and has as much to lose as we do.

She might as well know everything." He turned toward the naiad. "No one outside this room knows of my presence on Olympos, and it is very important that no one else learn of it. Lord Kronos is plotting to depose both our father, Lord Okeanos, and Lord Nereus, the husband of our sister, Queen Doris. The situation is very grave. Our little expedition this morning has complicated matters greatly, and we have to try to find some way to salvage the situation."

"Brother," Philyra interrupted, "Lord Kronos is expecting me for breakfast. I dare not keep him waiting."

"Can you stay a few minutes longer? I'll try to make this as brief as I can."

She shrugged. "No time was specified, but breakfast must have begun by now."

"Thanatos is a minion of Kronos," Proteus continued. "We know that. The things we found in his locked room would not be tolerated were they not there by Kronos's expressed consent. A dead nymph, a decapitated god, a kidnapped nymph—Kronos would not want the other gods to know about them. Now the secret is no longer a secret. The nymph has been rescued, the head of Oizys has been carried away.

"When Thanatos awakens, if he hasn't awakened already, he will inform Kronos. Kronos will feel threatened and do everything within his power to prevent his secret from being revealed. Nalassa will be hunted. The little godlike mortals disappeared from the room, too, and that implicates Metis, who is known to have an interest in them. This room will be the first searched. Metis will be closely questioned."

"Then she and Nalassa will have to leave Olympos," Philyra said.

"If they have to leave, then you do too," Proteus said. "And it wouldn't end there. Klymene and her children would be in danger, too, because Kronos will presume that Metis shares her secrets with those close to her. It may come to that; if so, then so be it. But it would be better to try first to smooth things over if we can. Remember, you and Metis and Klymene are all daughters of Okeanos; if you leave Olympos now—carrying Kronos's secrets with you back to our father— you could make it impossible for Kronos to abandon his plot. He might very well feel compelled to act, even before the wedding of Eurybie and Crios."

"What do you suggest, then?" Philyra asked.

"Nalassa might have escaped by herself. Her bonds were tight and well tied, but Thanatos can't be certain she couldn't free herself."

"But what about the men?" Metis asked. "She couldn't have carried all of them away by herself. And there's Oizys . . ."

"The cage door was left open. The doors to Thanatos's bedroom and from the apartment to the outer corridor were left slightly ajar. I saw to that, to distract Thanatos from Ophion's tunnel."

"Then you want Thanatos to think I freed myself," Nalassa said, "that I opened the cage for the mortals and let them escape the apartment?"

Proteus nodded. "And that you carried away the head of Oizys. You're a compassionate female who would never leave them to the tortures Thanatos obviously intended. It stretches credulity more than a bit that the mortals could have disappeared without a trace, but it's far more likely that you escaped alone than that someone crept past Thanatos while he slept and managed to open the lock on that door from the outside."

"I still don't see what you're getting at," Philyra said.

"It's this. Kronos doesn't really care about Nalassa or Metis or the mortals. His interest is in keeping secret the work of Thanatos. It would greatly embarrass him if the other gods, particularly the Titans, were to learn of it. It might hamper his plot against our father—though we can't trust in that outcome, unfortunately. The existence of that room must be kept a secret, and that is Kronos's main concern. If he thinks his secret safe, then we're safe."

"But how can we make him think that?" Nalassa asked.

"You can do it, with your words and actions. You have only two choices—to flee, or stay here openly. If you hide here, you'll be found. You can't conceal yourself in a different form, as Metis or Philyra might do temporarily. If you flee, Kronos will search across the face of the earth for you. But if you stay here openly—in plain sight of the other gods—and make it clear that Kronos has nothing to fear from you, he may leave you in peace."

Nalassa considered for a few moments. "That does make sense, in a way. Still—"

"I'm afraid it's our only chance. Metis can only avoid

suspicion if you are here to convince Kronos that you acted alone."

"I've caused so much trouble," the naiad said. "I'm very sorry. Of course I'll do anything I can to help."

"Can you do it convincingly?" Proteus demanded.

"I—I think so. Yes, I will!"

"Good. Then what I want you to do now is go eat breakfast. Philyra can lead you, but you must be careful that the two of you aren't seen together. At breakfast, while all the other gods are nearby, let Kronos and Thanatos see you. Act as though you arrived on Olympos during the night, didn't want to wake anyone, found an empty room to sleep in. Whatever you do, don't let Kronos or Thanatos get you out of sight of the other gods. As long as you're in public, you should be safe. Everything you say and do should carry the unspoken message that as long as Kronos leaves you alone you will remain silent. Do you think you can do that?"

Nalassa nodded.

"I don't like it," Philyra said. "I don't think it will work."

"Have you a better idea, sister?"

"But what if it doesn't work? All the gods knew Aigaion was here, and that didn't stop Kronos from making a prisoner of him. She can't avoid being alone at some point if she stays."

Proteus was silent for a moment. Then he said, "I won't let anything happen to her. If it comes to that, I'll rescue her again and take her away from Olympos—even if it means revealing my presence here and abandoning my mission."

Philyra considered his statement, then said, "I guess it's worth a try." She did not sound enthusiastic.

"Good. You're already late for your breakfast engagement. Take Nalassa with you, to show her the way. But remember, don't let anyone see you together. Metis and I still have a lot to discuss. We have to find someplace to safely hide Oizys and the mortals."

Metis waited until her sister and the naiad had left the room, then said, "Brother, you haven't been candid with them."

Proteus's eyebrows rose. "Really, Metis?"

She nodded, looking very serious. "You don't really think

Kronos will let her stay here on Olympos unmolested. You and I have both seen that room.''

"It is a gamble.''

'It's a desperate gamble to buy time,'' Metis continued. "When she falls into Kronos's hands—unless she's an excellent liar—he will force the whole story out of her. And then Kronos will know you are here, and you will have failed.''

"We have no good options in this situation. Perhaps she will manage to keep him at bay long enough for me to find Aigaion, or maybe she'll turn out to be a great little liar. I really don't see anything else we can do.''

TWENTY-TWO

Most of the ground floor of the palace was given over to the great hall of Olympos, in which were held the council meetings of the gods and over which presided the massive ivory throne of Kronos. Opposite the throne, at the other end of the hall, enormous golden doors opened onto a wide portico. Beyond the portico began a series of terraces, the nearest of which had been turned into a broad, grassy patio.

It was here, beneath the golden sun or silver moon, that the gods partook of their formal meals, surrounded by blooming flowers and festooning garden shrubs. Farther away and continuing to the very edge of the precipitous cliffs that ringed the mountaintop, began the orchards of Olympos, where the gods grew fruit and nuts of divine proportions. Springs of red nectar bubbled up from deep within the mountain to irrigate the god-size trees and bushes.

Near the portico but off to one side, partially encircled by a bower of myrtle, the Lord of the Titans sat in a high-backed armchair, a golden, three-legged table within easy reach of his right hand. Queen Rhea sat beside him in a smaller chair. She had barely touched her food and spoken no more than a half-dozen words. Occasionally she glanced at her husband, but he seemed to have no need of conversation. One hand resting on his goblet, he surveyed his subjects.

The patio was now a hubbub of divine noise and motion. All across it other high-backed chairs and three-legged tables had been pulled together in larger or smaller circles. Lesser gods and goddesses brought baskets of freshly collected fruit and nuts from the orchard, or carried huge jars of nectar balanced on their shoulders as they returned from one of the springs. Immortal children scurried about, serving as cupbearers or attendants.

As Kronos watched, his brother Hyperion returned from his morning hunt, gliding down out of the sky. He folded his magnificent wings and reabsorbed them into his body as he strode forward, his shoulder-length blond hair swaying with each step and his long, slender spear swinging lightly in his hand. Walking directly toward the open hearth near the middle of the patio, he slung from his shoulder and handed to Koios—who was presiding as roastmaster—a slender rope from which dangled more than a dozen red deer.

Eurybie was wending her way among the tables, tossing flippant greetings to those she passed. She caught Kronos's eyes and began to make her way toward him.

"Good morning, my lord," she said as she reached the bower. "Good morning, Lady Rhea. I see I'm not late, after all." She nodded toward the barely touched platters beside each of them.

Kronos frowned ever so slightly. Rhea smiled stiffly.

"May I join you?" Eurybie asked, looking about for an attendant before either could answer. She spotted a young god and signaled him to bring table and chair.

Rhea began to stir. "Tell him not to bother," she said, rising. "I'm not hungry. You may have my place."

Kronos did not even look up at his wife.

"What a shame," Eurybie said, examining Rhea's plate more carefully. "The food looks wonderful this morning. Or perhaps I'm just very hungry."

Eurybie waited until Rhea entered the portico, then slipped into the vacated chair. She signaled an attendant.

"Good morning, Lady Eurybie," the boy said. "What may I bring you?"

"Take these away first," she said, motioning disdainfully toward the food and drink Rhea had left. "What meats are we having? I just saw Hyperion bring red deer."

"Yes, my lady, but it'll be a short while before any is ready. We still have a little of the aurochs Iapetos killed.

Everyone says it's very good. There's some chamois, too, if it's not all gone.''

She stroked his cheek affectionately. "Do your best for me, my young fellow; a little of this and a little of that."

As the first boy left, a second arrived, placing a fresh goblet beside her and filling it from a flagon. Eurybie took a long, slow drink, then turned her attention back to Kronos.

"I must say," she told him, "you don't look very well this morning."

He glared at her. "I don't feel all that well. I didn't sleep half the night."

"I always sleep well. Very soundly. Nothing ever troubles me."

"Sometimes, Eurybie, I think you have no insides at all— that you're nothing but a hollow shell."

She laughed softly. "If you're determined to offend me, at least wait until I've finished my meal."

She looked up to find the Muse Thalia setting a basket of fruit and nuts on the table beside her. "Thank you, dear. By the way, is it true the Hesperides are going to sing this morning—have I missed it? Isn't that rather risky, with all the empty stomachs?"

Thalia grinned back maliciously. "Singing is what they *say* they're going to do!" she said as she turned away to continue on to another table.

Before Eurybie could begin on the basket, the boy returned with a heaping platter for her. She thanked him with a wide smile and began to eat heartily. After a few minutes she looked over at Kronos, who was still staring out over the assemblage of gods. "You're ignoring delicious food," she said, still chewing. "Good food is more important than any of them."

"I'm responsible for all of this," Kronos said softly, still not looking at her.

"What did you say?"

His cold gray eyes turned slowly to appraise her. "I said that I am responsible for what you see here. For the very food in your mouth. Had I not done the things I have done, you would be breakfasting on raw fish and seaweed."

Eurybie swallowed, then laughed. "You certainly did sleep poorly!"

His eyes turned back toward the other gods. "I brought all

of this to the gods—by the strength of my arms and the swiftness of my brain.''

Eurybie started to giggle. She followed his gaze. Gold and silver glittered all across the patio in the brilliant, pure rays of the morning sun.

''None of this would exist without me. Everything you see on Olympos is the result of my work—the child of my mind if not of my arm. I've given it all to them—and yet they oppose me. . . . Must it always come back to brute force? I should have their loyalty, their gratitude. I led them to this life of ease and plenty. . . .''

His tone had become musing, and Eurybie began to eat again. ''Those things don't really exist,'' she said after a minute or two. ''Loyalty and gratitude are just ideas in your head, that you haven't been able to make real yet.''

He shrugged. ''Perhaps so.''

''What you really want,'' she said, ''is for them to love you.''

He faced her. ''Why shouldn't they love me? Haven't I done everything for them?''

''That will only get you envy and hate.'' She cracked a large nut and began to pick out its meat with her fingers. For some time she had been searching for a way to distract Kronos from his increasingly irksome topic of conversation. Now she saw Nalassa standing on the steps leading down from the portico to the patio.

''Who's that?'' she asked.

Kronos shrugged.

''I've never seen her before,'' Eurybie continued. ''She looks a bit lost, don't you think? Shall I invite her over? She might be the breath of fresh air you need.''

Kronos was looking at the nymph now, becoming increasingly aware of her physical charm. Still he hesitated. ''I'm waiting for someone to join me.''

''What does that matter? Who is it, male or female?''

''Philyra, the Okeanid.''

Eurybie smiled, remembering his remarks of the night before. ''Oh, yes, the one you were so anxious to learn about. Still, two young nymphs are better than one. I'll snare this one for you.''

Before he could object, she had left her place and gone to the naiad. Philyra had sent Nalassa on ahead of her, and

Nalassa was still standing on the steps, trying to find a friendly face before venturing farther. She smiled as Eurybie approached her.

"Are you looking for someone to breakfast with?" Eurybie asked.

"Well . . . well, yes, in a way. I'm afraid I don't—"

"Look no further. Come right this way." Eurybie took her by the arm.

Nalassa smiled back, but no sooner had they taken a few short steps than she found herself looking into the face of the King of the Gods. Her heart sank. Eurybie's invitation could have only a single interpretation. Kronos knew her as the nymph who had escaped from Thanatos—who knew the secret of Thanatos's room. She fought to conceal her inner turmoil.

Attendants brought table and chair, while others scampered off to procure food and drink for the newest arrival. Within moments Nalassa found herself settled between Kronos and Eurybie.

"It's always good to see a new face on Olympos," Eurybie said. "Especially a face as lovely as yours. She is lovely, is she not, Lord Kronos?"

"Indeed she is lov— There she is!" Kronos said as he spotted Philyra coming down the steps from the portico. "Pardon me." He had already risen and now edged his way around the two goddesses to go to meet Philyra. Taking her by the hand, he brought her back toward the bower. Once again attendants were called, so that soon Philyra took her place as near as possible to Kronos on one side, while Nalassa and Eurybie sat on the other.

"I'm afraid I overslept," Philyra said. "I hope I haven't kept you waiting." She looked around the table and caught Nalassa's eyes, without being able to gain any clue to the situation.

The food began to arrive and Kronos to engage her in trivial conversation, leaning toward her, his hand settling on her with unnerving frequency. Meanwhile Eurybie kept Nalassa talking. Philyra found herself trying to listen to them while listening to Kronos and fending off his advances.

"I arrived in the middle of the night, with no one to greet me," Nalassa was saying.

Nalassa's eyes flashed to Kronos's face to see if he was listening. His face betrayed no hint of interest.

The meal continued, neither the Okeanid nor the naiad really tasting her food. Philyra found herself incapable of following both conversations, nodding her head and making affable, agreeing noises to whatever it was that Kronos was telling her.

"Good," he said, "you'll find it well worth the visit. There is not another like it in the world."

Philyra looked up, startled. "I'm sorry. What did you say?"

He smiled. "Just that you won't be sorry you accepted my invitation."

"Invitation?"

"Look," Eurybie said, interrupting. "The Hesperides are going to sing."

Four beautiful maidens had walked to an open spot on the grass. The various attendants stood in clusters to watch and listen.

"They're really quite good," Eurybie continued to Nalassa, "but they have to compete with the Muses and . . . well, no one can compete with them. They know that, of course, and . . . there's no love lost between the two families, I can tell you." Eurybie laughed gaily.

"What invitation?" Philyra whispered as the goddesses began to sing. "My mind must have wandered while you were talking."

"I want to show you my garden. You've agreed to come."

"Isn't this your garden?"

He shook his head. "I mean my private garden, atop the palace. Not everyone gets to see it."

"But my lord—"

"Shh!" Eurybie admonished them.

Philyra fell into silence as the Hesperides began to perform. The four sisters sang a lilting ballad, accompanying it with a pantomime dance that managed to maintain beauty and dignity while illustrating the song. The entire assemblage listened in silence until the last note and movement had been completed, then applauded and cheered loudly.

"Well!" Eurybie exclaimed. "They've certainly improved. Did you really kill such a monster?" she asked Kronos, who had been the subject of the composition.

He hesitated, then said, "I make it a point never to cast doubt on a lady's veracity."

Thalia, the Muse, was going back to work, but Eurybie waved her over to their table. "We were very unkind to them," she said as the maiden drew near. "If they keep practicing, you'll have some very strong competition."

Thalia drew herself up to her full height, momentarily losing her normal good humor. "As long as it's taken for them to become this good, we won't have to worry for quite some time." She turned and walked quickly away.

Philyra returned to the interrupted matter of Kronos's invitation. "I'm sorry, my lord, but I seemed to have agreed to something without realizing I was doing so. When would you like me to visit your garden?"

"After breakfast. In a few minutes."

She shook her head. "Oh, I'm sorry, but I really can't. I told my sister Klymene that I would work with her this morning. She has a great deal of fabric that must be dyed and—"

"I'm sure she can make do without you for an hour or two," he answered firmly. "We'll leave as soon as you finish eating." He laid his hand upon her thigh.

Philyra cast a hopeless look at Nalassa.

"Lord Kronos is going to show you his private garden?" she asked ingenuously. "I do hope I may be privileged to see it while here on Olympos." She had momentarily forgotten Proteus's admonition to stay in sight of the other gods.

Kronos started to answer, but Eurybie spoke before him. "I'll see to it that you do. But I was thinking that after we finish eating I ought to give you a tour of the palace myself. The garden, at least in a sense, is the most impressive of all the sights here. Lord Kronos has been kind enough to take me there many times, and I never tire of it." She shot a look laden with amused irony at him. "But to see it first would spoil all the other sights. Let Philyra go with Kronos now, while I serve as your guide to the rest of Olympos."

"But it would be nice to make a party of it," Philyra said, "the four of us—"

She stopped mid-sentence. Thanatos was approaching them, rubbing sleep from his eyes and brushing back his hair. He came up to the group and bowed his head toward the King of the Gods.

"Good morning, Lord Kronos. Lady Eurybie, Lady—" He froze as his eyes fell upon Nalassa. His brow knit in a deep frown. His eyes darted upward, toward his suite of rooms on the topmost floor, then back to the naiad.

"Yes, yes, good morning, if you insist," Kronos said crossly. "If you have anything else to say, then by all means say it and get it done. Otherwise go away."

Thanatos began to stammer. "L-l-lord Kr-Kronos—" His eyes now darted back and forth between his king and Nalassa.

Kronos passed a hand across his face, gently rubbing his eyes. "I'm losing what little patience I have for you. Say what you want!"

Thanatos stopped trying to talk. He turned and stared directly into Nalassa's face, scrutinizing every detail of it. Then he turned back to Kronos. "Pa-pa-pardon me, I-I-I've just remembered . . ." He backed rapidly away, turned, and ran up the steps and across the portico toward the inner stairway.

Kronos shook his head slowly. "Shall we go now?" he asked Philyra as he rose and extended a hand toward her. He bowed toward the other goddesses, then slipping an arm about Philyra's waist, led her toward the palace.

They had only taken a few steps when Kronos glimpsed Crios sitting by himself off to one side. He excused himself momentarily and went to him.

"Brother," he told the Titan, "I've decided that you and Koios and I have been taking life too easy. The three of us shall hunt the evening meal. Tell Iapetos and Hyperion not to bother today, and Koios that you and he are to meet me here this afternoon. Dress for the trail and bring your weapons."

Kronos rejoined Philyra and led her inside. Behind him an ashen-faced Crios watched him leave. Slowly he lowered himself back into his seat. He was no longer hungry, and the food already eaten turned heavy inside him.

What was Kronos planning? he wondered.

TWENTY-THREE

As Lady Rhea, Queen of the Gods, left her husband on the patio terrace of Olympos and climbed the stairs toward the portico that led into the palace, she became aware of the dull weariness that had descended upon her. Her overwhelming passions of the night before had consumed themselves through their own intensity, leaving her incapable of pain or grief. Even Eurybie's studied callousness could not find a single ember that could be stirred into renewed life. Her emotional exhaustion had now been translated into physical fatigue.

Barely thinking, letting her feet find the way, she entered the great hall and headed toward the far side, where a doorway would lead to one of the many staircases within the palace. She was neatly and tastefully dressed in an almost unadorned peplos, a light veil covering her head. Her eyes took in the familiar surroundings of the huge room without really seeing them; the gold and silver and precious jewels that gleamed and sparkled from every direction seemed as distant and as dimly perceived as stars viewed through the haze of a foggy night.

Now she became aware that her feet had stopped walking and that, for some moments at least, she had been standing directly in front of the enormous throne, staring sightlessly up at the imposing mass of carved ivory upon its plinth of gold. Shaped in interlocking segments, the tusks of ten thousand mammoths came together so perfectly that not a single seam could be discerned. Like an ivory mountain the throne loomed over everything.

She stared up at it, as though seeing it for the first time. A trickle of memory brought long-forgotten images of herself and her lord. She saw him as he had looked during their courtship, when his entire being seemed wrapped in grandeur and marvel, when the promise of the future gleamed from his deep eyes and smiling lips. She remembered their wedding, when he stood beside her before their brothers and sisters. All around them the valley lay carpeted in thickly strewn flowers. She remembered, too, the bed of pansies to which her new husband had carried her.

Her hands clenched as she remembered another scene, more recent. She had come to him at night, blushing despite their long years of marriage, her lips unable to conceal the pride and self-satisfaction she felt. Looking into his eyes, she sought a reflection of her own proud jubilance as she told him that she was with child, with his child.

Instead she met a face that grew pale and stony, eyes that grew fierce in outrage. For centuries she had thought herself barren, had yearned to give him a son. Her smile froze on her lips, unable to keep pace with her emotions.

She turned suddenly away from the throne now.

Sobbing, Rhea rushed from the great hall, pulling her veil across her face to shield it from view. She climbed the stairs so rapidly that more than once she had to cling to the railing when her foot slipped. Her suppressed emotions rushed up within her at each step. Other scenes, scenes she had not allowed herself to remember, flooded her mind.

Her chambers occupied the entire floor of the palace directly below that of her husband. In order to reach it she had to climb eight flights of steep stairs. Normally she would have gone slowly, possibly stopping briefly on one of the landings. Today she rushed all the way without even a momentary pause, so that when she reached her room, she was completely out of breath and her sobs came in broken wheezes.

She threw open the door to the room that, for practical purposes, served as her sole dwelling. All of the other rooms on the floor remained empty, or nearly so. She had no need of them. Immaculately neat and sparsely furnished, the small chamber— little bigger than a cell—was more than adequate for her needs. She had long since tired of the wealthy splendor Kronos had once showered upon her.

Running across the room, she threw herself down on her bed. Weeping uncontrollably, her body thrashed back and forth and her small fists pounded against the thin mattress.

In time her body refused to cry any longer. She sat up, wiping her eyes. Grief and hatred possessed her alternately. The bareness of her room seemed to symbolize the barrenness of her life. Lady Rhea, Queen of the Gods—she had nothing, nothing that mattered to her.

After a while she rose and began to pace the room, her hands twisting together. Had he always been that way? Had she only been blind to it in the beginning? Or had that awful throne—all that the throne stood for—coaxed and corrupted him?

She came to an abrupt halt. And what of her, who had allowed him to impose his awful will upon her, who had allowed him to make her his partner, his *conspirator* in this hideous crime? Why had she not rebelled, no matter the penalty, no matter the hopelessness of her position? Why had she not fled to the farthest reaches of the earth? Had she not been seduced, corrupted by that same throne, by all it symbolized in wealth and power and prestige to the goddess who shared it with him?

She felt a movement within her body and her hands moved to gently clutch her abdomen. Her child—her child within her, moving! So tiny in comparison to her fully grown body, so tiny and helpless. . . . She could feel it moving, moving vigorously now, and that meant that the day of its birth was fast approaching. It would be sooner than she had guessed, perhaps very soon. And then she would have to bring it to her lord, hand it to Kronos. What would he do with it? What thing too horrible for him to admit would happen to this child, as it had to her others?

"My child, my child!" she cried, her voice raw and shrill. "What must I do to save you? By the Earth and starry Heaven, what must I do?"

He was invulnerable; there was absolutely nothing she could do against him. Even revealing his crime to the other gods would probably have no effect—except to earn her perpetual banishment in the never-ending darkness of Tartaros.

They would sympathize, they would be horrified; but they would do nothing to oppose him. She could flee, but eventually he would find her and the child.

Holding her abdomen and gently rocking herself from side to side, she began to sing a lullaby to her unborn infant.

She had now wandered toward the one window of the room. It looked down over the broad terraces below, and she had a clear view of the patio. Kronos was still there, accompanied by three goddesses rather than the one she had left him with. Curious, she drew closer to the window, watching for some time as her husband betrayed his interest in one of the goddesses through the innumerable little mannerisms she knew so well.

Who was the goddess he found so interesting today? Rhea had seen her before, but could not remember her name. Now Kronos was rising, helping her to her feet. They were leaving together.

She drew away from the window. Where would he take her? she wondered. To the garden atop the palace, probably; he often took his new conquests there.

She realized, with surprise, that she felt no jealousy. Last night, when she had interrupted him with Eurybie, she could not have said that. But now she felt nothing.

Can you be *jealous* without being in love? she wondered. Perhaps the last shards of her love had finally died. She tried to decide exactly what she did feel, if not jealousy.

Her hands were trembling. While her heart—her mother's heart—was being torn apart, he could think of nothing but trivialities, and that was exactly what the young goddess was. A triviality without any significance beyond the next hour, a new toy for the husband responsible for all her anguish.

She screamed, a long, piercing wail, and turned to pound her fists against the limestone wall. Why should he have his trivial little pleasure while she had nothing? She was his wife, his queen! Spinning around, she walked determinedly toward the door, intent upon accosting him and the young goddess.

Almost immediately, though, her steps halted. Very slowly she turned and walked back toward the window. Again she stared downward, not toward the patio but across the broad world below Olympos.

She would gain nothing by creating a scene with her husband. Only one thing mattered now—the child within her. A sudden resolve took hold of her. Stepping back from the window, she loosed her peplos and let it slip to the floor. Transforming herself into a dove, she flitted out the window, across the many terraces, and then downward from the mountain.

Timbered hills and jagged peaks swept by beneath her as she flew directly south, traveling far faster than any true bird. Small white wings concealing Titanic power beat incessantly, sending her darting across the sky.

At last the twin peaks of Mount Parnassos rose ahead of her. Beyond them sunlight glinted from the Corinthian Gulf, and still farther away, from the turquoise waters of the Mediterranean. Alighting on a steep slope, she reassumed her natural form and quickly caused phantom garments made of mist to clothe her body.

All around her was solitude and almost absolute silence, as though nature held itself in abeyance, listening. A pleasant moistness clung to the air, and as she started to descend, the soft sounds of her feet echoed back from the rocks. Many narrow gorges cut the face of the mountain; mist eddied within them like ghostly rivers.

As she reached the cliff she sought, a figure stirred nearby, rising from the rock shadows and coming toward her. It was the nymph Daphnis, who spent her life in pleasant solitude attending the sacred place the gods called the center of the world. She came forward, smiling as she recognized the Titaness.

"Lady Rhea," she said, bowing her head slightly. "It is very good to see you again, after so long. How may I serve you?"

Drawing a phantom veil across her face, Rhea replied, "I wish to speak with my mother."

"Shall I withdraw, that you may be alone?"

Rhea nodded, and the nymph turned and walked some distance down the mountainside. They had awakened a lone bird somewhere below; it began to sing, its voice ringing out in the stillness.

The Titaness approached the gaping cleft that in later years would be the focus of the shrine of Delphoi. At the very edge of the crevice she dropped to her knees and bent forward, pounding her hands against the ground.

"Mother! Mother, help me!" she cried.

Again and again she pounded her hands against the ground, calling up Gaia, the earth, mother of all. She began to weep again, so that her eyes started to sting.

"Help me, Gaia. Mother! Mother! What shall I do?"

A mist began to rise from the cleft, at first tenuous, but growing thicker. Rhea drew herself up, her senses reeling.

"Must this be? Tell me, Gaia—oh, please tell me—is there nothing I can do to save my baby—my unborn baby, who has done no crime but to be sired by a hateful father?"

A shape took form in the mist. Troubled, tender eyes looked down upon the Queen of the Gods. Soft, maternal lips smiled reassuringly.

"Tell me—tell me what I must do, Mother," Rhea cried, reaching out toward the image. Tears flowed down her cheeks.

Now there were tears in the eyes of the image too. A hand reached toward Rhea, settled softly on her forehead. The Titaness sank forward on the ground, unconscious at the touch.

As unconsciousness claimed her, Rhea found peace. A soothing voice seemed to be whispering in her ear. Before her eyes came visions of startling clarity. A vast panorama swept before her, rushing by like the waters of a swift-moving stream. For more than an hour she lay unconscious at the edge of the gaping chasm, and during that time the future of the world was revealed to her.

When finally she came to her senses again, she arose a new person. All her fears and anguish were gone. Her entire appearance radiated serenity. Straightening her hair and clothing, she moved away from the opening.

Daphnis had been watching from a distance and now came toward her. "May I assist you now, my lady? I hope you have learned all you desired to learn."

"Yes, I have." Rhea's smile proclaimed the inner peace that had come upon her. She turned to leave, but before she had taken a half-dozen steps, the sound of footsteps drew both her attention and Daphnis's to the approach of a third party.

Themis, Rhea's Titaness sister, was walking slowly up the slope toward them. As she saw Rhea her eyes darted about in embarrassed confusion.

"Good morning, sister," Rhea said as she drew near. "I see that more than one of us is troubled this morning."

Themis, who had once been the wife of Iapetos, averted her eyes.

Rhea touched her arm gently. "May our mother help you, as she has helped me."

Turning, the Queen of the Gods began to walk back up the mountain, leaving her sister in the privacy she obviously desired.

TWENTY-FOUR

A separate staircase, accessible only from within the personal chambers of Kronos, led to the rooftop garden above the palace of Olympos. Something very close to panic swept through Philyra as Kronos led her up this final flight of stairs.

Since yesterday morning, when the Lord of the Titans seemed to notice her for the first time, she had spent much of her time fretting over the coming breakfast engagement. His reputation had left little doubt concerning the motive behind his sudden interest. She had feared just such a development as this, that he would maneuver her to a secluded rendezvous and force her to openly rebuke his advances.

She dreaded the coming confrontation. In the three months she had lived on Olympos, she had come to sense the atmosphere of tension that surrounded the king. She feared him for his physical strength and power, and for the eccentric swings of temper that were only alluded to in the most veiled ways. That he might try to take her by force was very unlikely. The true danger lay in offending him and thereby inciting his enmity against her and her sisters. She realized this more than ever now, after all that Proteus had told her.

The staircase ended in a little, roofed enclosure. From there Kronos led her out into the garden.

"These are the true riches of the world," he said, waving his arm toward the wonderland of color and fragrance that suddenly surrounded them. "They have been brought from the farthest corners of the earth."

Philyra came to an abrupt halt, staring at the beauty that sprouted and blossomed on every side. Despite her high pitch of nervous anxiety, she recognized the truly stunning splendor that had been achieved here; at the same time she saw an excuse to avoid close contact with her escort.

She ran forward, gasping in amazement at the enormous plants. Lilies and lilacs, towering ferns, gardenias and geraniums, roses of every variety—carefully cultivated and irrigated with nectar, they grew to a size and resplendence never seen below Olympos. The combined smell seemed almost intoxicating in its headiness.

"Come this way," he told her, taking her trembling hand. She followed him down a narrow, twisting path, pausing every few steps as he pointed out each new growth they passed. Each time they stopped, she pulled her hand free from his, but he always reclaimed it to lead her along.

"I come here to think," he said. "The quiet and solitude, surrounded by all this beauty, relaxes me."

"I don't know how it would be possible to think here," she said. "The eyes and nose are too dazzled."

He studied her delicate beauty, trying to determine if her admission that her senses were overwhelmed was also intended to carry the message that she could not be held too strictly accountable for what her body might do in such a keyed-up, overwrought state.

Long dark hair tumbled in ringlets about her shoulders and down her back. Her emerald eyes, so striking in contrast to her hair, sparkled as she examined each new sight. Her fine, straight nose crinkled appealingly at each fresh smell. Each seemingly thoughtless, natural movement of her slender body sent out waves of attraction, so that he felt as though he were being pulled toward her. He brought his hand to rest in the hollow of her back as he guided her along, felt her tremble beneath his touch.

Her shyness had dropped away, replaced by girlish delight. Was she really so entranced by the lush spectacle of the garden, he wondered; or was this but the first of a series of steps that would allow her by degrees to become more and more approachable? Had she continued her overly demure demeanor even when they were alone, he might have interpreted it as genuine disinterest. The garden, he realized, had provided just the excuse she needed to abruptly drop her proper feminine reserve.

She leaned toward a pink and purple blossom and darted a quick glance at him as she inhaled its perfume—was the glance to gauge his reaction to her display of feminine charm?

He studied her every expression, trying to read her innermost thoughts. There were still traces of diffidence—her eyes never met his for more than a moment—but most nymphs and goddesses wore that guise, though few if any were unwilling to shed it at an opportune time. He had long since learned to discount such appearances. They all seemed to delight in displaying their innocence, however little might remain. That Philyra might actually be the fresh, untouched thing she proclaimed was a prospect barely worthy of consideration, however pleasant a novelty it might be. The odds were decidedly against it, innocence being a negative quality—the absence of experience. Given enough time, life inevitably wore it away.

"Are you glad you came?" he asked.

"Oh, yes. It's more lovely than I could possibly imagine. Lady Rhea must be very happy here. Does she come here often?"

"Not often. She has many interests. This garden, beautiful as it is, isn't one of them."

Kronos interpreted the question as two-pronged. The Okeanid had neatly determined that they were unlikely to be interrupted. At the same time she opened negotiations, with a high asking price, by reminding him of his wife.

To him all life was a series of bartering: One traded what he had for what he wanted. Just now he wanted Philyra, quite strongly too; he needed to discover what she would require in return. He and the other male gods sought good looks above almost everything else; the females, while not adverse to that commodity, more often fell victim to subtler, less comprehensible appeals. They traded for security or prestige, wealth or power.

He let his hand slip around her back to gently stroke the firm flesh of her upper hip. She turned away from him to examine another flower, so that his hand slipped from her. He recognized the movement immediately as a coy female maneuver. If it had been translated into words, it might have said, "Not now—not yet . . . We don't know each other well enough, yet. . . ." Or, less tactfully, "We still haven't come to terms. . . ." Its true purpose and effect were to tantalize him, allowing him but the slightest taste of the banquet her body promised.

Now he led her down an adjoining path till they came to an open area. A wide pond rimmed by polished stones was fed by an artificial waterfall. There were benches nearby, and he brought her toward them.

"You're trembling," he said as he took her hand again, holding it in both of his. Her bosom was rising and falling rapidly, in obvious agitation. Had the combination of the garden and his attention already brought about this extreme agitation? She was obviously controlling her emotions only with great difficulty.

"You're very quiet," he said.

"I'm sorry, my lord. The wonders here are beyond words. I was just thinking that in nature you seldom see so much beauty side by side. There is always ugliness mixed in."

He sat down beside her, and she edged away a little. She was very aware of how nervous she was. Light sweat had begun to form in the palms of her hands. Despite all her efforts to avoid close contact with him, to keep their attention centered on the garden, he kept finding ways to get near her. Every time he had taken her hand or slipped his arm about her, she had found some plausible reason to reach out or twist out of his reach, politely but firmly indicating that she was not interested. He should have been able to tell as much from the apprehensive glances she found herself giving him every few seconds.

Normally the most guileless of creatures, she found herself mentally cursing him. He was the King of the Gods. How dare he misuse his power and position like this, pressuring her into a romantic situation she obviously wished to avoid? Oh, he was attractive enough, in an objective sense—and obviously knew it. But she was frightened of him, and now that she knew what he planned to do to her father, she felt only loathing toward him. Did he think she would submit to him simply because he was her king? Each time he touched her, something akin to terror shrieked through her.

To make matters worse, she had to try to conceal the true repugnance she felt, lest she offend him. Her heart was pounding fiercely, her face felt hot and flushed, and it took a conscious effort to keep her breathing from becoming panicky. His arm came around her again, pressing her toward his chest.

A fish leaped in the pond.

"Oh," she exclaimed, jumping up and rushing forward a few steps. "I didn't realize there were fish here!"

He followed her. "Yes, a number of interesting varieties. Come a little closer so you can see those below the surface."

For some moments she peered downward, seeming deeply interested. Finally she looked up. Kronos had been awaiting that moment. Stepping closer, his arms encircled her slender waist and his lips descended on hers. Startled, her head drew away, but he had only to lean a little farther toward her to bring their lips in contact.

He could feel the wild pounding of her heart, and she was almost burning hot to his touch. Her passions seemed to be aroused to the bursting point. His lips pressed hungrily against hers, but now her tiny hands were on his chest, pushing him away.

She stepped back as he released her. A hand moved to cover her face, and her bosom was heaving. Was she really so overcome with emotion that she could barely control herself? he wondered. He was already coming to the conclusion that she was highly passionate, but she was reacting very strongly to what, after all, was only a kiss.

Tossing her hair back and laughing self-consciously, she started down another path. "Where does this one lead?" she asked.

"Follow it and see."

He walked behind her, giving her time to recover her composure. After some time he asked, "What do you want, Philyra? Of all the things in the world, what would you most like to have?"

She considered for some moments, not looking at him. Finally she said, "Happiness, I suppose. For myself and my family." She turned away again, realizing belatedly that it was not wise to refer to her father in any way. Kronos seemed not to notice the possible significance of her words.

"We all want our loved ones to be happy, but what about you? Isn't there something you especially desire? Jewelry? Finery? Did you like the mirror I sent you?"

A resolve was growing within her. She would have to face him and let him know how she felt. The best she could hope was to do it as painlessly as possible for both of them. "It was beautiful," she said, seeing in this new topic a way of approaching the subject; "far more beautiful and ornate than need be, Lord Kronos. My sister Klymene, who is the wife of your brother Iapetos, has nothing so fine."

"Does it give you pleasure?"

"Yes, my lord, but . . ."

Her hands were clenched together in front of her. The tension was becoming intolerable. Even at risk of offending him, she had to set matters straight before they went any further.

"But . . .?" he asked, smiling at her.

"But I think I shall return it to you."

"Why would you do that?"

She forced herself to look directly into his eyes. "Let me answer with a question. Why did you send it to me?"

"Why? So that you can look at yourself in it and discover just how beautiful you are! That's a lesson every goddess needs to learn."

"It seems to me," she said slowly, "that a gift such as that must have other reasons as well, that something might be expected in return. If that were the case, I could not accept it, for the value is more than I am able or willing to reciprocate."

"On the contrary, the mirror is valueless in itself, only a cold slab of polished metal. If it seems rich and beautiful, that's because of the richness and beauty it reflects."

"You expect nothing in return?" she asked, forcing herself to continue despite his evasion.

He shook his head. "I gave it to you because I wished you to have it. I wanted to see you smile. That's ample repayment for me. Will you smile for me?"

She did not know whether to be relieved or flabbergasted. Had he understood what she was trying to say? He touched her chin gently, lifting it so that she faced him directly.

"Good," he said. "Now I've had all the payment I desire. Shall we continue walking?"

"I really think I should be going soon. Klymene will be wondering where I am. Thank you so much for letting me see this marvelous place."

He nodded in consent. "This path leads back to the stairs."

They walked in silence, reaching the small enclosure and descending to his apartments below. Kronos escorted her to the corridor.

"I shall be looking forward to seeing you again. Now that you've seen the garden above, perhaps you'll wish to visit it again."

"It's indeed very compelling. Good-bye, Lord Kronos," she said, letting him squeeze her hands gently in his before turning to make her way down the corridor toward the stairs.

As she walked, her heart began to lift. She had avoided disaster. He must have understood and taken her at her word. She sighed inwardly. It had really been very easy. All she had to do was tell him clearly that she was not interested in his romantic advances.

Behind her Kronos watched as she walked away, his eyes following each movement of her slender, girlish form. He had understood her very well. She was not to be acquired with anything as insignificant as a mirror. She was fully aware of her charms and intent upon obtaining the very best price they could command. Her almost convincing innocence, her trembling, suppressed passion—these were the opening rounds of the bargaining. She had his interest and had refused his first bid as too low. Now he would have to raise his offer.

From down the corridor in the opposite direction Thanatos was coming toward him. He had waited until Philyra disappeared down the stairs before approaching. Now he ran forward.

"Lord Kronos, I must talk to you. Something very important has happened."

Kronos turned toward him with a frown, his mood shattered by the intrusion.

TWENTY-FIVE

Thanatos had awakened late that morning, still tired and very hungry from his excursion of the night before. With great reluctance, he decided to eat breakfast immediately rather than interrupt his work later in the day. His inventive mind had already formulated a large number of experiments to be conducted upon his new subjects, and he was anxious to begin.

What he discovered on the terrace outside the palace, however, banished from his mind all thought of food and sent him racing back up the stairs to confirm or deny the evidence of his eyes. Calmly seated beside the King of the Gods, to all appearances a convivial member of the king's party, was the nymph he had kidnapped the previous night.

By the time he regained his apartment, he had nearly convinced himself that he must be mistaken. The nymph he had abducted and the one he had just seen breakfasting with Kronos could not be the same. His heart skipped a beat as he reached the door to the laboratory—it was not only unlocked, but had been left slightly ajar. He pushed it open and rushed into the room, eyes blinking in the dim light. Hens began to flutter about their cages. Pigs squealed.

The nymph was gone. The long strips of cloth that had bound her lay upon the floor. He moved slowly toward them, disbelieving. How could she have escaped? The bonds had been tight, the knots well tied. He had been sleeping in the very next room. Could she have unlocked the door and crossed his bedroom without awakening him?

He looked aimlessly about the room, his eyes settling now on the open lid of the cage in which the mortals had been confined. With a cry he leaped toward it. The cage was empty.

Stunned, he backed toward the door and out into his bedroom. He collapsed in a chair, unable to comprehend what had happened. He was not angry. He desired no revenge. All he could think of was how near he had been to discovering something of real importance—and what a setback to his work this loss represented.

Gradually his overwhelming disappointment gave way to a fuller realization of his situation. Did Kronos know who the nymph was—that she had been brought to Olympos by force and had seen the room in which he conducted his experiments? This morning she was well dressed and fully groomed, though the night before she had been dirty and clothed in rags. Who had befriended her? And why was the Okeanid Philyra—sister of that troublesome Metis—also at breakfast with Kronos? Did she or the child goddess play some role in the mystery?

His mind was too dazed to sort out all the elements of the puzzle. He had to talk with Kronos.

As he neared the chambers of his king, sounds from the stairwell informed him that someone was approaching. A soft female voice kept him from rushing forward. Reluctantly he stepped into the shadows and watched as Kronos and Philyra came into sight. Thanatos gnawed his lower lip in frustration. He dared not accost his master now, with an assignation in progress. He would have to wait still longer.

More than an hour passed, each minute increasing Thanatos's nervous anxiety. He knew Kronos would be angry with him for not somehow preventing the nymph's escape—but how could he have prevented it? The degree of his anger would depend on how much damage had been done, on whether or not the nymph had told anyone what had happened to her and what she had seen.

Kronos's insistence on secrecy was not only irksome, but incomprehensible. Why should the King of the Gods care what the others thought? For that matter, why should anyone disapprove? The work was messy and noisome, he realized—

but he did it, not they. All he was doing was seeking answers, answers to very interesting and important questions. A single nymph seemed very insignificant when weighed against such knowledge.

Finally a door opened and Kronos stood in the doorway, saying good-bye to the Okeanid. Thanatos waited until the goddess reached the stairs, then rushed toward his master.

A frown formed on the king's lips as he recognized him. Sighing in exasperation, Kronos said, "God of carrion, why do you dog my path? Haven't I made it clear that I wish to see you as seldom as possible?"

Thanatos came to an abrupt halt, drawing himself up and consciously slowing the flood of words about to pour from his mouth. "Has she told anyone?" he asked, his voice shrill with excitement despite his efforts. "What have you done with her?"

Kronos stared at him blankly, not understanding.

"How did she escape? Has she told anyone what happened?"

Kronos's expression moved from perplexity toward indignation. "What business is it of yours?" he asked, concluding that Thanatos was talking about Philyra. "How does she concern you?"

It was Thanatos's turn to be puzzled. "Don't you know? Didn't she tell you? She didn't tell you about me?"

"About *you*!" Kronos's eyes narrowed as he tried to untangle what the other god was saying. In his own mind Philyra was associated with but a single idea—romance. It was almost unthinkable that Thanatos, this despicable creature, could have romantic feelings of any kind, yet Kronos could find no other interpretation for the things he was saying.

"Yes, about me," Thanatos continued. "I brought her to my room last ni—"

"You *what*?"

"I can't understand it," Thanatos went on, shaking his head and exuding relief. "I thought she would run screaming to the first person she met."

Kronos's mouth had become a grim, straight line. He glared at him. "Stop babbling! Tell me what you're talking about, and tell me plainly. What did you do to her?" He was quivering with suppressed rage.

"She escaped from my room last night. I was sure she'd

tell you about it. But who gave her fresh clothes—was it you, or someone else?''

Kronos exploded, surging toward him and bellowing an awful oath. ''What did you do to her? Tell me or I'll tear the truth from your wretched mouth!''

Thanatos stumbled backward to escape the powerful hands of his master. ''I did her no harm, my lord! You told me I could have a nymph for my work, so I brought her to—''

''A nymph—for your work!'' Kronos's eyes had grown very wide. ''I said a nymph—one of the countless solitary creatures of the wilds—not a goddess! She's a full-blooded Titan, the daughter of a Titan father and Titan mother. How dare you lay your unclean hands upon her!''

''A Titan?'' Thanatos said, bewildered. ''No, you are mistaken, my lord. She is only a nymph. I brought her from the hills below Olympos.''

''You brought Philyra from the earth below? Are you mad? She's been here for months.''

''Philyra? I'm not talking about Philyra—I'm talking about the nymph at your table this morning, who had breakfast with you and Philyra and Eurybie.''

''This morning . . .? You must mean Nalassa. She's a naiad. She said she arrived here last night, by herself.''

''She did. I found her while searching for the creatures discovered by the Muses. I captured her and carried her back, bound and gagged, to my laboratory.''

''Your laboratory! She's been inside that room? But she said nothing about it, not even a hint. She gave no indication that anything unusual had happened to her.''

''The men are gone too—the little godlike creatures. I captured many of them, perhaps all, though I couldn't be certain in the dark. They also are gone.''

''The men and the nymph were locked in that room?''

Thanatos nodded. ''She was bound securely, and the mortals—they are mortal; I found that out before I went to bed—''

''Was the door *locked*?''

''I think so. I always lock it.''

''You aren't certain?''

''I'm almost certain.''

Kronos frowned deeply. ''The nymph was tied up and the men were . . .?''

"Inside a large cage, with the lid latched shut. It was open in the morning. The door to the room was unlocked and not completely closed."

"But why should she pretend nothing happened?" Kronos asked, almost to himself.

Thanatos shrugged.

"Why would she pretend, unless she had some reason to?"

"What reason could she have?"

"Only one," Kronos said. "To protect herself. And that means she had to know that what she had seen and what had happened to her were not safe to talk about."

"How could she have known that?"

"*That* I would very much like to know. You said she had changed clothes?"

Thanatos nodded. "She had been dressed in a dirty, torn tunic. You saw her this morning."

"I think she said something about changing clothes to Eurybie."

"I must get the mortals back," Thanatos said. "I can always get another nymph, but I may not be able to replace them. They're very important to my work—creatures so like us, but not deathless. They will provide insights impossible to attain otherwise."

Kronos was not listening. He was mulling over the facts concerning Nalassa's escape. Even if she had not confided in anyone yet—and that seemed unlikely—she would talk eventually. She had to be silenced, and along with her anyone else who knew of the work going on in Thanatos's laboratory.

A massive hand shot out and closed around Thanatos's throat. Fingers tightened. Gasping for breath, Thanatos felt himself being lifted upward. His eyes began to bulge from their sockets as the grip on his throat grew still tighter.

Kronos held him so that their faces were close together. The eyes of the Lord of the Titans showed only coldness—no anger, no deep emotion. When he spoke, his voice was calm and unwavering.

"Son of Nyx, I warned you what would happen if you embarrassed me. You begged for more subjects for your experiments. You got your nymph and you allowed her to escape. She is your responsibility. You will find her and bring her to me. Do you understand?"

Thanatos was unable to answer. The words could not pass through his constricted throat. He nodded his head frantically.

The fingers loosened, lowered him back to his feet.

"You understand," Kronos continued, "that you are in very serious difficulty. Your only hope is to do exactly as I tell you. The nymph was to go with Eurybie, to be shown the sights of the palace. You will find her and bring her here. You will say that I wish to show her my garden. You will stay with her—not let her out of your sight—until you deliver her to me.

"Probably she and Eurybie will still be together," Kronos continued. "If they are not, and if you do not stumble upon the sea goddess during your search for the naiad, you will seek her out after you have brought Nalassa to me. You will tell Eurybie that I command her immediate presence. Do you understand this too?"

Thanatos nodded, rubbing his injured neck.

"Good. Then go."

Thanatos obeyed, more than happy to escape the company of his master.

After he had left, Kronos brooded for some time upon Nalassa and Thanatos. When he had plumbed the matter as deeply as possible without further information, he let his thoughts turn to more pleasant matters.

He remembered a necklace, a really fine work of craftsmanship that glittered with opals and garnets and large white pearls. It would make a good present for Philyra—a good way to open the second round of bargaining. She would expect more, he knew, but the necklace would make a fine beginning, neither too little nor too much.

TWENTY-SIX

However pleasant his reveries, he could not allow them to continue indefinitely. Other matters demanded the attention of the Lord of the Titans.

Arising from the enormous couch on which he had been reclining, he went to look out a window. The sun had already passed zenith. Nearly an hour and a half had elapsed and Thanatos had still not returned. Frowning, Kronos shook himself and stretched his massive body. His brothers, Crios and Koios, would be awaiting him below. For a moment he considered postponing his plan for them. Through the window his eyes sought out a distant range of mountains, and he found himself yearning for the cold, moist air and dizzying open spaces. Olympos seemed very confining.

He decided suddenly that the nymph and the problems she posed could wait two or three more hours. Stretching again, he could feel the pent-up strength of his bulging muscles. Going to an adjoining room, he began to dress, substituting a tough leather loincloth for the ornate linen he had worn. On his feet he strapped high-ankled hunting boots, and over his shoulders he draped a long, heavy cloak of bear skins. Belting a small dagger to his side, he went to a rack against one wall and chose three long, slender spears, each with tapering points of gleaming bronze.

The two Titans were waiting for him on the otherwise deserted patio, Koios seated in sullen dejection, Crios pacing. Both came forward as he descended the steps from the portico, Koios in the lead, Crios hanging back.

He surveyed them critically. "Simple leather and plain furs would serve you better today than ornate garments more suited to a council of the gods." He held all three spears in his huge right hand, their butts planted on the ground and their points bristling toward the sky. The suggestion of a smile played upon his lips and his eyes gleamed.

"It was you who first encouraged us to dress well," Koios said, looking down at the short chiton of purple silk he wore. A jewel-studded girdle circled his waist and a thin cloak, bordered with thread of silver and gold, lay draped over his arm.

Kronos laughed. "It's been a long time since you killed your own meal. Hyperion and Iapetos would never hunt in such clothes."

"They *like* to hunt," Crios said. His own garments were nearly as ill-chosen as Koios's. "Why not let them do it? We have other things to do."

"We all have our own preoccupations, but too often they make us forget our basic needs. We've grown soft, brothers—in need of a little vigorous exercise. And when the body is continually pampered, the mind becomes dull and sleepy. It needs invigoration too. Come. We have far to travel, much to do."

Draping his cloak over one arm, he caused wings to grow from his shoulder blades. Koios and Crios followed his example, and within moments the three were flying from Olympos. Kronos led the way, his huge wings beating in slow, measured strokes. His brothers had to exert themselves to keep pace with his effortless speed.

For some time they flew toward the north, alighting at last on the steep slopes of a high mountain. All around them jutted other craggy peaks of the same range.

"Why have we come here?" Crios asked. "There isn't any game up here." He pulled his thin cloak about himself in an effort to keep the icy wind from his body.

"Exactly right, brother. The game is below us, but from here we can see anything that moves down there. We are Titans, not lesser gods. We must have game suited to our rank. From here we can more easily spot our quarry."

"Just what do you propose to hunt?" Koios asked.

"I haven't decided definitely. Perhaps we can locate a group of wild boar. That would present a little excitement."

Koios frowned and Crios groaned. The prehistoric wild boar, more than four feet high at the shoulders, would attack anything, even a god. Lions retreated from their towering presence, but the boar almost always stood its ground until the last moment, concealed by bushes, then charged forward to gore and slash the feet of the unwary god. Hunting such creatures often resulted in very painful injuries.

Kronos led them along a mountain path. For Crios and Koios the trip was a nightmare. Mist floated among the rocks, often making it difficult to see. The trail was narrow and winding. Sheer walls and gaping chasms met them at every turn. When the route dipped lower they passed the remains of a solitary dead tree, its bare branches stretched out forlornly like frozen arms. The snow-covered walkway, strewn with easily dislodged rocks, narrowed in places to a width that forced them to edge along with their backs to the mountain, hands clinging to any available support.

They watched Kronos with amazement and growing terror. His sure footing never failed him. While they crept along, convinced that the next step might send them careening downward, Kronos followed the tortuous path with perfect self-assurance. Fully erect, his chest expanded and his shoulders thrust back, he seemed to relish the frigid air and awesome danger of this world of stark precipices and looming chasms. He seemed completely at home here, among the wild, jutting rocks, the ice and snow and drifting mist.

Occasionally they stopped to peer down at the world below. On the lower slopes of the mountain a saber-tooth stalked a cave goat, inching forward behind the concealment of rocks and shrubs. A great bear scratched its back against a boulder.

At last Kronos brought them to a halt, pointing down from a high cliff toward a herd of mammoths on a distant plain. "There, that's fitting game for Titans."

"But how can we get close enough?" Koios asked. "The plain is wide, with nothing to conceal us."

"There's no need of concealment," Kronos said. "We shall kill them from here."

Both Crios and Koios stared at him in disbelief.

"Shall I take the first cast, or one of you?"

They looked at each other. Finally Koios said, "I don't see that it matters. Nobody could hit a target at this distance."

Kronos smiled. "We are brothers. We have lived together on Olympos for countless ages. Yet there are still things about each other we don't know."

"I know you were once very skilled with your spear, my brother and lord," Koios said. "But I also know that Olympos occupies too much of your time for you to hunt very often. I know, too, that such a thing is impossible."

"You're wrong on two counts. I still hunt occasionally, though not nearly as often as I would like; and it is not impossible. Have you ever tried it?"

Koios shook his head.

Kronos gestured with the point of a spear toward the rocks that surrounded them. "Much of my youth was spent in these mountains, in the days when our father still ruled the earth and we all lived separately, like beasts. I roamed these paths, spear in hand, loving the stark majesty I found here. I was the master of these high, wild places where no one else ever ventured. I still come here every now and then, to get the stale air of Olympos out of my lungs."

"But no one can throw a spear that far, or hit so small a target," Koios said.

"I could once. I learned to hunt from these peaks. I sharpened my eyes and trained my muscles. I may be a little out of practice, but it is most definitely not impossible. Try it with me; you may surprise yourself. We should all throw at the same time. After the first strike, the herd will bolt."

"I'll just watch, I think," Crios said, a whine in his voice.

"And you?" Kronos asked Koios.

"As you wish."

"Good, then throw with me." He stepped toward the edge of the sheer cliff, Koios doing the same a little distance away. Holding two of the spears in his left hand, Kronos balanced the third in his right. He studied the wind, measured the distance, then drew back his arm.

The spear, as large as a full-grown pine, shot downward from the mountain, the air screaming and roaring around it. A bull mammoth, looking smaller than a child's wooden toy in the distance, had time to look up from its grazing toward the deafening sound. Before it could move, the shaft pierced it through and buried itself in the ground, radiating shock waves through the earth that shook other members of the herd to their knees.

Koios had flung his own spear downward only a fraction of a moment after Kronos, but it fell short by at least half a mile.

"They're on the run now," Kronos said, "and far more difficult targets."

The herd had broken into a number of small groups, which were now running in different directions. Kronos threw his second spear, aiming ahead of the lead animal of one of the groups. It roared downward with deadly accuracy, once again cleanly impaling the creature. Impact tremors sent the other mammoths skidding among the high grass.

"Very impressive," Koios said coldly. "Whatever you're trying to prove, brother, you have proven it."

Crios was trembling, both from cold and from fear. He cursed the circumstances that had made him a party to Kronos's schemes.

"This way," Kronos said. "We may find more game on the other side of the mountain."

"What about the kill and our spears?" Koios asked.

"I still have one left, and Crios has his. We'll collect the others and the game on our way home."

Reluctantly they followed him along the narrow trail. The path grew even more rugged. Mist hung all around them as they climbed upward; snow and ice crunched under their feet.

With a thought and a gesture of his hand, Kronos commanded a part of the mist, sending it on ahead to a place he knew. Obeying, it moved past them in unnoticed wisps and swirls.

"Years beyond number have come and gone," Kronos said softly, "and yet these rocks are all but unaffected by the passage of time. It seems odd—for we have changed so much."

He spoke as they walked, glancing around occasionally to look at them. "So much has happened over the ages that our memories of those earliest of times have grown dim. A place like this makes me remember—reawakens those dim memories. I come here for a few hours, and when I return to Olympos, my problems there seem small and manageable, insignificant beside the vast forces of nature that have already been tamed."

The path had broadened, and they were now approaching a wide, relatively flat area ringed by lower peaks. Kronos slowed, moving in such a way that his brothers went on ahead of him, stopping near the open area. They turned to face him as he stood with his back to a wall of rock.

"It's very easy on Olympos to forget the way things were. Most of us no longer hunt our own food. We're never hungry. We not only have clothes to keep us warm, but fine clothes, the work of hands more skilled than our own. The rain and the cold no longer touch us, and there is always beauty within sight, if we care to look for it. Comfort and luxury surround us, and we forget how long it took to acquire all that. We forget that once we lived like the animals that teem upon the world below.

"No—worse than animals," he continued, eyeing them narrowly, "for we fought with each other for the wealth of those days, food and skins and comfortable patches of grass upon which to sleep. We cared only for ourselves, instead of working for our mutual good. . . ."

"We haven't forgotten," Koios said. "You've reminded us often enough how much we owe you. What are you getting at? We've already sworn to obey you."

Kronos nodded. "What was needed was organization—a brain to direct the many hands. I became that directing brain, and I wrested cooperation from even the most unwilling. For the most part I did it by making it worthwhile to do as I wished. Only occasionally had I to resort to violence to impose my will."

Koios was becoming angry. "What are you saying? That you won't spit us upon your spears as you did the mammoths—unless we make it necessary?"

Kronos smiled. "No, brother, I am trying to make you understand the absolute folly of opposing me. I never flaunt my skill and power. I use it sparingly, only when—"

"Your demonstration was quite impressive. You can strike us down from unimaginable distances, when we think ourselves perfectly safe. You've made your point very well and—"

"No, I haven't." Kronos's face became implacable. "I need no spear to deal with traitors. You have not the slightest conception of the powers I am capable of wielding. At my command the very earth will swallow you up!"

He pointed past them as he spoke, toward the wide, plateaulike area. As he pointed he issued a mental command.

The mist, which had formed itself into a phantom landscape, gave up its deceitful form and drifted away. A gaping chasm, nearly six thousand feet deep, yawned almost at their heels, its sides toothed with jagged points of rock.

Crios screamed, throwing himself forward. Gasping for breath, he lurched toward a boulder, his knees shaking so wildly that he could hardly stand. Koios's face turned ashen as the magnitude of the act and the nearness of danger became clear. He walked stiffly away from the edge, trembling.

The illusion was complete. An entire section of mountain seemed to have vanished. Had Kronos wanted to punish them, they thought, he could have made the chasm appear a few inches nearer. Before they could cause wings to grow, they would have been ripped apart upon the ragged cliffs. To varying degrees most of the gods were capable of altering matter, but it required intense concentration and usually could be performed only piecemeal, or on small objects. Such an act as this was beyond anything they had thought possible.

"I have no wish to harm you," Kronos said slowly, standing above them now that Koios had collapsed upon a boulder near his brother. "My purpose is simple and straightforward. I must have your complete and unquestioning obedience."

It took several moments for either of them to recover enough composure to answer.

"Only a fool would oppose you," Koios finally said, his mouth dry and his lips quivering. "I will obey you in everything."

"I will obey, I will obey!" Crios almost shrieked, covering his face with his hands.

He gave them a few minutes to steady themselves, then said, "Shall we continue? We need more game for the larder. The way is impassible now. We will have to detour."

They followed in silence as he led them up the frozen face of the cliff to another path. His eyes were gleaming. His bulging muscles carried him effortlessly over every obstacle. Tall and unbending against the bitter wind, he glanced back to watch as they struggled to keep up.

He need no longer be concerned about their obedience; he was certain of that now. He only wished Iapetos could be brought to heel as easily.

TWENTY-SEVEN

Thanatos's search proved lengthy and frustrating. He went first to the patio, but found neither the naiad nor the sea goddess. Neither were they in any of the communal areas of the palace. Finally he went to the apartment of Eurybie. No one answered his knock, but the door was unlatched. He searched within, still in vain. Only one other possibility suggested itself. He went to the chambers of Iapetos.

He intended to question Philyra. He was suspicious of the Okeanid both because she had eaten breakfast with Nalassa and because she was Metis's sister. Even if she had no connection to the escape of the naiad and the mortals, she might have invited Nalassa to visit her. At the same time he hoped to interrogate Metis about the missing mortals.

He found Prometheus and Epimetheus playing in the atrium. The boys looked up in surprise as he entered without announcing himself.

"Oh, it's you," Prometheus said acidly, standing up from the game he had been playing on the floor and taking a bold step forward. "What do you want? I'm going to tell my father how you keep sneaking in here."

"Where is the Okeanid Philyra?"

Prometheus hesitated before answering. Finally he nodded in the direction of her room. Thanatos started to move in that direction, but Prometheus ran in front of him.

"I'll get her," he said. "I'll bring her here."

Thanatos took two or three more steps, but then changed his mind and came to a halt. He preferred to surprise the goddess, possibly hearing or seeing something that she would otherwise try to hide from him. Nevertheless the boy's firm voice and prompt action made him wait in the atrium.

Philyra returned with Prometheus. "You wish to see me?" she asked.

"I wish to see the nymph Nalassa. Is she here?"

Philyra concealed her uneasiness as best she could. "You mean the nymph I met at breakfast? No, I haven't seen her since."

"Do you know where she might be?"

"I believe Lady Eurybie was going to show her about the palace."

Thanatos listened without discernable reaction. "Is Metis in her room? I wish to speak with her." He stepped quickly around the divine maiden and moved down the short hall before Prometheus could intervene. A few quick steps brought him to the door.

He stepped inside, looking around the cluttered room. Instead of Metis he found Iapetos.

"Good morning, Thanatos," the god said, coming toward him. "Are you seeking me?"

Prometheus had followed behind Thanatos. The unexpected presence of his father in Metis's room puzzled him as he edged his way to a corner to watch.

Thanatos was puzzled, too, and surprised. "But I thought you were going—" He had passed Iapetos not long before and expected him by now to be in his workshop.

"He's looking for Metis," Prometheus said. "This is the second time he's entered our apartment without being invited. He pushed his way past us."

Iapetos listened to the boy, then looked at the god. "Does he speak the truth? Such conduct is very questionable. I'm sure you have a good reason to act in such a way, but you risk being thought discourteous."

"P-p-pardon, Lord Iapetos," Thanatos said, starting to stammer as he backed toward the door. "I'm on an e-e-errand for L-L-Lord K-K-Kronos."

"An errand for my brother? It concerns Metis? Tell me about it. Perhaps I can assist you."

"I won't t-t-trouble you any l-l-longer. I'll come b-bback. . . .'' He continued backing toward the door, so that Philyra and Epimetheus had to stand aside to let him pass back out into the hallway.

''As you wish,'' Iapetos said, following as Thanatos retreated. ''Come whenever you like, though I trust you'll remember to properly announce yourself before entering.''

''Y-y-yes, my l-l-lord,'' Thanatos said, bowing as he backed down the hall. They all followed him to the atrium.

When he left the apartment, Prometheus and Epimetheus began laughing. ''Oh, Father,'' Prometheus said. ''I'm so glad you were here. I thought you had gone out. But why were you in Metis's room?''

''I was looking for Metis,'' he answered with a smile.

''Is she in trouble?'' Epimetheus asked.

''Back to your toys, children. Philyra, come tell me exactly what happened here.''

Philyra followed him back to Metis's room. ''Perhaps Thanatos will think twice in the future before being so rude,'' he said as the door closed behind them. The features of Iapetos blurred, and a moment later Proteus stood before his sister.

''That was very close,'' she said, grinning.

''Luckily I heard you talking to him outside. His voice is rather loud, and quite distinctive.''

''How long have you been here? You weren't around when I returned from breakfast. And where's Metis?''

''I arrived only a few minutes ago, by way of the tunnels. They interlink much of the palace. Metis is getting the mortals settled and will probably be busy for quite a while yet.''

''Where are they?''

''We decided Thanatos would search every room in the palace for them, starting here and then proceeding through all the unoccupied apartments before tackling the occupied ones.'' He paused, grinning. ''I have a riddle for you, sister. Which apartment is both occupied and unoccupied at the same time?''

She frowned. ''I'm no good at riddles. Just tell me—wait! Our parents have rooms here, even though they never visit. Is that it?''

He shook his head. ''Too obvious. Thanatos will think of that right off. This is a standing joke in the palace, Metis tells me. Momos—Thanatos's brother, you realize—has chambers of his own, but almost never uses them.''

Philyra laughed. "He always falls asleep on the benches in the corridor. He's probably forgotten where his rooms are!"

"So Metis tells me. We've moved Oizys and the mortals to his apartment. One of the rooms has an entrance to the system of tunnels, so it will be relatively easy to come and go between it and this room."

He pulled a chair from the wall and sat down. "How did your engagement with our amorous king go this morning?"

She blushed slightly. "Much better than I had hoped, though for a while I thought I was going to have a rough time. I told him as gently as I could that I wasn't interested, and he let me leave."

Proteus's eyebrows rose. "I wouldn't have expected that."

"Neither did I. I'll tell you all about it when we have more time. Now you must know why Thanatos was here. He was looking for Nalassa."

Proteus considered her statement for a moment. "Our bluff hasn't worked then, though it did buy us a few extra hours. There really wasn't anything else we could have done. Where is she?"

"I don't know!" Philyra related quickly what had happened at breakfast.

"Then Kronos didn't recognize her," Proteus said. "Everything she said was lost on him."

"Thanatos must have told him by now."

Proteus nodded. "Very likely."

She had pulled a chair near his and leaned forward now to place a hand on his arm. "She's in danger—very grave danger, judging from everything I've been told. You promised to help her, brother."

"I will."

"But we don't even know where she is. She should be warned, before Thanatos finds her."

"We don't need to know wh—"

They were interrupted by a faint cry from the direction of the entrance to Ophion's tunnel. "Come on, you two," the voice called. "This isn't funny."

Proteus pulled away from the entrance the heavy chest he had pushed there seconds before Thanatos entered the room. A mortal-size figure jumped to the floor and immediately resumed its normal size.

"Metis!" Philyra exclaimed, blushing fiercely. "Where are your clothes?"

The child crossed the room and recovered her chiton from the place where she had tossed it. A few quick movements pulled it over her head and adjusted it properly.

"I'm starting to get the knack of staying small," the girl explained, "but I don't dare try to concentrate on something else—like phantom clothing—at the same time. You wouldn't want me to crush myself inside there, would you? And I haven't had time to make little clothing for myself yet."

"Don't bother," Philyra said. "I'll make some for you!"

"That reminds me," Proteus said, turning to Philyra, "can you change size yourself?"

"You mean become as small as she was? I suppose so. I can't impersonate others the way you do, but I can change shapes. I often became a dolphin when I swam."

"Can you hold the shape for a long time?"

"As long as I've ever wanted to. I have good concentration. I used to tease sharks and let them chase me."

"You!" Metis said.

Proteus smiled. "She wasn't always prissy and proper," he told the child. Turning back to Philyra, he said, "Practice becoming the size of a man. You may have to travel through the tunnels yourself. We can't have you seen coming and going from Momos's rooms."

"You should see Alalkomeneus," Metis said. "He's taking charge of the other men, keeping them from wandering too far or getting into trouble. Some of them are already starting to imitate his speech, making sounds that are almost words."

"But what about Nalassa?" Philyra demanded. "Aren't you going to do anything?"

"What happened?" Metis asked.

They told her of Thanatos's visit. The child's face radiated outrage. "He came here to find Alalkomeneus and the other men. He may have hoped to find Nalassa, but he was really looking for them."

"And, I fear, he may suspect more than he realizes yet. He must have seen Iapetos shortly before coming here. He certainly didn't expect to find him at home. If he thinks very much about it . . ."

He threw himself into a chair, slumping deep into its

cushions. "I'm afraid our time is almost up. Before long Nalassa will be a prisoner, and even if Kronos doesn't force from her all that she knows, I shall have to rescue her—and that will certainly stir up a caldron of activity. At least you two will not be implicated and will be able to remain here on Olympos and work for our father's interests. I spent the afternoon searching the lower levels of the palace for Aigaion's cell, but it's useless. The palace is far too large."

"Have you no clue at all?" Philyra asked.

"Only what little I overheard Kronos telling Eurybie. He is safe—under Kronos's personal protection—and will arrive in the Kingdom of Nereus with Kronos's entourage."

"Then you don't even know for sure that he's still here on Olympos," Philyra said.

"Oh, he's here. I'm certain of that. I can feel it. I've been searching for a room designed to hold a god prisoner, but if there is such a cell, it's probably so well concealed that I could never find it. If Kronos simply has him under full-time guard, I might locate him eventually, but it would mean searching every apartment. Worse still, Kronos might be keeping him in a state of perpetual unconsciousness—by denying him all food and drink, for instance. Then he might be concealed in almost any compartment large enough to accommodate him. I fear it's hopeless."

"You could try to rescue him when he joins the entourage," Metis suggested.

"I suspect Kronos will be prepared for such a contingency." He sighed, then rose to his feet. "I'd better see about Nalassa now."

"But you don't know where to find her," Philyra objected.

"She'll be brought either to the chambers of Kronos or of Thanatos." He turned to Metis. "Will you be where I can find you later?"

The child goddess wore a look of angry determination. "I'll be here until supper. Brother, don't worry very much about Thanatos. I have a score to settle with him." Her expression discouraged inquiry.

Proteus threw off the cloak that had been wrapped about his body. A moment later he assumed the form of a bat and flew into the open mouth of Ophion's tunnel.

Metis moved to one side of the room, near the gallery.

Squatting on the floor, she spread a number of plants before her.

"What are you doing?" Philyra asked, standing behind her now.

Metis held in her hand a small plant. "I'm keeping a promise to myself. Please don't talk. I need to concentrate."

She turned her attention back to the herb, staring fiercely down at it. Philyra watched from above her. The plant began to change, a small, mushroomlike bulb sprouting from the tip of one of the stalks.

Philyra started to object, but then changed her mind. She had a glimmer of what her young sister planned. Smiling, she returned to her own room.

TWENTY-EIGHT

Thanatos grumbled to himself as he left the chambers of Iapetos. Trying to locate a single individual among the innumerable rooms and passages of Olympos was an almost hopeless undertaking. He cursed the nymph for the trouble she was causing him.

Actually the odds of his finding Nalassa were even worse than he suspected. Eurybie and the naiad had finished their tour of the palace before Thanatos began searching for them. Realizing that Nalassa was in need of rest, Eurybie suggested they postpone the lesser sights for a later day and proposed instead that they find an apartment for her. Suitable quarters were available on the same floor that Eurybie occupied. Most of the time that Thanatos was searching for them, they were in the new apartment, chatting and putting the rooms in order.

Eurybie had taken the nymph under her wing to separate her from Philyra—so that Kronos could have the Okeanid all to himself. But the sea goddess had a secondary motive as well. She made a point of learning all she could about each of the inhabitants of the palace. She used information as a weapon and worked very hard to keep her arsenal fully stocked.

To her surprise she found herself enjoying the company of the naiad. Nalassa's low-key, friendly personality made it easy to forget the passage of time. Her homely stories of her parents and sisters had both humor and charm. Eurybie finally left her, having thoroughly enjoyed the hours they had spent together.

Thanatos was waiting for the sea goddess as she reached her own apartment.

"Where is the nymph?" he demanded, stepping out of the shadows.

"Nalassa? I just left her. Why do you ask?"

"I must bring her to Lord Kronos. Will you lead me to her?"

Eurybie laughed cynically. "Her education begins even sooner than I thought. . . . Such charming simplicity here on Olympos—sooner might the moth nest untouched within the flame!"

"I don't know what you're talking about. I am to bring her to Lord Kronos as soon as I find her, and you are to go to him also, as soon as you have led me to her."

She pursed her lips. "That's peculiar. There may be more afoot than I suspected. She's down the corridor, around the corner. Come."

They reached the door and Thanatos entered immediately. Already curious, Eurybie became even more so as she watched the god. He crept across the atrium, listened, then headed toward one of the adjoining rooms. She followed him at a distance.

Nalassa was in her new bedchamber, arranging the bed in preparation for a much needed nap. She had spent the last few minutes trying to decide how she could go about informing Proteus and Philyra of her whereabouts. If she went to the apartment of Iapetos, she risked linking Philyra to herself, thereby putting her in jeopardy. The only other option she could think of was to wait until dinner and hope to reestablish contact then. This left her in some danger but was preferable to endangering others. With that settled, however unsatisfactorily, she decided to try to sleep for an hour or two.

A slight sound made her swing suddenly around. Thanatos was only a few steps away, and she caught a glimpse of Eurybie in the doorway. A startled cry escaped her lips. She twisted first one way and then the other, seeking some avenue of escape as she backed away from him.

Thanatos came to a stop and stood upright. "I come from Lord Kronos," he said stiffly. "He wishes to see you."

Calming herself now that she had retreated partway across the room, she said, "I'll be happy to see Lord Kronos again. I'll go to him as soon as I've had time to prepare myself. Where does he expect me?"

"He wishes you to come immediately to his chambers."

"It'll take only a few minutes for me to adjust my hair and clothing. Tell him I will be there very shortly."

"My instructions are to bring you as soon as I find you," Thanatos said, annoyed at the delay. He started toward her, but stopped again when she immediately began backing toward the entrance of an adjoining room.

Nalassa glanced past him, toward Eurybie. "This is really quite impossible," she said. "I must have a few minutes to prepare myself. I could have been nearly finished by now. Please deliver my message. Lady Eurybie can lead me to the king."

Thanatos turned toward the sea goddess, surprised to find her behind him. "You were to go to Lord Kronos without delay. Why are you here?"

Eurybie came forward into the room now. "This is far too interesting to miss. I'll go up with Nalassa."

"Kronos commands you to go immediately. This is none of your concern."

Eurybie shrugged her shoulders and turned her back upon the god. She retreated only as far as the atrium, then crept back to listen and watch.

"I won't go with you," Nalassa was saying.

"You defy the King of the Gods?"

"I do not defy him. I will go to him—but not with *you!*" Her eyes flitted past him, toward the open doorway. Behind her in the other room lay only a dead end.

"I have no time for this," the god said. "You will come—"

She bolted around him, toward the atrium. He lunged after her, clutching her around the waist. Twisting to face him, she thrust the palms of her hands into his face. He lost his grip, and she ran into the next room. As she passed, Eurybie stepped back from the doorway and flattened herself against the wall.

Thanatos caught the nymph before she could open the outer door to the corridor. Turning on him again, she kicked and scratched. Real fear gripped her, and she was determined not to fall into his hands again. At last he managed to twist one of her arms up behind her back. She continued to struggle until the pain became excruciating, then suddenly became limp.

Relaxing his hold, he opened the door and shoved her toward it. "Now we will go."

She spun around and pushed him away, then ran into the corridor. He picked himself up and stumbled after her.

Eurybie crossed the room and peered out after them, watching in amazement as the god and the naiad battled their way down the corridor. Each time Thanatos caught her, she squirmed and struggled free of his grasp. It was an astonishing display, unlike anything Eurybie had witnessed in the three years she had lived in the palace. It fascinated her at the same time that it inspired feelings of sympathy for the nymph, whose terror was obviously genuine; she even felt a momentary inclination to intercede on Nalassa's behalf. Instead she followed along behind them, by turns amused and concerned.

Finally Thanatos was able to deliver a stunning blow to the naiad's face. He struck her twice more, then threw her over his shoulder, ignoring the gawking stares of the lesser gods and goddesses who had stopped to watch. He carried her toward the stairs.

Eurybie followed, determined to satisfy her curiosity.

Thanatos took the most direct route he could find to the chambers of Kronos. Time and again he passed gods and goddesses who turned to stare at him and the attractive female slung across his shoulder. At last they reached the top floor of the palace and he deposited the unconscious Nalassa on a divan in the outermost room of Kronos's personal quarters. He went to the adjoining doorways and called aloud, receiving no response.

Eurybie stood just inside the room as he returned. "Well," she said, "you've got us both here. Now where is my lord?"

"I don't know."

She stared at him in astonishment, then began to laugh almost uncontrollably. "You beat her unconscious because she wouldn't come immediately—and he isn't even here!"

"He must have gone out. It took me a long time to find you."

Shaking her head, she moved toward Nalassa. She arranged her more comfortably on the divan, then brought nectar and let a few drops touch her lips. The naiad began to stir, then slowly sat up.

"I don't know what's going on here," Eurybie said, "but it certainly has relieved my boredom. Are you all right?"

Nalassa stretched her limbs tentatively, then began to rub her jaw.

"Relatively speaking, I mean," Eurybie said.

Nalassa smiled slightly. "I suppose I could feel worse. Where are we?"

"In the chambers of the king. Thanatos was very determined to fulfill his mission—and made quite a spectacle of himself in the process. Unfortunately, Lord Kronos is not at home."

"Yes he is," a deep voice said from behind them.

Kronos entered the room, still dressed for the hunt, carrying his three spears. His eyes swept from Eurybie to Nalassa to Thanatos. Glaring at the god, he said, "So you made a spectacle of yourself, did you? And beat the nymph as well?"

"It'd be more precise to say he made a spectacle of himself by beating her—and being beaten by her!" Eurybie said gaily.

Thanatos's eyes could not meet the unflinching gaze of his master. His fingers were tenderly stroking the long, painful scratches that ran down his face.

"Wait in the hall," Kronos told him. "I'll call you when I want you." He turned to Eurybie. "You too. Both of you stay in the corridor until I call."

Eurybie rose, straightening her peplos and smiling politely. "As my lord commands."

Kronos carried his spears to a nearby room and placed them in a rack, then returned to the nymph. She was standing. He brought two chairs from their places near the wall and motioned to her to be seated. She complied, and he sat across from her, leaning forward as he spoke. He smiled to put her at ease.

"I shall not lull you with sly words, Nalassa—that is your name, is it not?"

She nodded, her large brown eyes unable to completely conceal the fear she felt.

"Thanatos's overenthusiasm has made that unnecessary. You know why you are here. Tell me all I want to know, and I will treat you as kindly as I can."

"What do you wish to know?"

"How you escaped from Thanatos's room, who helped you, and whom you have told."

"No one helped me. I managed to free my hands from their bonds, though it took much of the night. The door to his bedroom was locked, but the bolt is easy to work from the inside. He was asleep, and I crept out into the corridor. No one was about, so—''

"What about the mortals—the little, godlike creatures?"

"Oh," she said, as though she had forgotten them until reminded. "He had brought them to Olympos at the same time that he brought me. The first thing he did was to . . . to cut off the head of one of them. It was terrible! Before I left the room, I opened their cage. I . . . I hoped they would escape, that he would kill no more of them. I left all the doors open—from that room to his bedroom, from the apartment to the corridor—that they might have a chance to get away. Did . . . did any of them manage to escape?"

"All of them escaped."

"All! Oh, I dared not hope as much. . . ." Her mind was working very fast. He had not asked about the head of Oizys. Should she mention it, or wait for him to question her concerning it?

"What did you do then? After reaching the corridor?"

"I didn't know what to do. I had only been to Olympos once before, when I was very young and my father brought me. I am one of the daughters of Asopos, the river god. When I found no one about—it was very late by then—I decided to try to awaken someone. I had descended a number of flights of stairs, to get far from him. No one answered at the first apartment I tried, but the door opened when I pushed on it, and I went inside. Soon I realized that no one was living there. Under the circumstances, I decided to stay until morning. One of the rooms had a number of chests—being stored there, I suppose. In the morning I cleaned myself up and found this gown. I dressed and went downstairs. Breakfast was being served and—"

"Whom did you expect to find there?"

"No one. I know no one here on Olympos."

He studied her face as she spoke, trying to determine if she were lying. "And whom have you told of your adventure?"

"No one."

"Not even Eurybie? You have been with her most of the time since breakfast, have you not?"

"I've been with no one else, until Thanatos came to get me. We spoke of many things, but I told her nothing about what had happened to me."

"Why have you told no one?" he asked. "Something

extraordinary had befallen you. Why did you not come to me and tell me that Thanatos had abducted you?''

"I was afraid to," she said softly. "I was afraid that I might offend you."

"How would that offend me?"

"I thought that you, the Lord of Olympos, must know what he was doing—if not that he had abducted me, then at least of the terrible things in his room. It did not seem reasonable that he could do such things on Olympos without your being aware of it and tolerating it. It seemed better to keep my own counsel until I could learn more about Olympos."

His face was unreadable. "I ask you again, whom have you told?"

"No one, my lord!" Her eyes became very large, looking straight into his. "You heard me at breakfast, and I had not spoken to anyone until then. I spoke to Eurybie about many things, but not that, and I have spoken to no one but you and Thanatos since." She paused, her expression suggesting that a new idea had just occurred to her. "Lord Kronos, Eurybie does not know of the room? Is it a secret from the gods who live on Olympos? Is that why you are concerned?"

He did not answer.

"If that is the case, you need have no fear. I'll tell no one. I'm very good at minding my own business."

He stared at her, trying to decide if she was telling the truth. As long as no one else knew of Thanatos's work, the rest of her story did not really matter. She could not be allowed to go free in any event. Finally he rose and went to the door, calling to Thanatos.

"Take her to your room," he told him when he had entered the apartment. "Keep her there until I tell you otherwise."

"May I begin my experiments?" the god asked anxiously.

The Lord of the Titans sighed. "Do as you are told—no more or less. You are responsible for all of this. Keep her in your quarters. Let no one talk to her. Treat her well, and dare not harm her."

"But my experiments—I must have a nymph—"

"Do as you are told," Kronos said firmly. He turned to Nalassa. "Go with him. If he harms you, I will punish him. You are to see and speak with no one until I decide what must be done."

He waited until they disappeared down the corridor, then called in Eurybie. He interrogated her at length, dismissing her only when he had satisfied himself that Nalassa had told the truth, at least concerning the sea goddess.

He sat alone for some minutes, head cradled in his hands, then rose and made his way to the garden atop the palace. The naiad must be kept silent, he thought as he strolled among the frolicking blossoms. He could send her to Tartaros, or he could let Thanatos have her for his experiments. He had to be assured of her silence, and one solution was no crueler than the other. She was a pretty thing, and he had no desire to see her harmed, yet necessity was always the final arbiter of such matters.

He would let Thanatos have her, he decided reluctantly. It was better than to sacrifice another nymph to him while this one languished in Tartaros. But not here. He would have to take her someplace else to do his work, someplace far away. The disappearance of the mortals, however, still puzzled him.

As Kronos weighed the fate of the naiad, his other prisoner steeled himself for a terrible ordeal. He was determined to concentrate all his remaining energy in an effort to extend his consciousness outward from his mind toward the rest of his body. He would force it downward, into his arms and hands. He knew he could not move them, but he wanted to reassure himself that they were still there, that they still existed.

He sought the familiar feel of his neck and shoulders. Instead he found—strangeness. The muscles felt different somehow. The firm hardness of the bones eluded him. He forced himself to continue. Instead of arms and hands he found—

And then Aigaion remembered. He remembered what he was and how he had become that way, and mixed with that recollection was a vagrant memory that sent shudders through him.

He had once heard the story, amusing but unlikely, of a god who had retained an alien form so long that he could never again change back. In that instant he knew that the story was true, and that the same thing was happening to him.

TWENTY-NINE

Proteus, the shape changer, flew through the inky blackness, his membranous bat wings thrashing the still air and his ultrasonic cries guiding him unerringly through the mazelike twists and turns of Ophion's tunnel toward the topmost level of the palace. Though he had traveled the route but once, his quick eyes and sure memory had noted every detail, so that now he had no difficulty in finding the way—even flying at top speed, in a strange form.

Within minutes he reached the secret room of Thanatos. He paused only to assure himself that no one would see him, then resumed his normal form as he alighted upon the floor. The caged animals began to stir at his presence. Moving slowly so that he would not frighten them, he crept toward the door and pressed an ear to the cold metal.

From without he could hear nothing. Opening the door, he peered out through a narrow crack, then moved into the bedchamber. He made his way slowly and cautiously from one room to the next, finally reaching the door that led out into the main corridor.

Twenty or thirty minutes had passed since Thanatos had left the chambers of Iapetos. He was not in his own quarters; therefore he had not yet found Nalassa, or he had taken her to Kronos—probably to the suite of rooms at the other end of the corridor. Rather than risk discovery, Proteus retreated to a room that opened onto the gallery. Assuming the form of a bird, he flew around the outside of the building.

He could hear voices even as he climbed over the high sill into one of the rear rooms of the apartment. Within moments he reached a point from which he could proceed confidently; his clandestine visit of the night before had left him familiar with the important details of the suite. He had no difficulty locating the room in which Kronos had entertained both Eurybie and Lady Rhea.

He crept cautiously toward the doorway, hugging the wall as he stepped over open chests bulging with silk and linen, around tables heaped with golden plates and platters, then darted across the room to slip behind the amphorae and bulging skin flasks that had concealed him last night. Once again he could see clearly into the adjoining room.

Nalassa lay upon a divan, just recovering from unconsciousness. Thanatos was there, too, and to Proteus's surprise, Eurybie bent over the naiad, comforting her.

Soon Kronos appeared, and Proteus followed with interest all that was said. He remained in concealment after Nalassa and Thanatos were sent away, listening as Kronos questioned Eurybie. Even after she was dismissed, he waited. He knew the Titan was considering her story and hoped to gain some clue to what he thought. In this, however, he was unsuccessful.

After Kronos, too, departed, Proteus came out of his hiding place and moved toward the doorway. Before passing through it, however, he hesitated. In the darkness and haste of the previous night he had not noticed the nature of the items that filled the room. Now he stood studying the stacked chests, the open casks of jewels, the silks and linens and golden implements. Together they constituted a truly royal gift from the King of the Gods to the newly married—and newly installed—Queen of the Aegean.

He started again to leave, but turned back instead to stare at the heaped riches. He could not escape the feeling that somehow these gifts held some significance for him. But what could it be, other than that they were gathered here by Kronos—in his safekeeping, one might say? And these wedding presents, certainly, would be carried to the Kingdom of Nereus with Kronos's entourage.

But none of the items was large enough to contain a god.

Still he hesitated, troubled. These gifts suggested something to him, something elusive . . . As he stood thinking, he noticed the floor in front of one of the chests. Kneeling, he touched a finger to the floor, then to his tongue.

He went to work immediately, quickly and quietly, since Kronos could return at any moment. He opened the chests one by one, unfastening their catches and unstacking them as necessary. At the very bottom of the stack he found the chest he sought, filled to the brim with salt.

Why would Kronos give salt to a sea goddess?

He thrust his arm into the chest, sifting the contents. When he brought it back out, he held a crab. He brushed the salt from the creature, then shook it slightly. In response it moved its limbs feebly.

Why would Kronos give a crab to a sea goddess, unless the crab was not a crab at all, but a god somehow trapped in that form? Proteus could imagine no other explanation. He shook the crustacean again in hope of reviving the god, then cleaned up the spilled salt and replaced the chests as he had found them.

Before entering Kronos's chambers he had draped himself in a phantom cloak; now he reshaped it into a garment suitable to the King of the Gods and concealed the creature beneath it. Assuming the form of Kronos, he went quickly to the outer corridor and followed it to Thanatos's chambers.

He threw open the door and entered, perfectly mimicking the natural, regal bearing of the Titan. Thanatos leaped to his feet as his king entered.

"She is here, just as you commanded," he said, bowing slightly.

Nalassa, on edge from the mere company of Thanatos, gripped the arms of her chair. She feared that Kronos's sudden appearance indicated that he had reached a decision concerning her.

"You've decided?" Thanatos asked, thinking the same thing. "How soon may I resume my work?"

"I have not decided." The god turned toward the river nymph. "Come. I wish to question you further. You need not be frightened."

Nalassa rose, and he gestured to her to precede him. She was apprehensive, but more than happy to escape the presence of Thanatos. The door closed behind them and Thanatos was left to his frustrations.

Cursing the nymph, Thanatos slumped into his chair. Delay and disappointment met him at every turn. Nalassa promised the most interesting results, but even a single mortal would have satisfied him.

He sat up suddenly. What a fool he had been! He'd had the nymph to himself and forgotten to ask her what she had done with the mortals. He stood up, hesitating. Perhaps he could still find out, before she and Kronos entered the king's chambers. He dared not interrupt once they were inside, but they had not yet had time to reach the rooms.

Opening the door, he saw that they were still in sight. He could still catch them if he tried. Holding up the hem of his long chiton, he rushed after them. They were farther ahead than he had thought; they reached the entrance before he caught up with them, but instead of entering Kronos's chambers, they continued down the hall.

Thanatos slowed to a stop, watching as his master and the river nymph disappeared into the stairwell. Why had they gone that way? Kronos had said he wanted to talk to her. Why was he taking her downstairs?

Thanatos began to walk again, slowly increasing his speed as he followed them.

As soon as they left Thanatos's quarters, Nalassa was surprised to have Kronos take her hand and squeeze it gently. She looked questioningly into his face.

"Quiet, Nalassa," the god said. "You are safe—or nearly so. Appearances are often deceiving."

"What do you mean, Lord Kronos?" She had hoped that Proteus would somehow learn of her predicament and come for her. She dared not let herself believe that this hope had already been gratified. Again and again she darted quick glances at the god who accompanied her.

"Yes, it is I—Proteus," he whispered, smiling.

"Oh, Proteus! I knew you would come if you knew where I was—but I didn't think you could know."

"Quiet," he repeated.

They descended the stairs, the naiad almost heady with relief after the fear and tension of the last hours. The touch of his hand seemed like the most wonderful thing in the world.

She knew of his unequaled abilities and felt a complete trust in them. He was with her, and nothing could go wrong now.

"Someone's coming up toward us," he said.

He was leading her toward the chambers of Momos. They had descended three floors and had four more to go.

"Walk ahead of me," he told her. Once more he changed shapes. As Kronos he would attract attention; not only would he be noticed, but many of the gods they passed would want to talk briefly with him. Thanatos was safely behind them, and no one wanted to talk to him. He assumed the tall, emaciated form of the son of Nyx.

Nalassa was now nearly ten steps below him as Momos came into sight, climbing slowly and grumbling to himself. The nymph moved far to one side to avoid him; nevertheless he managed to bump against her as he passed.

"Too narrow too!" the god said. "Too many steps and far too narrow."

Proteus—now in the form of Thanatos—edged to one side as Momos squinted at him.

"Most unpleasant," the rumpled god continued to himself. "Pressed up tight with the most unpleasant company imaginable . . ."

The real Thanatos, puzzled and growing more and more suspicious, had increased his pace to the point that he was quickly drawing closer to those he followed. Now he found Momos coming upward toward him, weaving from one side of the staircase to the other.

"Out of my way, fool," he snapped as they drew near each other.

Momos blinked at him, slowing almost to a stop and blocking the way so that Thanatos could only squeeze past him with difficulty.

"There should be a law," Momos was saying, shaking a finger in his brother's face. "I'm going to talk to Lord Kronos. Nobody should be allowed to come down without going back up first."

"Move," Thanatos said in exasperation, taking him by the shoulders and shoving him roughly against one of the walls.

"No wonder the stairs are always crowded," Momos said. "No wonder at all, when you go down twice while I'm still trying to go up once."

Thanatos pushed past him and continued downward. Long years had accustomed him to completely ignoring everything his brother said. What a fool Momos was. Of course you had to go up the stairs before you could come back down again.

Proteus, hearing voices behind them but unaware that they were being followed, caught up with Nalassa and changed forms again, this time assuming the shape of Iapetos, whose floor they had just passed. It occurred to him that Thanatos or Kronos himself could be just behind them. Gesturing toward the nymph, he sent her on ahead. He planned to follow at a slight distance in case some problem developed.

Instead she ran back toward him. "I don't know the way," she whispered. "Where are we going?"

Now Thanatos reached a point from which he could see them. He had expected Kronos and Nalassa. Instead he found Iapetos and the nymph. This unexpected sight made him hesitate before joining them.

"Pardon, my lord," he said, short of breath. "Where is Lord Kronos? I thought he would be with the nymph."

Proteus, perfectly mimicking the manner of the Titan he impersonated, turned to face him. "My brother is still above. I believe he's gone to see Lady Rhea."

Puzzlement was evident on Thanatos's face. "But the nymph? How does she come to be with you?"

Proteus, thinking quickly, answered, "Lord Kronos asked me to escort her to supper. He is to join us as soon as he is free."

Thanatos looked from Iapetos to Nalassa and back again.

"Is there anything else?" Proteus asked.

Thanatos shook his head slowly, still deeply puzzled. "No, my lord. Pardon me for detaining you." He turned and began climbing back toward his own quarters.

Why would Kronos entrust the nymph to Iapetos? Iapetos was one of the gods Kronos particularly wanted to keep in ignorance of Thanatos's experiments. It would have been easier and less dangerous to leave the nymph with Thanatos until after visiting Rhea.

Thanatos halted just out of sight. Something peculiar was going on, and although he normally would have been completely uninterested in any such mystery, this one concerned his prize experimental subject. He crept back down the stairs after her, this time moving more slowly and being very quiet.

As soon as Thanatos had passed from sight, Proteus began casting about for another form to assume. They were now two floors above the chamber of Momos, and the lower they descended, the more likely they were to pass others on the stairs. It was risky to remain in the form of Iapetos, whose wife or children might come face to face with them at any moment. Above him, definitely, were Thanatos and Momos. Neither pleased him as choices, but after a moment's consideration he took on the rumpled appearance of the latter. They were, after all, making their way toward that god's apartment.

Thanatos came down toward them, increasing his speed while remaining as silent as possible. They had a single flight yet to descend when he got close enough to see them. Now Nalassa seemed to be alone, with his fool of a brother doddering downward eight or ten steps behind her.

Where was Iapetos? Why was the nymph alone? He rushed after her, shouldering Momos to one side.

"What's going on?" he demanded, grabbing her by the wrist.

She struggled to pull free, but his grip was firm.

"Answer me. Where is Lord Iapetos? Why are you alone?"

She continued to struggle, but he grabbed her other wrist. She glanced up the stairs and he followed her look, seeing only Momos.

"Answer me or—" He stopped short, looking back at Momos. What was he doing here? Hadn't he passed him a few minutes before, on a higher level? The words his brother had mumbled came back to him—something about going downstairs twice, without first going back up.

Nalassa jerked her hands free and ran a short distance, but stopped to look back up.

"H-how . . ." Thanatos said, staring at the approaching god. "You were up—"

Momos had now reached him, head bowed, lips constantly moving, shoulders slumped.

"You can't be down here and up there. . . ." He shoved the rumpled figure backward a step, and something fell from under his cloak. Thanatos stared down in total befuddlement at the crab.

Suddenly sharp, clear eyes looked up at him from the wrinkled, puffy face of Momos. Two plump hands reached out and took him by the shoulders with incomprehensible strength. The hands shook him, lifted and then flung him upward, to land in a crumpled heap a dozen steps above where he had been.

"Run!" Proteus called to Nalassa. He recovered what he had dropped, then followed her three steps at a time, still retaining the form of Momos but propelling the paunchy body with all his natural strength. Taking her hand, he pulled her along after him.

At first Thanatos was too stunned to stir. Another minute passed as he tried to sort out what had happened. At last he regained his feet and forced himself to try to follow them, but by now it was too late. They were gone, and he turned to retrace his steps toward the uppermost level of the palace, intent on turning the mystery over to Lord Kronos for a solution.

Obviously it had not been his brother who had dealt with him so effectively and efficiently. But who was it—who was it who looked so much like Momos? Then he remembered Iapetos. Had it truly been Iapetos accompanying the nymph, or . . .? The thoughts all came together at once. Momos—the real Momos—must have been saying that he had seen Thanatos twice on the stairs, just as Thanatos had seen Momos twice. That was what his curious statement had meant. Kronos had taken the nymph and led her away, but it must have been a false Kronos, someone impersonating the King of the Gods. This same impostor had become Thanatos when passing Momos, then Iapetos when Thanatos caught up with him. . . .

Iapetos—he remembered his earlier, unexpected meeting with the Titan, when he had entered Metis's room. Had that been the real Iapetos, or the impostor? And why did everything keep coming back to Metis, the Okeanid?

Okeanid! Metis was an Okeanid, a daughter of Okeanos—a sister of the most famous of shape changers. Even Thanatos had heard of him. Proteus, the eldest son of Okeanos, was secretly here on Olympos—that was the only possible answer.

The eldest and most powerful son of Kronos's most steadfast enemy! Thanatos had heard the King of the Gods rail against his brother time and again. This was information his master would be anxious to know. He forced himself to climb faster.

Kronos was not in his chambers. Thanatos searched for him, but did not think to go up to the rooftop garden. Supper would have begun by now; perhaps, he thought, the Lord of the Titans was already dining. Once again he returned to the stairs.

By the time he reached the patio his legs were beginning to wobble from fatigue. Stopping on the broad steps, he surveyed the assemblage. Kronos might be seated anywhere on the wide, grassy terrace. Finally he spotted Eurybie and staggered toward her. She was sitting alone.

"Is Lord Kronos here?" he asked, so short of breath that he had trouble speaking.

She shook her head, chewing and swallowing while he awaited her answer. "Not yet. He should be down soon. Why? Is something wrong?"

An attendant brought a chair, and Thanatos dropped into it. "I must speak with him. Something has hap— I have very important information for him."

"Hmm. Sounds interesting." She deposited a final morsel in her mouth, licked her fingers, and chewed with unabashed enjoyment.

He twisted around in his chair, craning his neck to look for Kronos.

Metis, who was serving her turn as an attendant, had seen him as he entered. She began preparing a plate of food, ladling out a large serving of sauce and carefully mixing something into it.

"Thalia," she called, waving to the Muse as she passed nearby. "I'm running behind. Will you deliver this for me— over there, to the thin god with Eurybie."

"At once, dear child," Thalia said, taking the plate and carrying it to the god Metis had indicated.

Thanatos barely noticed as she set it on the table by his side. He was looking toward the portico, expecting Kronos to appear at any moment. He glanced at the food, then began to pick at it absentmindedly, dipping the meat into the sauce before each bite. He continued to watch for Kronos.

"I've finished eating," Eurybie said, "and I don't have anyone interesting to talk to. I think I'll go find Lord Kronos for you. Did you look in his chambers?'' Her curiosity had been aroused by the earlier incident with Nalassa, and she hoped to at least partly satisfy it. Acting as messenger might help achieve that goal.

Thanatos was too exhausted to object. ''Yes, I suppose that's a good idea. Please tell him where I am and—''

''And that you have *very important information* for him,'' she said mockingly. ''I shall.'' She glided across the lawn, up the stairs, and into the palace.

He continued to wait, idly eating. His mind was racing, and he barely tasted the food. At first the peculiar sensations were so slight that he scarcely noticed them, but they soon became clearly unpleasant. He rubbed his hand over his stomach, wondering if Eurybie had found Kronos yet.

From across the patio Metis watched him, noting the sequence of his reactions. She had spent almost two hours perfecting the herb, altering it bit by bit until it exactly suited her requirements.

By now discomfort had become pain. He clutched his belly, bending far forward. His head seemed to be spinning and he wanted to lie down. With difficulty he rose to his feet. As he reached the portico, Kronos was coming in his direction.

Kronos saw him too—and was displeased. Thanatos was supposed to be guarding Nalassa. Why had he deserted his post?

''Lord Kronos!'' Thanatos managed to call out, heading toward him. He was intent upon telling his master what he had learned, but just as he reached him, the pain in his stomach became even more extreme. Doubling over, he began to vomit.

Kronos drew back in revulsion.

''Lord Kro—'' His stomach heaved again.

Kronos stepped wide around him, disgust clearly evident on his face.

Eyes running and mouth drooling, Thanatos abandoned his attempt and once again started toward his own quarters. Every few steps he stopped, heaving uncontrollably.

Metis smiled and turned her attention back to her work.

Kronos sat at a table and tried to eat when his food was brought, but his mind was on Nalassa. He had to know why Thanatos had left her. Reluctantly he abandoned his meal and went back upstairs. The stairway reeked with the evidence of the sick god's passage.

The nymph was gone. He found Thanatos, still dressed, lying in his bed.

"Where is she?" Kronos demanded. "You've let her escape a second time!"

Thanatos only moaned in answer, barely able to open his eyes.

Kronos started to reach for him, intent upon shaking him by the throat. He reconsidered before touching him. As he backed from the room, Thanatos gave out another low, gurgling moan and began to retch.

THIRTY

Proteus and Nalassa reached the chambers of Momos without further difficulty. Small by comparison with the apartment of Iapetos, it was nevertheless of fair size, with four major rooms in addition to the large entrance hall and a number of small storage rooms.

"Greetings, Lord Proteus," Alalkomeneus cried as they entered one of the rear chambers. The man stepped forward from amid a number of his fellows and bowed stiffly. All around him the naked mortals scurried to hide themselves or crept forward with wide, curious eyes, depending on their individual temperaments.

"We have awaited your presence as the flower awaits the sun," Alalkomeneus continued, obviously pleased with his own eloquence.

"And we are pleased to be with you," Proteus answered. "Have the rest of your people been behaving? Has anyone been here since Metis left?"

"We've seen no one, my lord Proteus, since the Goddess of the Dark Curls departed. As to the men, I've had my hands full with them. None of them understands very much, but as long as they are confined in this room, little harm can befall them. Will Lady Metis, the Laughing Goddess of Many Smiles, be returning soon?"

"I hope so," Proteus said distractedly.

Nalassa moved about the room, looking for a place to sit.

She avoided the chair occupied by the head of Oizys, which was propped up by pillows, watching them. The mortals had settled all over the room; she lifted one out of the way and sat down, immediately beginning to tend to her appearance.

Proteus removed the crab from beneath his clothes and set it on the floor, then brought a decanter from a nearby table and doused the creature with nectar. For a long moment nothing happened, but then the form of the crustacean blurred and began to enlarge. A moment later the sea god Aigaion stood before them, tall, thin, and naked, his long hair as wild as a bramble thicket. Proteus stepped quickly toward him to stop him from falling.

"Sit, friend of my father," Proteus said, assisting him into a chair. He brought a goblet, and the god gulped down the nectar, moaning softly and rubbing his eyes. "You're free now, Aigaion, thanks to the concern of Okeanos."

"Is that you, Proteus?" Aigaion asked weakly. "Yes, I see now that it is you, Son of Okeanos. I have done a terrible thing, a despicable thing. I let Kronos force me to tell evil lies about your father and my brother Nereus. He beat me terribly, and I was too weak to resist him." His hands trembled as Proteus refilled his goblet.

"I know. That doesn't matter. You did your best, and now you are free. But how did Kronos trap you in such a manner?"

"He would not let me eat or sleep, even after I had said all he wanted me to say. At last, when I could stand no more, I transformed myself into the form in which you found me— not to escape, which was impossible, but to avoid the blows. I tried to scuttle away, but was too slow. He threw me into some container and poured some substance over me, so that I was frozen still and could not move at all."

Proteus nodded. "I suspected something like that. Rest now and gather strength, while there is time." He turned to Nalassa. "I'm going to get Philyra and Metis and bring them back here. The two of you should be safe until I return."

Her smile and nod could not conceal that she did not want him to go.

The entrance to Ophion's tunnel lay near the floor. Proteus had pried out its circular stone seal earlier in the day, when he and Metis had agreed to make this room the center of their clandestine activities. Two large amphorae stood in front of the entrance to conceal it from casual view.

Metamorphosing himself, he flew through the tunnel to Metis's room. The child goddess was not there, and Philyra was not in sight. Risking discovery, he assumed the form of Iapetos to seek the older sister in her room. He found her without difficulty and returned to his own form.

"We must talk," he told her, "all of us. We have little time. Where is Metis?"

"She's downstairs, at supper."

"Good. Find her and let her lead you to Momos's quarters. We'll have to chance your being seen. Be very careful."

He returned to Nalassa and Aigaion. Twenty minutes passed before they heard the Okeanids entering the outer rooms of the apartment. When they arrived, Alalkomeneus ran toward the child goddess with a cry of joy; she swooped him up and amply returned his affection.

"No one saw you coming here?" Proteus demanded. "No one, particularly Kronos or Thanatos?"

Metis grinned. "Thanatos certainly didn't see us, nor Kronos."

Proteus quickly told his sisters of the rescue of Aigaion and Nalassa and how Thanatos had followed them. "Even if Thanatos didn't recognize me," he concluded, "Kronos certainly will know whom to suspect. By this time he knows I'm on Olympos, and that means none of us is safe."

"He doesn't know yet," Metis said quietly.

Everyone stared at her. "What do you mean?" Proteus asked. "Why are you smiling?"

"Thanatos hasn't told anyone anything. I told you not to worry about him, brother."

Proteus and Philyra exchanged glances. Philyra was smiling despite her efforts to remain impassive. "Let her tell you," she said.

Metis explained how she had transmuted one of her plants, ground some of it into fine powder, and added the powder to the god's meal. She described in detail what she had seen of Thanatos's reaction to eating it.

"Then he's too sick to talk?" Proteus asked.

The child nodded. "Too sick to do anything."

"Are you certain?"

"Almost certain. From the time he started to vomit, he shouldn't have been able to put three words together. By now he's probably so weak he can barely move. He's forgotten all about you.''

Proteus looked at Philyra.

"She knows plants," Philyra said. "If that's what she says, I'd believe her."

"How long will he stay that way?"

Metis shrugged. "A day or two. Maybe three."

Proteus laughed softly. "The daughters of Okeanos are not to be trifled with! But our situation has not really changed. When Thanatos recovers, Kronos will know everything, or guess it. Both of you will be in danger."

"What if he doesn't recover?" Metis asked. "Then Kronos wouldn't be able to link Nalassa to you or us. Besides, I'd like to keep Thanatos sick."

"You have a previously unsuspected malicious streak, little sister. Could you do that?"

"I think so. I'd like to try. I could reach his apartment through Ophion's tunnel and force more of my herb into him while he sleeps."

"Kronos will still be suspicious, now that Nalassa has disappeared. He knows that peculiar things have been happening, and he'll make an effort to discover what it's all about. Still, he might not learn that Aigaion is missing, and if he doesn't learn that in time, his plot against Okeanos and Nereus may be impaired."

Philyra leaned forward. "Impaired? If he has no witness, haven't we won? Haven't you defeated him?"

Proteus shook his head. "You didn't see and hear Kronos as I did. This won't stop him. At best it may weaken the support of his accomplices. I fear we've won only a small victory today."

"Then what shall we do?" Philyra asked.

"I have to warn Lord Nereus, and Nalassa will need help escaping the palace, since she can't fly. I'll take her to some safe place, then continue on to the Kingdom of Nereus. If Metis can keep Thanatos from talking to Kronos, then you both should be safe here."

"I can do it," Metis said. "Besides, there may be more to be learned. We can work for our father here on Olympos."

Proteus looked skeptical. "Metis, you've seen what the King of the Gods is capable of. Don't think for a moment that he'll spare you because you're a child or Philyra because he finds her attractive.''

"Brother," Philyra said, "none of us is safe as long as Lord Kronos plots against our father. In times like these we must all face danger. Metis and I must do all we can until you return.''

"Bravely said. Will you promise to be careful? Should Kronos suspect you, you must flee Olympos immediately. Come to the Kingdom of Nereus. You'll be safe there until the wedding.''

"Good," Philyra said. "It's settled. When do you leave?''

"Tonight, as soon as it's dark. Nothing can be gained by waiting longer, and the danger to Aigaion and Nalassa can only increase.''

"Where will you take me?" Nalassa asked.

"Where would you like to go?''

She hesitated, then answered without looking at him, "I've never seen the Kingdom of Nereus.''

"You may come with me, if you like. You'll probably be safer there—for the present, anyway—than with your family. What about you, Aigaion?''

The sea god looked markedly better now. "Far, far away," he said. "As soon as night falls I'll become a bird—the smallest, most inconspicuous of birds—and fly as far as my wings will carry me.''

A short time later they all went out on the gallery. It was night now, and the moon had not yet risen. Standing together, Nalassa and the children of Okeanos watched as Aigaion assumed a tiny, dull gray form, and flitted away into the darkness. As best they could tell, no one followed him.

Philyra stepped forward and kissed her brother tenderly on the cheek. "Perhaps someday you'll visit for more than a few hours," she told him. "Be careful, brother.''

Metis hugged him enthusiastically. He whispered in her ear, "Philyra is very brave and will do her best, but your temperament better suits you to this sort of adventure. You must try to be wise beyond your years.''

Nalassa had been standing to one side. Now Proteus caused wings to grow from his back and stepped toward her. He lifted her in his arms and carried her toward the railing, his great wings stretched and beginning to beat. The naiad closed her eyes and let her arms tighten around him as they plunged out into the night. A few moments later, they too had vanished.

Behind them, elsewhere in the palace, the King of the Gods crouched beside an overturned chest. Salt lay scattered all around him upon the floor.

Finally he rose and went to a neighboring room. From a cupboard he withdrew a weapon, weighing it in his hand and testing its edge as he carried it to a chamber lit by many lamps. Here for a long time he sat and thought, brooding upon the many things that had happened.

The nymph, the mortals, Thanatos and Aigaion . . . There was a mystery here—a mystery to be plumbed and an enemy to be crushed. He was angry, but he was intrigued, too—intrigued and invigorated. He sensed the hand of an uncommon adversary, and a rare challenge to his unexcelled strength and intelligence.

Holding the great curved sword forged for him by Iapetos, the Lord of the Titans began to plan, cunning thoughts crowding the labyrinth of his mind.